UNDETECTED

Suzy is a black widow who has married into a new family. Can they unearth her past before she strikes again?

By Jeffrey Marshall

Undetected
Copyright © 2020 by Jeffrey Marshall

Library of Congress Control Number: 2020904895
ISBN-13: Paperback: 978-1-64749-082-9
          ePub: 978-1-64749-083-6

All rights reserved. No part of this publication may be reproduced, distributed, or transmitted in any form or by any means, including photocopying, recording, or other electronic or mechanical methods, without the prior written permission of the publisher or author, except in the case of brief quotations embodied in critical reviews and certain other noncommercial uses permitted by copyright law.

Although every precaution has been taken to verify the accuracy of the information contained herein, the author and publisher assume no responsibility for any errors or omissions.No liability is assumed for damages that may result from the use of information contained within.

Printed in the United States of America

GoToPublish LLC
1-888-337-1724
www.gotopublish.com
info@gotopublish.com

1.

She could almost smell the inside of the motel before she went in. With its whitewash fading and the vacancy sign missing an "n", it would have the scent of cheap disinfectant and perhaps a slight mustiness. Suzy Perry remembered that smell, but it had been years since she'd experienced it. She never thought she'd have to revisit it, but things were desperate now, she was on the run, and she had no choice. Enjoying the comforts of an upscale motel was out of the question.

She had left Rye in mid-morning, steering the Mercedes west across the car-choked George Washington Bridge and into New Jersey. Passing the shimmering high-rise apartment towers in Fort Lee, she'd stopped in Parsippany to rent a car, leaving the Mercedes skewed at an ungainly angle against the chain-link fence in the back of the lot. Her rented Ford Focus, she knew, would be far less conspicuous – but she realized unhappily that having to rent the car with a credit card would link her to it.

From here on, she would be paying only in cash. She'd made two large withdrawals from the bank's ATM, gathering enough, she thought, that would easily get her to Little Rock and have plenty on hand to keep going, wherever her flight would take her.

Approaching Nashville, Suzy eased off I-40 just after the airport and headed north to the old Lebanon Pike, which meandered like a lazy gray river west into the city. She knew it just well enough from a previous trip to sense it was what she was looking for: an old commercial strip, peeling at the edges, graced – well, that wasn't exactly the word – with warehouses, storage rental units and motels that had long ago ceded any claim to prominence to the chain properties huddled just off the interstate.

The motel clerk, a thin young man with close-cropped hair, a scraggly brown goatee and ear piercings, looked up with a crooked smile. Suzy didn't know it, but the motel, in business for 62 years, had a local reputation as a spot for traveling salesmen on a budget and for daytime trysts for surreptitious lovers.

"Is this just for tonight?" he asked.

"Yes, just tonight." She seemed a bit uneasy, looking about, but calm.

"That'll be fifty-four dollars and forty-five cents, including tax."

"Fine." She reached into her wallet and brought out three twenties. As she'd suspected, she didn't need to fill out any form or write down the make and license plate of her car.

He reached into the till, hidden from her view, and gave her change and handed her a key card. "Room 221 – it's on the second floor. Just go down to your right a little ways and you'll see the stairs going up there." He seems sharp enough, she thought to herself, but I certainly don't care for the look; maybe he's an aspiring country artist, like so many in Nashville, and this is his idea of hip.

"Thank you." She didn't seem interested in making small talk, and so he simply smiled. She turned on her heels and walked toward the door, and he noticed that she limped perceptibly.

The room was only marginally better than Suzy had feared. It had a tired patina of the 70s, with dark brown curtains, a dark orange spread on the queen bed, and a window air conditioner, listing slightly, that seemed to be on its last legs. At least the room seemed clean. She set the suitcase on the bed, sat down beside it and sighed, and then her brain started working, plotting out the next day.

She glanced to her left and took in the upholstered chair. What struck her wasn't the shape, which was utterly conventional, or even the condition – a sagging cushion and a slight rip in the seat – as much as the color, a deep burgundy.

It was the color of the tie Avery had been buried in – a favorite that his children had insisted on. Suzy had wanted him cremated: dust to dust. But a stipulation in his will she had been unware of required a burial, and it was in a fine mahogany box, burnished to a rich sheen, with a creamy velvet interior and with gleaming brass handles. She'd lifted her eyebrows in surprise when she saw the price, but she paid it; some might have said it was the least Suzy could have done for a man who gave her 20 very fine years before she decided to kill him.

She pulled her phone from her purse and saw that there were several missed calls and a message from Dean – no surprise there. He would be shocked and concerned that she'd taken the car and left without a word. She went to her email and composed a new message for Sally – she needed to let her know she was on her way. Little Rock, here I come, she thought a bit dispiritedly. Diving into the proverbial arms of her best friend, who would have no idea what she was getting into.

EIGHT MONTHS EARLIER
Westchester County, NY

2.

Walking into his son's room, Alex Perry had a *frisson* of angst. He remembered how hard it was to be a teenager dealing with the challenges of growing into one's body, finding the right (or at least, appropriate) crowd, asserting one's independence, coping with body image issues.

He sensed Jason has going through many of the same litany of challenges – but he couldn't be sure. In part, that was because he had repressed many of those himself, preferring to bury a good part of his high school years in a dark blanket of mis-remembrance. More so, it was that his son was unrelentingly uncommunicative, which Alex learned from friends was common for boys his age – and especially when so much of his son's time was spent in his room, listening to streaming music or slaying reams of enemy warriors on his Play Station.

Alex couldn't comprehend how the zeitgeist had changed so radically, how almost every kid in Jason's orbit spent so much time alone, on their phones and computers, and so little chasing footballs or soccer balls or basketballs or any of the sports he and his buddies had enjoyed in the great outdoors.

Not that everyone was indoors all the time. Half of the parents he knew were frantically crisscrossing Westchester County like crazed lemmings - driving ceaseless carpools to soccer games, lacrosse games, hockey games and – later – to summer camps focusing on certain sports.

Lacrosse had mushroomed into a near-obsession in some households because it had a widely credited record of helping talented players, boys and girls, get into elite schools.

No one knew that for a fact, but it didn't take a genius to make the connection, like water boiling after being put on a hot stove. He'd even read about faraway places like Phoenix being hooked on lacrosse, which in his day was a preppie sport rarely played west of Pittsburgh.

He had tried to steer Jason toward tennis years ago, and while he showed considerable aptitude, he had little interest; eventually, Alex more or less gave up and stopped paying for the lessons. His son would have to make it on his intellectual bona fides, not some outsized athletic ability.

Jennifer was a different story, as siblings often are. She was two years younger, and on the cusp of her teenage ordeal. Bright and outgoing, she wasn't as bookish – or Alex had to admit, nerdy – as her brother. She had taken up lacrosse and field hockey, and excelled in both; Lisa was a carpool mom for her teams. Long-legged and sturdy, Jennifer seemed as full of promise as a bright morning in May when the trees were coming into full leaf.

Alex had no idea what their future held, but he sensed that the whole high school scene would be a roller-coaster of sorts. And wasn't there a time, sooner or later, when his kids would make him and Lisa out as embarrassments, treat them as pariahs? Teenage rebellion wasn't a newly minted penny; it had certainly been a part of his generation – though somewhat muted in his own case – and it had flared dramatically for the Baby Boomers intent on free love and world peace.

Somehow, though, he thought things might be tougher with Jennifer. She was more outgoing, more engaged and more strong-willed; Jason seemed more content to go with the prevailing flow, and his periodic sullenness produced long periods of silence. That was only compounded by his retreat to his room and his full-on embrace of electronic media; it could be hard as hell to get his attention.

All in all, though, Alex felt he could count his blessings. He had a good job as a magazine editor, and Lisa did well as second-in-command at a nonprofit promoting education. Their home, which they had bought a dozen years earlier, was a comfortable retreat on a leafy street; like many others nearby, it was a white-framed colonial with an attached two-car garage and a half-acre studded with full-grown trees and a necklace of shrubs gracing the front.

Winters weren't easy in the Northeast, and he hated shoveling snow, but what else was new? It was all he had ever known, and people made do; winter was a passing nuisance - it wasn't like they were living in North Dakota. Westchester County was affluent and sophisticated, and it had been that way for a century, since rich Manhattanites had fled the city's concrete confines in search of space and greenery.

He climbed up the carpeted stairs and knocked on Jason's door, which was ajar. "Dinner in a few minutes, kiddo," he announced as he walked in.

Jason was on his bed, propped up against the pillows, typing on his laptop. "Okay, Dad." He barely glanced up. Alex took in his wardrobe: old sweatshirt, frayed jeans, Sketchers slip-ons. He knew Jason must have changed – that wasn't acceptable for school.

Alex briefly glanced around the room. It wasn't messy, exactly, but it had that rigorously lived-in look; a few clothes were strewn on an armchair, and there were some papers in a corner of the floor by the desk. There was only one poster, which celebrated the most recent rendition of X Men, hanging on the wall opposite the bed. It wasn't like the bedrooms of his day, with the posters of Farah Fawcett or Catherine Bach of The Dukes of Hazzard. Technology ruled, not hormones.

Alex sensed that his family was very similar to others just outside his orbit: two children seemed right for this era. Families in the 50s, a decade after the soul-numbing war, were larger, but a suburban woman working outside the home was a rare bird in that era. Lisa loved working, and it provided a critical piece of her identity. Besides, a second income in Westchester was more than welcome; to those not in the investment banking or venture capital firmament, it was practically a necessity.

He went back down the carpeted stairs and walked to the bright and open kitchen, where Lisa was putting together a salad in big wooden bowl. "Captain America will be coming down soon, I hope," he announced.

She flashed her slightly crooked smile, the one he loved. "Jennifer's taking a shower – the usual after field hockey practice." On the far side of the marble island, she paused and looked hard at him for a moment. "Are we pushing her too hard? She's got a lot on her plate, and with the travel team…"

"Oh, I don't know. She isn't complaining, is she?"

"No, no. But I wouldn't expect her to – not in her nature." Lisa's brown hair hung straight to her shoulders; there was a touch of gray near the temples, like a light frosting.

"I know." He scratched his hand where it was itching. "But I guess we need to monitor it as best we can. Burn-out is a bad thing. She's too young for that."

"Well, it's certainly nothing you and I ever faced," Lisa said, slicing a cucumber. "Sometimes I think we would have been lost, with all the noise and the distractions these kids have. We had it simpler." She glanced at him quickly, taking in the square face with the firm jaw, the wire-rimmed glasses, and the neatly trimmed hair, the color of damp straw. At just under six feet, he was about five inches taller than her, and he held himself erect; he always had.

Alex sighed almost inaudibly. "No shit. It wasn't exactly *Ozzie and Harriet*, but it wasn't *Modern Family*, either."

She chuckled. His dry wit snuck up on her now and then, in a beguiling way. "Right. Would you get out the plates?"

"'Course. Oh, and Dad called. He wants us to come over on Friday night."

Lisa nodded. "Is Suzy cooking?" she asked slyly.

"I honestly don't know." Alex smiled conspiratorially. "Stranger things have happened, I guess."

3.

Alex didn't care for the term "force of nature," but it fit Suzy like a fine suede glove. She was the center of her universe, the nucleus for orbiting electrons, and those around her often felt the waves emitted by her personality. Those could be subtle at times, and at others like a searchlight being trained in the dark of the night.

He found himself constantly trying to decipher, to understand her ways. From what he could tell from a handful of social occasions, women frequently reacted poorly to Suzy, who often acted like a peacock in a drab covey of hens; she flirted, she performed, and she seemed to revel in an audience, especially of men.

She had come into Alex's life just over a year ago, when his father introduced her over dinner at one of his favorite restaurants. His initial impressions were memorable: she was relatively tall and quite curvy – her dress was tight enough to suggest considerable endowment – and striking in the way that few women in their late 60s are. Her face was relatively unlined, and her smile (clearly the pride of some orthodontist somewhere) was little short of dazzling; her sea-blue eyes were penetrating. Even her arms looked relatively taut, with little loose skin around the elbows. She'd made quite the impression.

But now she was her father's new wife of seven months, and it was "Suzy this" and "Suzy that" whenever he and his father talked. And that was relatively often, since Dean Perry had moved into a plush townhouse in Rye three years ago; it was a short drive to Alex's house in Larchmont – too short, often, in Alex's view.

His father wasn't a diffident sort, either. He had always been an imposing force in Alex's life, seeming to be forever glancing over his son's shoulder and cataloging his impressions, which he was happy to share. Alex had an uneasy peace with all this; he was close to Dean, and he respected him as the pater familias, but often wished his father would give him more space to maneuver, a bigger corral with lower fences.

Some of that dated to his childhood in Connecticut, when Dean leaned hard on him to go to Yale, his alma mater. Alex balked at that, and ended up going to Brown. He never regretted it, but even now Dean would occasionally get in a little dig about his choice; at least, by this time and mercifully enough, it was mostly in jest.

In some ways, Suzy's arrival had been a welcome distraction. Dean was so besotted with her that he had less time to suggest, complain and – yes, meddle – in Alex and Lisa's life. Where Alex had once fielded calls every other day or so, that frequency was down to about once weekly.

Oddly, for someone who had spent his career in communications – albeit, advertising – Dean was a pronounced technophobe and refused to get onto email. He had a cellphone, of course, but had only gotten it a few years earlier – and he adamantly refused to learn how to text. When he was asked about it, he simply said gruffly, "That's for kids."

At bottom, though, Alex was happy for Dean. His father was almost 73, and his health was strong; he was sturdy and muscular still, and he had a headful of graying hair – Alex was forever grateful that he hadn't been bequeathed the early baldness genes so many men had. He had no use for the shaved-head look – didn't that used to be just for bikers? Dean's hair was thinning slightly, and liver spots had started to freckle his hands, but he could have passed for almost 10 years younger.

Dean did have a bit of a paunch now, like so many men his age – it seemed to be practically a rite of passage, or more likely an acknowledgement that a flat belly was no longer worth the effort. He had the same square face that Alex had, with a firm jaw and deep-set eyes under brows now dusted with white. Deep wrinkles, like miniature furrows, were etched outside his eyes.

Certainly, it was hard to detect any want in Dean's lifestyle. The house in Westport had been lovely and gracious, not far from the placid Saugatuck River. His new condo was large and beautifully appointed – ornamented with rock facing and Palladian windows - and overlooked the 14th fairway at Oak Highlands Country Club, where women had been granted membership only a generation earlier, like a royal dispensation.

It was definitely old school. Dean played golf there a couple of times a week with his buddies in the warmer months, and he drove a silver Mercedes C550, a gift he had given to Suzy (and himself) a few months earlier. For a retiree, Dean was doing very well indeed.

Dean had a thing for German cars: He'd had several BMWs, including a convertible many years earlier, and it seemed to comport with his vision of himself as an auto afficianado. "You know what they say about nice cars?" Dean had joked with Alex a few days after buying this latest one. "If it's not German, it's vermin." Alex remembered rolling his eyes at that one. He and Lisa easily made do with a Volvo wagon and a Mini Cooper, which Alex had bought because he liked the styling and sporty handling. They definitely weren't on a Mercedes budget.

I bet Suzy is accustomed to luxury, he thought; she just presented herself that way. Dean had told him that she'd left Atlanta after her husband died and moved to Westchester at the behest of old friends, also from Atlanta; that struck Alex as a bit odd, but she'd told them she needed a change of scene. Those old friends were acquaintances of Dean's who had more or less set them up at a country club dinner – and they quickly clicked.

Alex didn't remotely begrudge his father for marrying again: he was still vital, and the years leading up to his former wife's death had been hard on everyone and everything. Dementia is an awful disease, like a never-ending gale, and the family had battened themselves down as it raged. His mother, Marjorie, had failed to respond to various drugs dispensed by the best doctors, and her last days were three forlorn months in a high-end nursing home, then a hospice. At the end, she recognized no one.

Dean had done what he could, and what he knew he owed her, but her care – both at home and then outside it – was an ordeal. There was no other word for it. At first, she was confounded, then angry and frequently in denial. Dates and appointments slipped away; before long, she became too confused to drive. It was a downward spiral that slid inexorably into an abyss.

For several years after her death, Dean threw himself into activities like golf and teaching a course at the local community college. But a cloud hovered over him, no matter what, and it had taken Suzy's arrival to dissipate it. He was a new man, and as demonstrably proud of her as a child with a new toy.

Alex had talked to Lisa about it, and he had to agree: sporting the new woman so proudly was definitely a guy thing; a woman with a new beau would have been more discreet, more concerned about sharing him with the family and not the world at large. If Dean had carried a placard, "This Is My New Wife," it would have been only slightly more demonstrative.

Children are always curious about new companions for their parents – and especially new husbands or wives – and Alex was no different. He felt himself sizing Suzy up, weighing every word and action, like a juror assessing a defendant on the stand. Talking it over with Lisa now and then, he felt himself wanting to pull back, to dial down his antennae. But it was hard. His father was well off, and he could certainly leave his estate to Suzy – something Alex would never have dreamed of a year earlier.

His sister, Debra, was in no position to weigh in the same way. She lived in Portland, Oregon, and had recently been through a nasty divorce. She was lying low, and, as Alex learned, drinking considerably. Her first contact with Suzy was at the wedding, and that initial meeting was a bit strained – in part because Suzy sensed (as everyone could) that Debra was not doing well.

Yet it was Suzy who had reached out and tried to befriend her, which Alex took as a good sign; Debra's agitation put a bit of a strain on the ceremony and the reception, but when she was bundled off for LaGuardia the next day, the worst was forgotten.

4.

"Jason, you get let us know if you want seconds," Suzy said brightly from her spot at the head of the table. "There's plenty more of everything."

Alex watched as his son nodded and mumbled something he couldn't catch; Alex sensed that his son wilted at times under Suzy's megawatt smile. His mother - Jason's grandmother - who'd died four years earlier, had been a much more comforting soul.

"I'll take some more roast beef," Jennifer said brightly.

"Coming right up," Dean said, rising from his chair and moving to the sideboard.

For Alex, the setting was new but the routine was etched in his brain: Roast beef on Sunday nights, usually accompanied by potatoes and different vegetables – peas one time, carrots another, or maybe broccoli. Dean was a creature of habit, and he did most of the cooking, as he had for years.

Suzy, self-assured as always, wore a white ribbed turtleneck and black slacks. Her blonde hair was pulled back enough to see she had on a pair of diamond stud earrings; her ears were relatively small and set close to her head. Taking a sip of wine, she turned to Jennifer and asked, "How is your field hockey going, Jennifer?"

"Oh, good," Jennifer replied quickly. "Our team's really doing well, and I'm having fun."

"She scored two goals in the last game," Lisa said, smiling at her daughter.

"That's my girl," Dean exclaimed.

"Really? That's good," Suzy said, half-turning to Lisa as she spoke. If she's just feigning interest, Alex thought, she's doing it well. "How much longer does the season last?"

"A couple more weeks," Jennifer said. "Our last game is just before Thanksgiving, but we could go longer if we qualify for states – and I think we will. We're leading our division."

"That's wonderful." Suzy flashed her big smile. "And what about you, Jason? What have you been up to lately?" Her voice was an alto, smooth and unaccented; it would be difficult indeed, Alex thought, to figure out from listening to her just where she was from.

Alex saw his son flush quickly and look down at his hands before lifting his head. "Not much, really." He was silent for a moment. "I'm working on some set design for our school play."

"Really?" She did seem interested. "That sounds fascinating. What's the play?"

"Well, we're doing 'Rent,' but it's not the full Broadway play – it's scaled down some. But it will still mean having a lot of apartment buildings and street stuff."

"Hmmm." Suzy looked reflective. "That sounds like quite a challenge."

"I guess so. I've been sketching some things out on my computer, but we're a ways away from having to actually build the sets."

Alex spoke up. "Jason designed the sets last year, too. It was a little different – 'The Music Man.'"

"I can see that," Suzy mused aloud. "Urban and rural – quite different."

"But it was a smash – well, you know," Dean chimed in. "Especially good for those of us old enough to remember the original. The boy who did the lead role was really fine."

"Were you in a school play yourself, Granddy?" Lisa asked, using the name the kids had for their grandfather.

Dean smiled. "Oh, sure. But at Choate, like most prep schools, it was very proper – you know, Gilbert and Sullivan. In my senior year, it was 'Pirates of Penzance.' I was one of the pirates – not very memorable."

"I bet you were very piratical," Suzy said, grinning. "Eye patch and all?"

Dean pursed his lips for a moment, reflecting. "Actually, no. I think I just had a head scarf. I don't think I would have scared a four-year-old."

A chuckle rippled around the table, and Dean beamed as if he'd delivered a spectacular punch line. "And that was the end of my acting career – at least until I had to tell my bosses at work what they wanted to hear. That required some skill." They all laughed again. It was a warm family moment that lingered subtly, like moonglow on an open field.

The dishes were cleared, and the extended Perry family retreated into the living room. Dean had turned on the big-screen TV to a rerun of *Downton Abbey*, which he knew was one of Suzy's favorites. Maggie Smith, the family matriarch on the show, was declaiming on something or other. Suzy watched from an armchair, as did Alex; his family was seated on the red leather sofa in various stages of near-repose.

"It's hard to believe what the lords and ladies had in those days," Suzy said, her gaze fixed on the screen. "Imagine having servants waiting on you hand and foot – and even a ladies' maid to help you with your clothes!"

"It certainly wasn't good for your privacy," Lisa replied. "And obviously, the servants loved to gossip about anything going on upstairs."

"Well, there was plenty to gossip about," said Alex, rubbing his knee. "Rape, children out of wedlock, financial troubles – could be a modern soap opera – except this was done so much better."

"I really don't like their clothes," Jennifer exclaimed, as the others looked at her and chuckled. "They look uncomfortable, and silly."

"You're talking about the women, aren't you?" asked Suzy, grinning.

"Oh, yes. The men all wore boring tweeds and all." Jennifer paused, then exclaimed: "And those dumb little hats the women wore – ugh!"

They all laughed. "It was a different way of life," Lisa said softly. "And one that won't be coming back."

"But it had its good points, especially if you were in the money, so to speak," Suzy argued. "There weren't many rules for the upper classes. You know what they say is the difference between crazy and eccentric? Money."

Alex looked over and smiled at her. He'd heard that one a number of times, and it always struck him as dead-on. He studied her quickly, seeing the firm profile, a hint of a tan – she and Dean had been in Hilton Head the week earlier – and a general lightness, an ease with which she carried herself. She was always poised, seemingly alert; it was clear that slouching had been taboo in her childhood.

Dean was standing behind Suzy's chair with his hands on her shoulders. "Does that make me eccentric?" He smiled with his eyes, crinkling.

Suzy leaned back and stroked his arm as she half-turned and looked up at him. "No, dear man, you're not. You're as sane as the day is long."

Dean looked down at her tenderly. "Well, it's nice to get a seal of approval."

Suzy excused herself and went to the powder room, which carried some of her touches: plush towels, neatly arranged, that matched the general light green décor; a soap dish with a round bar of scented soap, big as a small avocado; a bouquet of silk orchids, arching in white and light pink.

She reached into her compact and added a little powder to her cheeks. She appraised herself, as she did several times daily; the ash-blonde hair, carefully cut, was thick but considerably shorter than it was when she was young and was pulled back from her face symmetrically. Her eyes were bright, with minimal mascara, and the brows carefully penciled in. She had an oval face with a thin nose and a sensuous mouth that she daubed lightly with lipstick, often in shades of red that carried a hint of orange.

She'd put on some weight in the last 20 years, but who hadn't? Maybe Jane Fonda, but Suzy had dismissed the exercise mania that had swept through her circle in middle age. She didn't like to work so hard, and it didn't matter to the men she met; they seemed to like women with a little meat on their bones and not the "skinny birds," as she dubbed them.

"Not bad, old girl," she muttered softly to herself, leaning in for a closeup. "You're holding up pretty well."

Suzy thought quickly about Jennifer and Jason. They seemed like good kids, well-mannered, but in general she had little use for children. Yet she knew how to talk to them; it was a skill she had acquired over the years, and she knew how to adjust the charm meter for the situation. It served her ends. She was in a new family now, and she wanted – no, needed – their approval. If her *bonhomie* was a little fake, what of it?

Suzy rinsed her hands quickly, looked to the mirror again with a half-smile, and turned to the door.

Pasadena, CA

5.

The low, sullen clouds and the spitting rain weren't what most people associated with Southern California, but it was January, and storms could roll in off the Pacific at any time. Alicia Tallman thrummed her hands on the steering wheel as the traffic ahead inched on to the Ventura Freeway. Another day, another dollar – no, it was certainly better than that, she had to admit. But rush hour was a horror in LA, and the rain made it so much worse.

The image of Velazquez's paintings of the Spanish *infanta* popped fully realized into her head; it would be among the next set of paintings she would be talking about in her class at Cal State Northridge. She'd modified the course slightly this semester, and wanted to emphasize Velazquez, Goya and other Iberian masters and not dwell so much on the French contemporaries like Watteau and his airy representations; Velazquez was much more real. And the *infanta* was truly ugly, not idealized at all. In comparison, the blithe figures of Ingres or Watteau were virtually one-dimensional.

When she turned off at the exit for Pasadena, she was still daydreaming a bit when the Audi ahead of her slammed on its brakes and she had to do the same, with a bit of a start. It seemed that several cars ahead on the ramp, someone had swerved to avoid the car ahead that was slow to get into the turn lane. Horns honked gratingly. Alicia glanced at her watch: 4:35. Alison, her oldest daughter, would be home from high school, while her youngest, Isabelle, was probably still en route from junior high after band practice, catching a ride from a classmate.

Five minutes later, driving the curving lanes past a series of Tudor and brick mansions, largely hidden by lush landscaping, she arrived at her beige ranch-style house on a straight street lined with tall palms. She tapped on the garage door opener and waited as the heavy door rose slowly; then she eased the brown Buick Encore in beside the girls' bikes and the red loveseat she kept meaning to unload.

Tomorrow would be Isabelle's birthday, and they would celebrate by going to La Reserva, her favorite restaurant. Isabelle was 13, too old for birthday parties, and she was a level-headed girl who understood such things. But birthdays always held a certain sadness for Alicia, like a dirge that could be heard only faintly.

Since the divorce, Brian was scarcely part of the girls' lives. He had taken a new job across the country in Charlotte, and while they would Facetime with him periodically and get gifts, they hadn't seen him since he made a quick visit the summer before. Alicia wondered about whether he was considering remarrying; she thought he must have a girlfriend. He was smart and handsome, working in financial management, and she sensed he might be thinking about a second family. A lot of men did.

But it wasn't just Brian that troubled her. Alicia was an only child, and the girls' only cousins were three from two of Brian's siblings that were on the other side of the country. More than that, however, there were no grandparents from her side. Her father had died tragically, of a heart attack, and not long after that her mother was no longer a part of her life – literally.

After the funeral, her mother had sold their house in suburban St. Louis and literally disappeared. Alicia had been in her third year of her Ph.D program at UCLA, and she was deep into her studies when her mother, Bettina, abruptly left their home, her bridge-club buddies and the neighborhood Alicia had grown up in. Left, gone, like the sun sinking below the horizon.

The two had never truly been close – Bettina (Tina to friends and family) doted on her husband, David, and it always seemed to Alicia that the love Tina had for him eclipsed any chance for her to feel the same warmth. Indeed, there was a perceptible coldness, tempered by a thin veneer of cheeriness, that Tina evinced to her – and it had been like that for as long as she could remember. Her mother simply wasn't *maternal*, not like her friends' moms.

As a child, she gradually came to accept it, but it had always tugged at her heart. She always felt she was competing for her father's love – and he clearly loved them both – but her mother always had her hand one rung higher on the ladder.

She could never forget the phone call that came that one brisk day in February after she had finished dinner in her rented apartment in Westwood. It was a month after the funeral, a wet-eyed affair that had been difficult for everyone. Bettina had called her – that was a rare event – and proceeded to tell her that she was selling the house and that there would be a substantial settlement for Alicia from the proceeds.

"Where are you going to go?" Alicia had asked.

"I don't know," her mother had replied with a chilly reserve.

"Close by, though?"

"No, I don't think so." There was a long pause. "Your father was my world here, and it won't be the same without him. I think I have to move on. I'll let you know when I decide." She coughed. "The lawyers are settling the estate, and you will be getting a check in the mail. Hopefully before long."

Money had never been a problem, and Alicia hadn't really thought much about what might be coming to her; she assumed her mother would essentially inherit it all and set up something for her in the future. She tossed Bettina an olive branch. "Would you come out and see me first?"

There was a pregnant pause. "I don't think so, dear. But I'll be in touch."

That was 21 years ago. There were no phone calls, no letters, no cards for Christmas or birthdays or any other occasion. Her mother had walked out of her life, seemingly without a backward glance. Alicia had indeed gotten a large six-figure check, along with a brief and formal letter from the family attorney, several months after the call; that allowed her to pay off all her student loans and buy a nicer car – and start an investment portfolio.

When she and Brian were dating, she was loath for months to tell him about her mother, until it could no longer be hidden. He was somewhat troubled by the situation – he had loving parents and two younger brothers – but he accepted her as a sort of orphan, a fledgling that had fallen from the nest, and it became something of a mission for him to cosset her, to keep her from further harm.

After 17 years of marriage, something had changed; perhaps both of them had changed. They lost patience with each other, and the things they shared didn't bring the same pleasure. The girls were growing fast, and Brian seemed to love them, she thought, but he grew more distant, spent longer hours at the office. Alicia wondered at times if he was having an affair – her mind was quick to suspect the worst – but there was never any evidence of that. If it had happened, he had wiped the prints clean.

In the end, the split had been fairly amicable. She wasn't given to tears, but it had been hard telling the girls about it, and she started sobbing as she watched the disquiet on their faces. Brian agreed to let her have the house and consented to what seemed like a generous level of child support, as well as a promise to fund much of the girls' college tuition.

A few months after the divorce was finalized, he landed a job across the country and made plans to leave. There was an awkward dinner at a fine restaurant the night before he left; it was one of those family moments that linger in memory in stark relief, like a woodcut. There was a moist embrace outside the restaurant for the girls, and a perfunctory peck on the cheek for Alicia. Then he was gone.

At first, his absence brought back memories or her mother's disappearance. Alicia had heard about siblings who were deeply estranged and never talked, but a parent? Now and then she racked her brain, trying to catalog what brought her mother to this separation, but she couldn't put her finger on it. As the years went by, her mother became only a remote memory, like a dream that dissolves into fleeting fragments on waking.

She never expected to hear from her again. Bettina was almost surely still alive – but how could she know? Her mother had probably remarried and changed her name, and she could be anywhere. She mused now and again about hiring a private detective to see if she could locate her, but she recoiled at the expense – and the notion that she didn't know where to start. St. Louis, probably, but that was just the first door; there could be others, and blind alleys as well.

These thoughts stole over Alicia now and then, most often late at night when the kids were asleep. She knew that she loved them far more than her mother had ever cared for her, and that gave her some solace, some reassurance that a family stain hadn't seeped into another generation.

For years, Alicia had kept a portrait of her parents in middle age on a bedside table – her father, beaming, and her mother, with her blonde hair pulled back and a smile that could have lit up the studio. Alicia knew she would never have her mother's looks or figure, but she knew she was attractive – the attention she had gotten from men over the years attested to that. But the photo had been relegated to a bureau drawer and she rarely looked at it anymore.

Westchester County, NY

6.

Dean and Suzy huddled for warmth like pigeons on a ledge. The afternoon was raw and windy, with rain having passed through in a motorcade of black clouds a few hours earlier. The open stands by the field offered no protection whatsoever, but there was a small and enthusiastic crowd watching the girls' field hockey game. Lisa sat a few feet away, wearing a fleece jacket, gloves and a ski cap – she would stand up now and then to cheer Jennifer on.

Lisa didn't really care that much for the sport – she had played it, not especially well, in high school – but she knew it was Jennifer's passion, and she tried to make as many home games as she could. As fall made its long retreat toward winter, that was less and less appealing; it was just damned uncomfortable at times. But there was always a group of other mothers, and Alex had cajoled Dean and Suzy into coming to watch this game. After all, it was a state playoff round.

So here they were, in the aluminum stands that schools everywhere set up for spectators. Comfort wasn't part of the equation: the stands were in long rows with no backs, with just a lower set of planks for resting one's feet. There were stands on both sides, for home and visitors, but the latter were much shorter, an acknowledgement that while parents might make the trip for the visitors, few others did. This wasn't high school football, for God's sake, which even in Westchester was an event, though hardly the religious rite that draws so many worshippers in Texas or Oklahoma.

"Fun, isn't it?" Lisa's smiled crinkled her face, and she drew in her arms to show she was shivering.

"Oh, yeah," Dean smiled back. "But not something you'd want to make a habit of."

"You can say that again," Suzy said, staring straight ahead. She had on a long camel hair coat with the collar turned up, a pair of leather gloves and boots – but nothing on her head, which let the wind rake her hair.

They turned their attention back to the game, which had none of the grace or elegance of soccer; it was more like a slow game of keep-away, with the girls bent over like hunchbacks, their sticks jabbing at the ball, moving it forward in short passes. Jennifer was a mid-fielder charged with distributing the ball to the forwards and breaking up any attacks from the other team. The turf was still damp and muddy in spots, which made progress that much harder; Alex had joked to Lisa that the games often plodded on like trench warfare.

The teams changed ends after the first quarter, still no score. Lisa looked over to the hill between the field and the red-brick school and watched the branches in the tall oaks dance in the breeze, the brown leaves that hadn't yet fallen twirling and shimmying. Then she shivered again. "Let's go, Wildcats!" she shouted.

She focused on Jennifer, who was more or less standing at attention while one of her teammates moved to take a shot on goal. In some ways, Jennifer was almost indistinguishable from the others, with her dark ponytail held in place with a gold headband, a long maroon jersey and tartan skirt. Above the knee socks, her legs were rosy with the cold.

Then the Wildcats scored – a lucky goal that deflected off the stick of a defender and into the goal. The team ran into a small huddle and congratulated the girl that had scored, a time-honored tradition, before the ball was brought back to the midfield circle for a face-off. Lisa saw Dean and Suzy cheering, though without a lot of enthusiasm, and Suzy stamped her feet, apparently reacting to the cold.

As they watched, Jennifer took a pass and feinted past one defender, then moved the ball toward the right wing. Two other defenders converged on her, and she deked the ball past the first one. As the second came up to her, the girl slipped and her feet shot out; one cleated foot caught Jennifer in mid-calf with an audible slap. Jennifer went down with a loud yelp, falling on her shoulder and side, and immediately reached for her leg, moaning. In a moment, her startled teammates came rushing to her.

Lisa had watched this transpire, almost in slow motion. "Oh no," she yelled, and started running – if that was the word – down the stands toward the field. Dean seemed dumbstruck, and mouthed "oh, my God." He glanced at Suzy and squeezed her hand, but what he saw startled him. She was staring at the field, expressionless.

"Do you think she's hurt?" Suzy said finally, almost matter-of-factly.

"Of course she is," Dean almost shouted. "Can't you see that?" The coach and two of the officials had joined the ring of players around Jennifer, who was grimacing and holding her leg.

Lisa stood anxiously on the sidelines as the trainer assigned to the game tested Jennifer's leg and eventually had her try to stand. She did so, but it was awkward, like an egret on one leg – she couldn't put her weight on it. She was clearly crying as the trainer and one of the officials put a shoulder under each of her arms and helped her off the field. Her left leg was almost straight, and her heel would now and then touch lightly on the turf as the slow procession inched its way off the field.

While the game continued shortly, it was over for Lisa. She hugged Jennifer on the sideline bench, and it was clear her daughter needed medical attention.

"Oh, honey, this is awful," Lisa said. She wanted to sound reassuring, but to a red-faced daughter in obvious pain, it was daunting. "I imagine they'll want to take you to the hospital and find out what's wrong."

"Okay, mom," Jennifer replied between sniffles. "It hurts a lot, and I hope it's not broken."

One of the assistant coaches, a smallish woman with her hair tied back in a severe ponytail, knelt by Jennifer and touched her leg, which brought a yelp of pain. A nurse practitioner who acted as a doctor for the home games – tall and raw-boned, with shaggy blonde hair that whipped in the wind – soon joined her and prodded several places on the leg, asking Jennifer for feedback on where it hurt.

"We need to take her for x-rays," the nurse said, turning to Lisa. "More of a precaution than anything else. I'll pull the car over and we'll put her in."

"Fine. I'd like to go with her."

"Of course. You can follow me to the hospital."

She left Jennifer on the bench and started walking around the stands toward the parking lot. Dean and Suzy were at the foot of the stands to intercept her.

"Is she okay? How bad is it?" Dean stared at her, hoping for good news.

"We don't know. She's obviously in a lot of pain. It could be a broken leg, but maybe not." She paused and looked at them. "They're going to take her to the emergency room."

"Do you want us to come?" Dean asked almost beseechingly.

"I don't think so – no need," Lisa said crisply. "It may take a while. Obviously, there's not much point in you guys staying at this point."

"Certainly not," Dean snorted. "You'll let us know how she is?"

"Of course."

"I do hope she's alright," Suzy said evenly. "Such a shame, and in an important game." Her arms were folded in front of her.

"I guess we'll find out soon enough," Lisa replied, and walked briskly toward the parking lot. Dean watched her go, but Suzy just looked at the field, impassively, as the game lumbered on.

7.

"I tell you, it was just weird. She showed almost no emotion at all." Lisa was painstakingly cutting up some plum tomatoes to put into a salad. She wore a black running suit that emphasized her slenderness; her hands, too, were slender, with long fingers and unpainted nails. Her hair was cut in front in a modified page boy that framed her face nicely and accentuated her hazel eyes. She looked at her husband almost quizzically.

Alex leaned against the granite island, speckled like a bird's egg, with his arms apart and sighed audibly. "Well, we know it's not her grandchild, but still… Was it completely obvious that she was badly hurt?"

"Completely. And Dean was very sympathetic, very concerned."

They were getting ready for dinner, four hours after Jennifer had been injured. She was seen quite quickly at the hospital and evaluated by a tall young resident with longish brown hair who smiled easily and tried to put them at ease. Lisa had accompanied her for x-rays, and was basically at her side through the whole sequence of tests.

In the end, the news was good: Jennifer had a bad bone bruise and a developing hematoma on her calf that promised to turn an ugly eggplant hue in the days ahead, but nothing broken. Still, she had difficulty putting weight on the leg and had been given a set of wooden crutches. When they made it home, Alex was waiting and helped Jennifer up the carpeted stairs to her room, touching her as lightly as if she were a wounded bird. She had smiled reflexively when she saw him and tried to make light of it.

"I really got it this time, Dad. I just hope the girl who did this sends me some flowers."

Alex smiled and shook his head. "Don't count on that, honey. At least you guys won the game." One of the other moms had called Lisa and reported on the outcome, 2-1 for Rye Country Day.

"I know. That's great, but I won't be part of whatever happens next."

"No, that's true. But you know what they say – there's always next year."

"Yeah, I guess so." She screwed up her face. "Now I just have to be sure I'm ready for lacrosse season."

"Oh, you will be." Alex grinned. "I know you. Nothing will keep you from that."

"I sure hope not."

"How's the pain?"

"Oh, it hurts a lot, but they've given me some painkillers."

Now Jennifer was lying down in her room, and the tall grandfather clock in the living room struck seven. Jason was up in his room as well, part of his customary after-school retreat. That included some homework, Alex believed, but social media and games like Mobile Strike loomed larger; Jason was also a heavy Instagram user, like his friends, and Alex had to periodically check the family data plan to make sure things were under some semblance of control.

Back in the kitchen, Alex reached into one of the cupboards and pulled out a set of dinner plates. Turning to Lisa, he asked, "D'you want me to talk to Dad about this? Not that he didn't see it first hand, of course. But in so many ways, for him, she can do no wrong."

Lisa was silent for a few moments. "I don't know. I'm not sure what good it would do. It's just one more thing we seem to have learned about Suzy."

Alex nodded. He trusted Lisa implicitly on many things: she was smart, level-headed and calm, sometimes almost preternaturally so. Her mode of exercise comported with that demeanor: yoga and pilates. She had tried biking with him years earlier, but didn't like the chafing from the seat or the tightness that stole over her calves after miles of pedaling.

Alex set the plates on the island. "Indeed, just one more item for the ledger, just like Rushmore." Rushmore was their eight-year-old black Lab, who had growled slightly when he first met Suzy – a highly unusual reaction. With most strangers, he would approach and then wade in to be petted, wagging his curved tail like a metronome.

Suzy, acting slightly flustered, had said that she and dogs didn't seem to get along. "We never had one growing up, and Avery and I never had one," she'd said. "I'm not around them that much at all. Maybe they sense that." She had shrugged and smiled almost apologetically, but Alex and Lisa had soon traded glances; it was awkward. Ever since then, Rushmore had kept his distance from her when Suzy was in the house.

Alex reached for the silverware drawer. "Oh, and remember that we have dinner with them at the club on Friday night."

Lisa's lips curled into a faint smile. "Don't worry – I'll be on my best behavior."

Suzy stepped into the closet and eyed her wardrobe, something she did every day, often more than once. Most of it she had acquired in Atlanta, where women in her circle dressed well and often in dresses when they went out, looking – well, trying to look - as sophisticated as they often dreamed they might be.

She fingered a navy dress with white trim, a Donna Karan cut just above the knee, where she liked it. Next to it was a Dolce & Gabbana suit with a ruffled skirt. A couple of Prada dresses hung together, both in subtle prints. Her eye moved slightly to the right, to a pair of wrap dresses from Diane von Furstenberg, so *de rigeur* in the 90s.

She looked down at the racks of shoes below. I do have a lot of sandals, she thought – probably too many for Westchester, where the weather was just too cold or wet too often for open-toed shoes. Red. Green. Blue. Black. Leather and fabric, low-heeled and cork-heeled, enough for a different look for weeks on end. Avery had let her spend whatever she wanted, and like an addict searching for a fix, she would drive to her favorite shops and emerge with two or three new pairs.

But high heels were a very minor part of the collection; she never took to the stiletto look of Jimmy Choos or Manolo Blahniks, and they hurt her ankles. And she didn't need the height – she wasn't some petite fashion plate looking for an extra five inches or a bustling executive who loved what high heels did for the look of her calves.

Suzy blew out some air from her lips and turned her gaze to her collection of coats. Dean had bought her a sheared mink during their first winter together; it was almost criminally soft, but it was safely ensconced in a white plastic cover and she could merely make out its shape, a ghostly rectangle suspended from a padded hanger. Well, it was getting cold enough to consider wearing it now – the nights were falling below freezing. She smiled. Wealth did indeed have its privileges.

8.

Alex settled into the Aeron chair at his office and picked up the yellow mug - one of several they had picked up at an art fair years earlier – and turned on his computer. He clicked on his Google calendar and looked at the entries for the day: Not bad – he had an interview in the morning and another in the afternoon for a story he was writing on the latest treadmills. One of the interviews was with a safety expert who was deeply concerned about the potential hazards of some of the more sophisticated machines.

He leaned back and gazed out the windows, which offered an expansive view of the parklike grounds, the tree branches now mostly bare, like gnarled fingers. Much of the grass was still a verdant green, but it, too, would be turning toward brown in December.

Julie Epstein, his managing editor, poked her head in. "'Morning." Shortish and a bit on the plump side, she had a lopsided smile and a shock of curly brown hair that could star in a hair-color ad. "What's your day like?"

"Oh, nothing big. A couple of interviews." Alex pursed his lips as he looked at her. "How're we doing on the cover story?"

"I think we're in good shape," she said, her arms crossed. "He and I had a good talk the other day, and he has some good sources. I think it will be here early next week."

"Good. How 'bout that contributed piece on the latest ellipticals?"

She shrugged slightly. "I don't really know. We'll have to see. I think it may come in tomorrow, but I don't really know what to expect." She paused. "The photos should be good, though."

"Okay. Lemme know when it comes in."

"Will do." She smiled and walked out, and Alex swiveled to look out the window again; a loose assembly of geese was ambling toward the pond while a sentinel stood guard, outlined against the water like a signpost.

It wasn't *The New York Times* or *The Wall Street Journal*, but *Recreational Equipment* magazine was a wonderful fit for Alex. The hours were regular, he was well-paid, and he was becoming something of a recognized expert on the industry. Better still, he was spared the long train rides and the enervating delays that went with commuting to Manhattan. Here, he could be at the office in 20 minutes, half an hour at the worst, if traffic snarled as it often did in pelting rain or snow.

He'd made his peace with working at a "trade" magazine, which he knew wasn't for everyone in journalism. Big-name publications were a siren song for many, even if egos and self-worth were on the chopping block practically every day. And the newspaper industry was an incipient basket case, endlessly consumed with losing circulation, money and influence amid the stampede to the Internet; a winning model was as elusive as Fermat's Last Theorem.

He'd done a stint at the *Westchester Herald,* years of sitting in endless town council meetings - with their preening small-time politicians and annoying gadflies - and interviewing city officials about the intricacies of sewer projects, before being promoted to regional editor. He was periodically forced to work weekends, and when a new owner came in and starting taking an ax to the budget, he felt himself with his back to a wall. After a few months of searching, and with the help of a recruiter, the magazine job beckoned, and he took it. Editor in chief, with a staff of four – he could certainly live with that.

What's more, Alex felt a certain weight lifted off his shoulders when he left the paper that was almost palpable. He didn't like the vagaries of the work shifts, the skinnying down of resources – and he didn't like what those did to his psyche. He was more short-tempered, more glum; he was drinking when he came home, and not just beer or wine. Lisa couldn't help but notice, and that troubled him.

It was around that time, late in his stint with the paper, that he had a brief fling with one of his co-workers. It started at a bar, after work, where a group of them had convened at the end of the day. Kate was a nice-looking, sandy-haired blonde who was outspoken and flirtatious, and after a couple of drinks, they had eyes only for each other.

But Alex was cautious, concerned about not hurting Lisa. Not for him the early morning homecoming and the lamely delivered excuse about working late that would only raise suspicions. When he and Kate finally did go to bed, it was during the afternoon, at her apartment; it was quick, eager and mutually satisfying. After two more such encounters, however, Alex started to get cold feet, and it was a relief when Kate told him she'd accepted a job in the city with a top magazine. A few weeks later, she was gone, and with it his wanderlust.

Now, his magazine office was in a park-type setting in White Plains; the building housed a number of other businesses – none of them in publishing. It was a comfortable, modern space, with soft neutral carpeting, small individual offices and lots of amenities nearby – and the technology was top-notch.

He also liked that "business casual" had taken over most American offices, like his, spreading over time from the cities outward like ripples in a pond; looking professional didn't entail wearing a coat and tie, as Dean had done all of his working life. Hell, he'd even worn suits most of the time. Things had come a long way since the dull uniformity of *The Man in the Gray Flannel Suit*, and Alex, for one, was mighty glad of it.

In the past few years, he had found himself turning more and more to the Internet for research. Yes, it was an enormous, messily disorganized warehouse that could be maddeningly obtuse, but if the search parameters were right, it was a marvel. He'd never had to navigate the newspaper libraries of long ago, when everything was in the form of news clips stuffed into paper folders housed in tall file cabinets. Now, that information could be there at the click of a mouse. Amazing.

Take the search he had done a few months ago in the office on Suzy – Suzy Rittenhouse, as she had been known when she set down in Westchester. Putting that name into a Google search had brought up nothing, but when he had wheedled her late husband's name,

Avery, from Dean, he tried that. Up came an obituary from the *Atlanta Constitution* from early in the previous year. Avery Rittenhouse had died of a heart attack at the age of 74.

The obituary mentioned his son and daughter, and his grandchildren, and his position, before his retirement, as president of Southern Property and Casualty, as well as his membership in various clubs, including Augusta National. Alex had almost whistled audibly at that one. Clearly, Avery was an A-lister. The address in Buckhead didn't mean that much to him, though he knew it was the swankiest neighborhood in the city.

That fit neatly, like a jigsaw puzzle piece with a unique shape, into his view of Suzy. She was clearly used to the finer things in life, and knew how to find them.

9.

Suzy slipped out from under the sheets and looked over at Dean as she did so. He was snoring lightly. She glided from the bedroom into the carpeted hallway, lit dimly by the sconce on the wall, and walked slowly to the study, the second door on the left. There was just enough light to navigate safely, and there wasn't any furniture to stumble into. She left the door just ajar as she walked in.

She moved to the desk on the left – his desk – and turned on the table lamp; even that seemed overly bright for a moment, but it was far better than the piercing glare from the overhead. She pulled out her reading glasses from her robe and set them on the bridge of her nose. Sitting down in the padded armchair, she opened the laptop, turned it on and sat back as the screen turned blue, then switched to the wallpaper, in this case a scene of a beautiful mountain lake reflecting an azure sky studded with puffy clouds. A popup asked for the password, which she duly typed in.

The digital clock on the desk cast a fluorescent green glow; it read 1:47.

Scrolling the cursor up to the bookmarks menu, Suzy found the "financials" folder and clicked on it. Up came a series of links, about a half dozen in all. She scrolled down to "Goldman Sachs" and clicked on it, drumming her fingers lightly as the portal screen appeared. It asked for the user name and password, and she went to her desk and pulled out a small yellow slip of paper from under a glass paperweight; on it was the information she'd gotten from Dean the day before.

When the screen came up, she typed in his username and password, noting to herself that they were just the kind that security specialists recommend against: combinations of family names and birthdays. His user name was "Deanper5" and his password was "alexdeb18." She dutifully typed those in and hit "submit."

After a moment, the summary accounts page came up, broken into the various subaccounts: IRAs, brokerage, and checking. But her eyes went quickly to the big number near the top of the screen that showed the total for all the accounts: $5,334,617.

She smiled and sat stock still for a moment, almost as if in meditation. Then she clicked the "x" on the screen to get out of it, and clicked on another bookmark, Dean's gmail account, before closing the laptop and padding back down the hall to the bedroom. As she slipped back under the covers, Dean rolled slightly but didn't wake.

10.

"Ah, that's good." Dean sipped his martini – with two olives, as always – and looked over at Alex. "How's your wine?"

"Very nice," Alex said appreciatively. "I always know they'll serve good stuff."

He and Lisa had met Dean and Suzy in the lobby of the country club and walked to the table that had been reserved for them. Oak Highlands was nothing if not conservatively decorated – some would say stuffy – with a heavy emphasis on oriental rugs, mahogany and subdued lighting. It announced men's club with all the subtlety of a Hemingway sentence. A massive glass chandelier in the center of the dining room presided like a sun, providing most of the light, though each upholstered booth had its own sconce.

He and Lisa sat together, facing Dean and Suzy. Scrolling through the leather-trimmed menu, Alex's eye went to the roast duck, always a favorite; Lisa settled on a Caesar salad with chicken. She had also ordered a white wine, a Sauvignon Blanc from New Zealand.

"How are things at the magazine?" Dean asked. It was now three weeks before Christmas, and he wore a striped Oxford shirt and navy sweater vest topped with a subtly patterned sport coat.

"Fine," Alex said matter-of-factly. "Advertising has been pretty strong, and I'm generally happy with the editorial."

"Yes, advertising helps pay the bills, doesn't it?" Dean chuckled at the sledgehammer-subtle allusion to his former life.

"It certainly does. But we're looking at hiring a new rep firm we think could do even better. They want to expand our classified section. It would be something of a hedge, too, if display ads fall off."

"I suppose. I don't know anything about that side of the house," Dean said.

"Lisa, how are things at your job?" Suzy asked after a moment. She wore a black-and-white print dress in a kind of Chinese pattern that looked especially stylish, complemented by a black onyx necklace and a pair of square black earrings. The dress was Prada, one of her favorites; indeed, she had a half-dozen in various shapes and colors that occupied a special niche in her closet.

"Oh, good, though I always wish we had a few more people and more resources," Lisa replied smoothly. "But that's the nonprofit world for you. We're too dependent on the kindness of strangers." She smiled a bit ruefully.

"Yes, dear, I'm sure that's true." Suzy became animated. "When I was on the board of the Atlanta Art Museum, we were always casting about for some kind of income sources apart from the usual donors. You know: parties, fund-raisers with artists, all that kind of thing."

Lisa nodded slightly. "I didn't realize you had done that. How many years were you on the board?"

"Oh, six or seven. This goes back a ways. I did it once the children were out of the house." She pulled her hair behind her ear with her left hand.

Alex and Lisa had heard from Dean that Suzy had two step-children, a boy and girl, Tom and Robin, who were about a decade younger than he and Lisa. Both still lived in the Atlanta area. Beyond that, they knew very little. Tom and Robin hadn't made it to the wedding, which had been a small ceremony, quickly put together – almost as casually as a dinner invitation among a select coterie of friends.

The waiter, a tall, dark-haired fellow with a tie and tartan plaid vest, came and asked for their orders, which he took with an almost exaggerated politeness. Ladies first, of course.

When he was gone, Lisa looked over at Suzy and asked, "Are you planning to go down to Atlanta over Christmas and visit with your children and grandchildren?"

Suzy returned her gaze. "Step-children," she said coolly. "No, not this year. Your father has promised us a special trip." She turned to Dean. "Do you want to tell them, dear?"

"Sure. We've booked two nights at the Ritz on Central Park. We'll take in the lights and the tree at Rockefeller Plaza, since Suzy has never seen it." He looked at them both in turn. "We would be there just before Christmas, and come back on Christmas eve in time to celebrate here."

"That sounds terrific," Alex murmured. "So, Suzy, you've never been to New York at Christmas? It really is very special." There was a light hum from other diners and the clinking of glasses and silverware, so he leaned forward slightly to make himself better understood.

"That's what I keep hearing," she said. "I asked Avery about it a few times, but he didn't like the idea of the cold weather and the crowds." She laughed lightly. "I understood. We've seen it on TV, of course, but there isn't anything like the real thing, I'm sure. I'm really looking forward to it."

"How many grandchildren do you have?" Lisa asked.

"Three." Suzy rubbed her arm reflexively. "Tom has two and Robin has one. They're all under 5, so I'll be looking at toys." She smiled, lifting the corners of her mouth slightly.

"I guess they're really too young to miss their grandfather," Lisa mused. She went on, as if she were picking at a thread. "I imagine you'll want to go for a visit next year."

"Oh, probably." To Lisa, Suzy's smile seemed a bit forced. "That depends on what your father has in store for me. I do know he wants to travel." She turned to Dean and squeezed his arm.

Dean returned her smile. "Not sure just where yet, but we'll be working on that, won't we?"

"Absolutely." She beamed as fulsomely as if she were posing for a family photo.

11.

It was two days after Christmas, and Alex was still on the holiday break the company gave everyone. Once again, he mused at the difference between his job and the newspaper business, where the paper had to get out and it was hard for lower-level editors to carve out vacation time; he recalled the time he had to push through a blizzard, the flakes seemingly as big as dimes and the wind blowing them sideways, to make it back from Boston in time for his shift. Never again.

Sitting casually in the family office, he checked his personal emails on the Sony laptop. As an avid bicyclist who rode with a well-organized group on warm-weather weekends, he was used to a flurry of bike-related messages – but not in winter, when the bike was securely stowed in its rack in the garage. Still, he usually had a slew of promotional emails that he looked at once or twice a day; they came from a host of sources: restaurant chains, nonprofits (even Lisa's), political parties and causes, concert promoters, catalog companies, newspapers and magazines – the list went on.

He blew some air out when he saw the message from LinkedIn. Why had he joined, anyway? He wasn't involved in networking in a major way, and he didn't give a whit about the connections the site reported for people he barely knew. But he had signed up when he was still at the *Herald*, when a colleague insisted the site was a vital cog in the networking machine. So, he'd dutifully enrolled and filled out his profile, but it had proved generally as useless to him as a dating website.

Clicking through the stories on *The New York Times* website, he spent maybe 40 minutes reading through items on politics, the arts, business and sports. He still subscribed to the Sunday *Times*, with its array of sections and esoterica – too much to ever get through – but he tried dutifully, and Lisa was a devotee of the Arts section and the magazine. Alex loved the Sunday crosswords, and finished most of them, but the acrostics were another story. They were just damned intimidating.

It was almost noon when he tossed a casual "Be back soon" to Lisa and set off for Dean's to have lunch. The Mini Cooper seats were cold, even in the garage, and the engine sputtered ever so briefly before it caught. He backed out into a largely empty street, where the modest snowfall of a few days earlier was relegated to frozen piles on the curbs, melting slowly in the sun. There would be some black ice at night as it refroze, he thought quickly.

Dean's complex was gated, and Alex punched in the four-digit entry code at the stone gatehouse and eased in. The townhouse was a few streets away, a look-alike in a sea of near uniformity clearly put up by a builder enamored of the British village scheme of gray fieldstone and dark shutters; the streets had ersatz Old World names like Canterbury Court and Sherwood Drive. Alex parked on the street in front of the unit. Dean had told him that Suzy had taken the car to get her nails done and they would have lunch alone.

He went up the flagstone steps to the door, adorned with a classic round Christmas wreath of fir branches with red metal balls. He rang the bell and folded his arms almost involuntarily; it was still chilly, and the sun could only do so much.

Ten minutes later, Dean and Alex were seated in two wrought iron stools at the island in the kitchen. Dean had fixed a couple of grilled cheese sandwiches and a salad of arugula, tomatoes and feta cheese – a sort of Greek salad without the black olives, which Dean had always disliked. Dean had on a black turtleneck and green corduroys; his gray hair was starting to get a bit long in the back, like tufts of crabgrass on an otherwise well-tended lawn. Alex saw a trace of dark circles under his eyes and his face seemed a bit puffy, which was unusual.

Alex took another bite and asked, "Are you and Suzy going to travel south for a while?" Dean had been going down to the Sarasota, Florida, area for years, renting a condo for up to a month at a time when the weather in the Northeast could be routinely expected to be at its worst. The condo was a few minutes' walk from long and curving Siesta Beach, one of the finest beaches in the world.

"I think so." He looked contemplative. "We have to nail it down, but probably in the first week in February. I mentioned Sarasota, but she has friends from Atlanta who are in Naples, and we may go there instead."

"Sounds good. I can look after the condo, as usual." Alex set his sandwich down and wiped his hands on a paper napkin. "Think it will be a month or so?"

"Again, I think so, but I'm not sure."

There was silence for some long moments, then Alex spoke up. "I gather Suzy enjoyed the stay at the Ritz and the big tree. Too bad it had to be so cold."

"Yes, well, that did put a damper on things. But we went to the Met for a half-day, and that was great. Suzy said she hadn't been there in many years." Alex immediately knew that Dean was referring to the Metropolitan Museum of Art and not the Metropolitan Opera; his father enjoyed the symphony but had no interest in opera and the notion of the human voice as a wonderful instrument.

Dean suddenly looked a bit downcast, and he pursed his lips. "Listen, Alex, there's something that happened in New York that has me a little troubled."

"What's that?"

Dean scratched his neck for a moment, distractedly. "Well, it happened the second day we were there. We were having lunch at the Ritz, and this woman came over and insisted she knew Suzy – except she didn't call her Suzy." He blew out a breath. "He called her Tina, Tina Tallman I think it was. She was very insistent."

Alex shrugged. "It certainly wouldn't be the first case of mistaken identity. It happens."

"But this woman wouldn't back off. She said she hadn't seen Suzy in many years, but that she recognized her right away. She said she was from Clayton, Missouri."

"Missouri?"

"But more than that, she said they were in the same bridge club."

Alex stared at his father. "Damn. What did Suzy do?"

"That's just it. She seemed a little flustered, and you know that's not her." He studied his hands for a moment. "She kept saying that the woman was mistaken and she hadn't lived in Missouri, but the woman – and I would say they were about the same age – got a little angry, almost. It certainly wasn't a typical reaction if you mistake someone. She wasn't remotely apologetic."

"So what happened? Surely she realized it was a mistake, and she left."

"Oh, she did, but it probably went on for least a minute, or it seemed that way. She kept staring at Suzy. She finally said something like, "'I'm sure I know you. It's been many years, but I can't forget someone like you.'"

"And Suzy essentially shrugged it off?"

"Oh, she did, but…." He paused again. "It seemed to bother her. I made all the appropriate noises about this happening to people all the time, but she seemed a little rattled. It did change the mood for our lunch, for sure. But a couple of hours later, all seemed forgotten."

"But it clearly seems to be bothering you," Alex said.

Dean cupped his chin in his left hand. "A little. It came out of the blue, and it was so uncharacteristic of her. I – uh – I wanted to tell you about it without her here. I think you can understand."

"Absolutely. Thanks for sharing, Dad." They ate the rest of their lunch in silence.

12.

The snow started wet and heavy, like flakes of laundry soap, before it turned finer and steadier as the temperature dropped. Forecasters had dubbed it the worst storm of the winter, the kind of Nor'easter that zigs and zags up the East Coast – dumping heavy rain in Virginia and the Carolinas – before venting its fury on the New York metropolitan area.

Forecasting here was more science than art, thanks to the advent of Doppler radar and sophisticated computers, but the timing and the quantity of snow was as much a guessing game as picking a trifecta at Belmont. Much relied on the infamous "rain-snow line" demarcating where rain (or sleet) turned to snow. In this case, that line had slid to the south, below Long Island, and the New York metro area was getting pounded with snow.

Alex decided to take the morning off, during what was predicted to be the worst of the storm. He called Julie at home and told her he'd try to make it in after lunch, after the phalanx of plows had done their best to open up the streets and the office parking lot had presumably been mostly cleared. He didn't like to venture out in heavy snow: the Mini Cooper was reasonably sure-footed, but visibility was poor and traffic was terrible.

The timing was bad, however. Deadlines were coming up later in the week, and he'd have to make up some time for every hour spent out of the office. While he could proof-read pages online by logging into the production portal, there was more editing and writing that needed to be done first, and that was better done in the office. He sighed and kept reading from his laptop. School had been called off, and the kids were upstairs; Lisa's office had also called off work for the day, and she was reading a novel in the living room.

Then she was at the study door looking in. "Are you going in later?" she asked.

"I think so," Alex replied. "I told Julie I would try to make it. But if it's still really ugly…"

"I know." Lisa had on jeans and a heavy gray sweater; it was clear she was settled in for the day. "But you'll have lunch here? I can heat up some soup, and maybe a sandwich?"

"Sounds good."

Suzy was in the kitchen, staring out the window as the snow fell softly, obscuring the trees. She had on flannel-lined slacks and a thick gray sweater with a shawl collar, warmer clothing than she would have needed in Atlanta. She sighed and went to the pantry to pull out some fettuccini; she told Dean she'd make spaghetti with mushrooms for dinner, one of the few dishes she felt comfortable making. It was a recipe she'd inherited, so to speak, from her mother, though she added a few things, like a pinch of thyme and basil, and she insisted on using portabella mushrooms, sliced thin.

She measured out the fettuccini and put a Revere ware pot on the stovetop and started the water, adding a splash of olive oil. Then she poured herself a glass of Malbec from a bottle that had been opened and plopped down in a chair at the island. Dean was watching television – probably the news, she thought. He rarely missed the PBS Newshour.

Her mind went suddenly to that encounter at the Ritz. Connie Waters – she had recognized her almost immediately. She was older and grayer, certainly, but she had that same hard slash of a mouth and the voice that was always a few decibels too loud. It has hard to play dumb, to draw her face into a blank and pretend she had never seen her before. But she had to. Connie was one of the four or five women she recalled the best from those St. Louis days. And Connie remembered her, and regrettably, her name.

It was an awkward encounter; in another circumstance, they might have embraced each other, and shared some memories, even with Dean by her side. Of course, that couldn't happen. She knew she could wait the woman out, deny any acquaintance, but the seconds stretched interminably before Connie strode away. Suzy credited the acting skills she had acquired over the years – the ability to conceal or alter her emotions, whatever the situation required.

Could Dean suspect anything? Not likely. He was besotted with her, and she milked that; he knew nothing of her past, and rarely asked about anything, apart from an occasional question about Atlanta. To him, she was like a gold bracelet that turned up at the bottom of an old steamer trunk – something lovely and wonderful, a discovery with no provenance.

And she told herself that the encounter was an extremely rare event, like sighting Halley's Comet. Unless she went back to St. Louis, the odds of running into people from there seemed remote. Yes, it had happened, but it might never happen again. Still, she had to be on her guard. She would do better next time, if there was one.

13.

Dean studied the menu. It was very busy, with little blocks of text and capital letters everywhere; it took a while to make sense of it. He wasn't surprised: seafood restaurants in Florida were often casual, with fish mounted on the wall, life rings with ship's names embossed on them and silly pirate allusions – the Jolly Roger was especially popular.

This restaurant, in downtown Naples, drew a pretty regular crowd, many of whom lifted their eyes from their beers periodically to stare at the oversized screens above the bar. There was a basketball game on now, in fact, but Dean didn't pay much attention to it. Basketball held just a tad more interest to him than cricket.

Sitting next to him in the booth, Suzy was deep in conversation with Ann Davis, one of her best friends from Atlanta. Her husband, Danny, was across from Dean and was certainly less talkative. He was a builder with a score of developments to his credit; chunky and somewhat ruddy, he had a thatch of silver hair that he kept cut short. Dean sensed that he was sometimes a bit unsure how to deal with Dean as the new man in Suzy's life. He and Avery had been good friends for something like 30 years.

It was the Davises who had found an apartment for the Perrys and acted as their unofficial hosts to Naples, which had grown like crazy in the two decades they had been coming down in the winter. Dean was fond of the winter weather in Florida, but he never liked the flatness and monotony of the land, the relentless swampiness and the sameness of many of the shopping centers, with their whitewashed fronts and orange tile roofs.

Dean studied the menu again and chuckled. "Fried alligator – now that's something you don't see every day."

Danny smiled. "Damned right. But I've had it a couple of times, and you'd be surprised – it's not bad." As he pronounced it, the word sounded like two syllables; "by-ad."

"Tastes like chicken, right?" Dean grinned.

"Ha – well, you're right, it actually does."

"Well, I think I'll pass." He looked down again for a few moments. "I bet the catfish platter is pretty good, though."

Danny was looking at his menu. "Yeah, that's a good bet. I may have the conch fritters. Always been one of my favorites."

Dean turned to Suzy. "What are you looking at, sweetheart?"

She smiled slightly. "Oh, I'm not sure just yet. Probably some fish, though."

Ann spoke up. "The mahi-mahi and the snapper are especially good." She was almost as tall as her husband, with salt-and-pepper hair, worn fairly short; she had a direct gaze softened by doe-brown eyes and a Georgia drawl heavy on "y'alls."

Suzy scanned the menu again for a few moments. "I've always liked snapper, so I think I'll go with that."

"Do you ever see pompano on the menus down here?" Dean asked. "It was always a special fish, but I don't seem to see it any more, almost like it's been fished out."

"You may be onto something, Dean," Danny replied. "It's true – you just don't see it. And that's a shame – it was wonderful."

They were finishing their entrees when the talk turned to the next day. Dean and Danny would be playing golf at one of the local public courses; the women were interested in driving somewhere and doing some sightseeing.

"How about Sanibel?" Dean asked. "It's a beautiful spot, and you know it has some of the best beaches anywhere. And then there's the shelling."

"Oh, honey, we're too old to be collecting shells," Suzy said with a slight shake of her head. "Aren't we, Ann?"

"Indeed we are. But I do like the idea. It is a great spot, and while I'm sure it'd be crowded, if we were there in the morning it might not be so bad."

"That's good for us," Danny piped in. "We have a tee time at 9:10."

"How long a drive is it?" Suzy asked.

"Oh, about an hour, probably," said Dean. "You'd take 41 North and take a cutoff most of the way there and work your way west to the water."

Suzy looked over at Ann. "What do you think?"

"I'm up for it."

"Okay." Suzy let the word linger in the air. "We'll probably leave about the time you do tomorrow, and we'll find someplace to eat up there."

"Sounds like a plan," Dean said, spreading his hands in the air. "We'll all be having fun."

Suzy and Ann had just finished their lunch – hers a Cobb salad, Ann's a seafood salad sprinkled with conch and shrimp. The breeze lifted the hem of the red umbrella at their table, showing its pale underside; the Gulf was no more than a thin blue line above the arch of the beach. The restaurant was predictably busy in high season, mostly with retired couples and a few younger families with restless children, and service had been desultory. No matter – they were in no hurry.

Suzy excused herself to use the restroom after telling Ann they would split the check. She followed the arrows to the "Gulls" door – another silly sight common in Florida, she thought – and sat down in one of the stalls. She hung her purse on the hook and brought out her iPhone.

After opening it, she looked at her messages. Yes, here was the most recent one from Roger Nathanson, the broker in Rye who handled Dean's accounts – and wanted to poach some of hers from Atlanta. He seemed nice enough, and competent, she thought, but she wasn't going to rush anything.

"Hi Suzy," it read. "I think you should buy Apple and Google on any sign of weakness. I can give you some more advice on timing."

She studied the message for a moment before typing back: "Maybe. You know I think some of these tech stocks are overpriced." She avoided the shortcuts, like "u," that millennials made part of any and all messages.

Less than a minute later, her phone beeped and she looked at the reply. "Well, we agree to disagree some there." He followed that with an emoticon of a smiley face. "Are you guys in town? I owe Dean an update on his positions. We should think about getting together for a lunch."

She composed a reply. "You just need to be patient. In Fla. now and back to Westchester next week." Her short nails clicked on the simulated keyboard. "Keep me apprised on stocks."

Suzy flushed the toilet and put the phone away without waiting for a reply, walked out of the stall and washed her hands at the white porcelain sink. Her leg was bothering her more than usual today, and she had felt herself limping noticeably. But she steadied herself and, looking into the mirror, swept her hair from her face with both hands in a well-practiced move and strolled back out the door.

Pasadena, CA

14.

The wind rattled the windows, and Alicia could see the tops of the palms across the street swaying like Hula dancers. It was unusual for the Santa Ana winds to pop up in March – they were more of a fall phenomenon – but here they were, rushing through the LA basin like a freight train that's behind schedule. Leaves and a few fronds littered the street like shrapnel.

Saturday was ordinarily a slow day at her household, down time after a busy week of teaching and the demands of the girls' school. It was late morning, and she had just come back from dropping off Isabelle at a friend's house for the day. Alicia was curled up on the upholstered living room couch, reading a thriller, while Jingles, their gray Siamese, was sleeping on an armchair nearby, legs outstretched.

Alison wandered in from the kitchen. It being a weekend, she had on her casual wear, ripped jeans and a powder blue sweatshirt with "UCLA" in modified script across the front.

She sat down on the couch and leaned back against the armrest. "Mom, you're lucky you didn't have to deal with social media while you were in high school."

Alicia lifted her head from the book and looked at her; clearly, her daughter wanted to talk, and she set the book down in her lap.

"I tell myself that all the time, honey. It was bad enough that it wasn't right for girls to bring backpacks to school. They might have allowed that here, but not in Missouri." She paused and looked harder at Alison, whose was staring down at her hands. "Why, is something going on?"

"Yeah, there is," Alison said, looking up. "My best friend – you know her, Suri – is getting trolled by some other girls on Facebook. All because she wanted to run for a class office. Um, you know, some people have prejudices against Indians."

"How bad is it?" Alicia asked.

"Pretty bad, I guess." She paused again. "It started about a week ago. They're calling her names, bad-mouthing Indian culture, stuff like that. I - I posted something really positive about her, but now a few of them are kinda coming after me for wanting to help her."

Alicia sighed. "You know, sweetie, some people are just narrow-minded. Unfortunately, a lot of that seems to start at home. And – of course – it's a heckuva lot easier to trash somebody online that say it to their face."

"That's for sure." She spread her hands and looked at her nails. "I was just wondering if you had any advice for me. Getting more involved probably won't do any good. But it's hard for me to see what they're doing to her."

"Well, I'm certainly not the best person to ask, certainly about Facebook. But I think, in general, that you have to stand up for your friends, be willing to swim against the tide if you have to. Sometimes, that takes a lot of courage."

"I guess." Alison paused. "It must have been hard for you, growing up, not to be able to talk to your mother like this."

Alicia felt like she'd been hit with a light punch in the chest – she wasn't sure she liked where this was going.

"Actually, I did have her around when I was your age – she didn't leave until I was well out of the house, in graduate school. But" – she looked at her daughter appraisingly – "it wasn't the kind of relationship that you and I have. She – she just wasn't there for me emotionally. I had to figure out a lot of things on my own."

Alison tossed her long brown hair back with her left hand. "That's so weird."

"I guess it is. But she loved my father, and I just came to understand that there wasn't another place set at the table for me."

Alison looked at her almost beseechingly, her brown eyes bright. "I know we haven't really talked about this much, but did you ever try hard to find her?"

Alicia sighed again, this time audibly. "Hard? Not really, I suppose. It seemed like she had abandoned me, and any attempt I made wouldn't have been welcome. Besides, I didn't know where to start, apart from going back to Missouri."

Alison drew up her knees to her chest and folded her hands over them. "So, she could be anywhere?"

"That's right, honey, though I think it's very unlikely she's anywhere near here. East Coast, perhaps – that would be the farthest away. I – I just have no clue. But something tells me she's still alive."

"How old would she be, again?"

"Sixty-eight. She had me when she was 23."

"And what if she changed her name?" Alison stared at her again.

"Oh, I bet she did. You can do that legally, you know, especially if you get remarried."

"You – you used to have a photo of your parents in your room, but I haven't seen it for a long time. Your mother was a beautiful woman."

"Well, I still have it, but I put it away. And yes, she was beautiful, and very refined in her own way." She scratched her knee again. "Sometimes I think of her like a piece of porcelain that had some cracks that nobody could see."

15.

February 23rd wasn't a special day in the life of the nation – it was a day after the traditional celebration of Washington's Birthday, which had morphed into President's Day and the obligatory three-day weekend and a landslide of bedding and mattress sales. Apart from that, in much of the country, it was just another day spent in the vagaries of winter.

But the date had special meaning to Suzy. It was her father's birthday, the father she had loathed for as long as she could remember until his death 20 years earlier. It was a milestone, a day to muse on avenging the sins of the father, whose death she learned about from her best friend. Suzy had cut off communication with her mother many years ago because her mother refused to leave her father, but what could her mother do? She had never worked, had only a high school education, and put up with her husband as a sort of security blanket, as tattered as it was.

Suzy had been thinking about this day for many months. It just felt right. Avery was slowing down noticeably, and he was no longer the man she'd married. He was considerably heavier: his paunch had widened, and his neck bulged at the collars of his shirts like a sausage straining at its casing. His weight, coupled with years of wear and his years as a college football lineman, had taken a toll on his knees, and he was starting to limp badly. His cholesterol, which had always been a concern, required careful monitoring.

She had plotted this out carefully. Dorothy, the family cook, had the morning off but would be coming in shortly before noon. Suzy had her regular bridge club meeting, which included lunch, at the country club. If all went according to plan, Dorothy would find Avery in his recliner. She'd try to rouse him, but would get no response.

Be calm, she told herself; this is in your hands.

She and Avery had their customary breakfast in the lovely semi-circular nook overlooking the garden, now mostly bare and as spare and clean viewed from the window as an Edward Hopper painting. She had a poached egg and toast; he had eggs and bacon, creamy grits and a couple of slabs of frozen French toast that he heated up in the microwave.

Avery had taken the obligatory retirement from Southern Property and Casualty at age 65, and his days were far different now. True, he still served on a couple of corporate boards, but they usually met quarterly and the demands were far from onerous. He played golf on weekends – usually Saturday – but not when the high temperatures dipped below the 50s. He spent much of his time puttering around the house, whistling softly to himself at times, reading the newspaper and novels – John Grisham was a particular favorite.

He swallowed a piece of French toast and looked at her fondly. "You have your bridge club today, don't you, sweetie?" His jowls bounced slightly as he talked. Behind his tortoise shell glasses, his eyes beamed.

"I do." She smiled levelly. "I'll be leaving just after 11, as usual. Dorothy will be coming in later."

"Right."

"What about you, more reading?"

He beamed, and the creases around his mouth deepened. "I think so. I'll be in my usual spot." The leather recliner was in the family room, across from the big-screen TV and close by a set of built-in bookshelves lined mostly with paperbacks that Avery had read over the years. He usually listened to classical music while he read and was particularly fond of Mozart and Haydn.

Three hours later, she stole into their bedroom and lifted the plastic baggie from its hiding place at the bottom of one of her drawers. She moved into the kitchen and found the mortar and pestle, brought them out on the counter and took a small bunch of the leaves and started grinding away. There was some noise, but the family room was a good distance away, and the music there was fairly loud.

It took her five minutes to grind the leaves into a greenish powder – perhaps as much as a tablespoonful. She reached into the refrigerator and brought out a can of Diet Dr. Pepper, Avery's favorite. Then she popped the tab and, taking a slim measuring spoon, carefully took the powder from the pestle and dropped it into the can. She felt a few beads of sweat on her forehead.

She could only guess at the right amount to use; it wasn't like she could find a recipe. But she had tested the *Gelsenium* a couple of weeks earlier, mixing some of the powder in a small dish of water she set out on their concrete birdbath, emptied for the winter. Starlings often swarmed the yard, and she was sure they would find the water.

A day later, she walked out and looked by the birdbath. Twenty feet away, near the back hedge, lay a dead starling, its beak half-open in rigor mortis. She'd ask Avery to remove it, but she smiled inwardly. It seemed clear that the powder was working.

Suzy secreted the baggie in its place in her drawer, then walked back to the kitchen and lifted the can from its spot on the counter. Holding one finger over the open tab, she swirled the can for some seconds to disburse the powder. Then she carried it into the family room and saw Avery deep in concentration, staring at the pages of the novel.

"I've brought you something, dear." She smiled and handed him the can. "I'm going off to the club."

"Thank you, honey." His eyes crinkled with affection. "Have a good time. And don't let Sheila Johnson win big again. I'm tired of hearing Ralph brag about her."

"I'll try not to." She leaned over, kissed him lightly on the forehead, looked at his face for a long moment, and walked out.

Westchester County, NY

16.

Dawn was seeping through the basement windows as Alex reached 15 minutes on the treadmill in his basement. Clad in gym shorts and a black t-shirt, he felt his armpits go damp and his throat a bit dry; he tried to do 15 to 20 minutes on the treadmill or the elliptical machine almost every day in the colder weather, before he could reasonably ride his bike.

At least it was getting light at 6:30. During the winter, he was exercising only by the fluorescent lights in the room, which they had converted into a modest exercise space: there were yoga mats, some free weights up to 20 pounds, a medicine ball, some elastic stretch bands. Lisa would join him at times, but most mornings she was preoccupied with prodding the kids and getting them off to school.

He wiped off the sweat from around his collar, put on his glasses again and trudged up the stairs toward the shower.

Through his office windows, Alex could see the first sign of spring emerging, like a toddler slowly rousing from a long slumber. The daffodils in the beds under the trees were out, nodding gently in the breeze. It was still too early for most of the trees to start leafing out, but here and there dabs of green marked where some were budding. An early magnolia, on the other hand, was starting to push out its broad white flowers almost brazenly.

He recalled the famous opening line from *The Wasteland* that "April is the cruelest month." He never quite bought into that notion: aside from income taxes, for so many people in cooler climates, it was a month of hope and the promise of longer days and warming breezes.

Sipping his coffee, which he always drank black, Alex logged into the proofing application and started scrolling through the magazine pages. He loved that he could see the magazine electronically, in full color, and flag any minor changes – typos, bad word breaks, whatever. Kerry, his art director, did a great job of layouts with minimal resources, and managed through photos or artwork – most obtained from Getty or another image bank – to make the pages visually appealing. Inviting the reader into a story was critical.

The full-color nature of a magazine and the variety of layout techniques fascinated him, coming from the far more limited array of choices at the newspaper. True, color had come to the newspaper world in the past generation, but the options were so much more limited. You could do a full-color bleed across two pages of a magazine and knock out the type against the color; you could run type around a square or a circle or some other geometric figure.

He yawned, took off his glasses and rubbed his eyes gently, looked at the ceiling and blew out a breath. After a moment, he took his coffee and walked two doors down to Julie's office. She was staring intently at her screen, so much so she didn't notice his presence at first. Alex always had her do the initial proofing; she was very conscientious, and not much got past her, but his was the final say.

"Hey, how's it looking?" He sipped his coffee.

"Good, good." She looked at him and smiled. "I've gotten as far as the jet ski feature and haven't found much at all." She paused. "The art for the jet ski piece is really nice, but I don't think that would be my cup of tea. Have you ever done it?"

"Just once, a few years ago up at Lake George, with the kids." He shrugged. "It was fun, but I didn't feel like it was something I needed to do often. But – hey – I would do it again."

She picked up her cup, which had her usual Earl Grey tea, heavily sweetened. "It's kind of like riding a motorcycle on the water, isn't it?"

"Well, yeah, I guess you could say that. But thank God you can't go as fast." He glanced at his watch, a diver's watch with a black analog face: 10:20. "Give me a shout when you're done. I'm still on the Briefs," he said, referring to a section in the front of the magazine.

"Will do."

Several hours later, after a modest lunch at his desk chased down by a can of green tea, Alex was most of the way through proofing the "book," as magazines are generically called. He'd found very little to correct, but there was always something; it was especially hard to pick up niggling issues in copy he had personally written. He'd been told that the brain tended to skip over words and phrases that were very familiar, the way an assembly line inspector might occasionally miss a flaw. Was that true? He didn't really know, but it made sense.

He decided to take a bit of a break and went to the Web and the *Times* site. Scrolling through the headlines, he read through a few stories on politics – a subject that fascinated but usually bothered him – and a couple on technology, including one on driverless cars. There was something disturbing: he really couldn't imagine sitting in a car like a ventriloquist's dummy while invisible hands turned the wheel. But it was coming, as sure as spring would morph into summer.

Then, under the "Arts" heading, he saw something that piqued his interest: a piece highlighting a retrospective on "The Merry Widow of Windy Nook" on BBC America. The narrative was arresting: Between 1955 and 1957, a British woman named Mary Elizabeth Wilson had lost four husbands, thereby earning herself that title. Some of her marriages lasted only weeks, he read – but long enough that she became the heir of their estates, and collected an inheritance after each one died.

Not surprisingly, she fell under suspicion. The authorities exhumed the bodies and found them laced with insecticide. But though she was sentenced to death in 1958 for two of the murders, her sentence was reduced to life in prison, he read, and she died in 1963; she was 70.

The notion of courting and then blithely killing husbands for their money was appalling to Alex; it was truly an amoral crime, in his mind only barely removed from men who preyed on woman and went on serial killing sprees. He sighed. This wasn't a show he wanted to see, but it held a certain fascination, like a lurid drawing or stealing a look at a woman's legs as she sat down. He might watch a few minutes of it to see if it was compelling, but he didn't think Lisa would join him.

Later, that night, Alex set down his book, the biography of Woodrow Wilson by A. Scott Berg, and found himself thinking back to his mother, and her illness. His mother, warm and gentle as a rule but now and then stubborn and as unexpectedly chilly as an ice treat in July, had left them on the worst possible terms – well, perhaps not; at least they had the opportunity to say goodbye, albeit to a woman on her deathbed who had failed to recognize anyone in her family for nine months or more. A fatal accident, he mused, would have been worse. At least as it was, they had some time to prepare.

He remembered in particular the final weeks in the white clapboard hospice, with its antiseptic feel, the beatifically smiling nurses in their light gray pantsuits and the motel-like anonymity of the room, dominated by the hospital bed and the monitors crowded around it. The TV mounted on the far wall was generally off; his mother was slipping in and out of consciousness and had no need for daytime fare, nor for prime time, either.

He'd come several times in the last weeks, once with Dean, once with Lisa and the kids and once alone. The deathly quiet of the carpeted hallways stayed with him; he could almost hear himself breathe as he went down the corridor toward her room. With Lisa, they took turns holding her hand and speaking softly to her, knowing that their words might as well have evaporated before they reached her. Still, they wanted to make the effort.

He was content to lean over and hold her hand as he spoke; Lisa also stroked her hair. It didn't matter – Marjorie was unresponsive to anything. Alex told her that he loved her and thanked her for putting him on the right path to adulthood, while Lisa reminded her of her grandchildren and all the memories they shared. Moist-eyed, she brought over Jennifer and Jason, shy and quiet in the presence of looming death. Both of them, in turn, knelt by the bed and held her hand as they spoke softly. Jennifer's eyes filled with tears, which inched down her cheeks like snowmelt. Jason was dry-eyed, but his voice broke audibly a few times. Five days after that visit, Marjorie was gone.

While Dean didn't talk about it, Alex fully sensed that his father had felt cheated – not only by her premature death, but the all-engrossing nature of dementia, which placed him, too, in a hard and implacable prison. He couldn't enjoy himself – that simply wouldn't be right – but he couldn't help her, either. The disease had taken him hostage, and there was no negotiation and no reprieve.

All of which made Alex understand more fully the joy and the enthusiasm that Suzy had brought into Dean's life. Here was a lovely, sophisticated woman who enjoyed doing things, yet was willing to give Dean space to play golf or whatever else he wanted to do. Alex's mother had been relatively independent, but Suzy was even more of a free agent, able to engage and disengage as either she or Dean wanted; she was never clinging and, at least as far as Alex could see, rarely demanding.

Yet there was an air of mystery to Suzy that he couldn't seem to penetrate. Some of that, he thought, was the natural product of a stranger arriving full-blown into an intimate core of the family. But it was more than that.

Suzy's past was a chain of unknowns and little-knowns; she was like a foster child that landed on their doorstep one morning with little more than the briefest of histories. Alex wanted to learn more, but he felt he had to observe customary social niceties. He couldn't interrogate her, for God's sake. More would eventually come out, he was sure, as she became a more permanent part of the family fabric. In the meantime, though, he'd just have to settle for any crumbs of information that fell from the proverbial table.

Little Rock, AR

17.

Sally Pritchard opened the latest email on her Dell desktop computer. She sat quietly in the alcove off the living room, which she and Harold had converted into a small office. She kept it neat, as she did the rest of the small white ranch house; nothing compulsive, really, but she swept and dusted at least once a week, going from room to room as thoroughly and monotonously as a night watchman making his rounds. The children had been out of the house for decades, but she kept their rooms as neat as if a drill sergeant was standing over her shoulder.

It had been close to 20 years since she and Suzy had started writing emails to each other, the logical follow-on to many years of letters and phone calls. There was still an occasional call, but they both liked the ease and privacy of emails. She confessed her frustrations to Suzy, but if hers were emotional – sometimes the equivalent of spilling blood on the figurative page – Suzy's were measured, succinct, more remote. But they were unequivocally Suzy.

Suzy's emails were sporadic – sometimes once a week, sometimes only once a month. Sally would usually reply within a few hours; on the other hand, Sally's emails occasionally went unanswered for long days. Sally had made her peace with that. She was firmly in Suzy's shadow – she always had been.

Growing up on the same street in Little Rock, the girls had been fast friends since age six. They had walked to school together, later sat beside each other in the back of the rumbling yellow school bus, eaten their lunches together on the school's smooth white formica tables.

Tina's mother, Josie, made sandwiches for Tina every day, often peanut butter and jelly on sticky Wonder Bread halves. Sally started asking for the same kind of sandwiches from her mother.

Their closeness had persisted into high school, where Tina Squires (as she was then) soared with the in crowd, her loveliness and budding sophistication separating her from the lesser girls like Sally Tate, her given name. Tina sported retainers on her teeth for a couple of years in junior high, but she wasn't alone, and she treated it more as a rite of passage than a disfigurement.

When Tina had developed her figure, really at age 14, the boys descended on her like bees to a fragrant flower. Even older boys – she had started dating a junior when she was just a freshman. She was the object of considerable admiration among her classmates, along with no small dollops of jealousy.

Like many pretty girls – in theory, and in real life – Tina was especially drawn to girls who were no threat to her standing. Sally wasn't mousy, but she had small eyes and a wide nose, and she was stocky, with thick arms and calves. Her parents had five other children, mostly older, and she was perpetually wearing hand-me-downs. Other girls did, too, but hers seemed especially obvious.

Sally had been with Tina on that most fateful of days, the night they came back from a double date, laughing conspiratorially and just a little tipsy, when Tina's father, Harlan – drunk and belligerent, spoiling for a "lesson," as he called them – chased her out of the house, down the wooden porch stairs and toward the ravine. That was when Tina had fallen, stumbling and wheeling, onto the rocks and shattered her left tibia. They were sixteen, and after that, things were never quite the same.

Oh, the shift wasn't dramatic, at least not after the initial few months. Tina had a couple of operations, and spent several months in a heavy plaster cast that reached past her knee. She came to be adept with her crutches, and had her cast signed by dozens of classmates, who wrote little messages embellished with hearts or flowers. But something inside Tina changed, and Sally was the one who saw it best.

On the surface, she was much the same – pretty, clever, outgoing. But Sally saw a new coldness sometimes in her eyes, in her mouth, as if anger had reset her face in new angles. Her limp, at first profound, had morphed into something merely noticeable. But her career as a cheerleader, and as a softball player, were over; Tina told her time and again that she felt much of the joy in her life had been stolen from her.

The accident also crushed her father's spirit, for he wasn't too unfeeling not to experience remorse. At first, he apologized to her almost daily, he beseeched her – not for forgiveness, since that wasn't attainable, but for understanding. He wrenched himself away from beer and bourbon, not an easy task for a man who saw drink as one of life's few pleasures; he rededicated himself to his job at the local bottling plant. And he never again came to her in the middle of the night, reeking of booze and whispering for the love "your mother doesn't give me."

That horror had started shortly after she turned 13. At least once a week, as she recalled it, he stole into her room in the middle of the night, commanded her to silence, and crawled into her bed. At first, he confined himself to fondling her body and her breasts, but before long, he had moved onto vaginal penetration, first with his finger. Then came the real thing. She lost her virginity to her father at 14, losing only a small bit of blood, as if it were simply a sin of little consequence.

But it was the shame of it; she felt like she needed a new skin, elastic, that she could slip over her own. Tina would have been shocked at the number of girls who had suffered a similar fate, from fathers and stepfathers. As it was, she felt alone and doubly assaulted, by her father and by her mother's acquiescence, for surely she must have known. For many years, the thought of it made her clench her teeth in anger.

Apart from Sally, she felt she really had no one to confide in, but even Sally could know nothing about her father's nighttime depredations. Tommy, Tina's only sibling, was three years younger and, she was sure, sensed nothing. He was a gawky, sullen boy who bore the brunt of their father's anger; he often withdrew to his room, where, starting probably at age 12, he listened to rock music night and day. Where Tina was a good student, and conscientious, Tommy was indifferent, lazy, piling up a record of mostly just passing grades.

They had never been close; it was a relationship marked by silences and angry outbursts. Tina felt all the superiority that older siblings feel, coupled with a certainty that Tommy would never amount to much; if she had been more capable of reflection and self-analysis, she might have realized that her attitude toward Tommy was bossy and condescending well beyond reason. And it galled her that as a boy, he would never suffer from their father's wayward attentions, never feel the need to conceal emotions like a cloistered nun who'd taken a vow of silence.

Tina collected a few boyfriends in her last two years of high school, the kind to be expected of a girl with her looks: a star football running back, the senior class president. It was the 60s, and sexual awakening was all around them like spring bulbs popping from the ground. But her father's maraudings had turned the notion of sex into something that troubled her, made her queasy; she was fine with kissing and even petting, but anything more was *verboten*.

Like every high school, hers had girls of what could politely called easy virtue – and everyone knew who they were. They weren't popular, as a rule, but they were well-known and the targets of endless gossip. Tina, on the other hand, had an unsullied reputation, which some girls thought was fabricated; how could she attract the top boys, who could have anyone, unless she "put out?" It was a conundrum that set the rumor mills churning. Little did most girls know that among certain boys, Tina was dubbed "the ice queen."

Two years after her accident, after their high school graduation, Tina left Little Rock for junior college in Memphis. She was determined to make something of herself, and she knew that she had looks and brains – and those would certainly take her somewhere, perhaps far away. The high school guidance counselor, not as dull as his crew cut and horn-rimmed glasses would suggest, told her she should try college. It wasn't advice he gave to many at the school.

Tina settled on marketing: it sounded exciting, and she knew she was good with people, knew her attributes would be helpful. Two years later, after getting her associate's degree, she told Sally in a long phone call that she was taking a job with a company in St. Louis. Sally, who had married Harold a year earlier and was six months' pregnant with her first child, wistfully wished her well.

Sally soon realized that Tina was serious about remaking herself: her accent, the soft drawl that some likened to light molasses and had been so much a part of her, had essentially vanished not long after the move to St. Louis. She told Sally that she didn't want to be pegged by her speech, burdened by assumptions that others would unconsciously make.

In the intervening years, Tina had lost two husbands and was now married to a third. That seemed a little confounding to Sally; she knew Tina had professed her love for both of them. On the other hand, Harold was all Sally had ever needed, and she loved him despite his physical issues: a gut that grew ever larger, lapping over his belts; a disappearing hairline and high cholesterol. He'd been put on statins a decade ago, and now she was on them, too. Too much barbeque, she thought.

She should have known better, an inner voice railed at her now and then. After all, she has a registered nurse, and nutrition was an area she had been exposed to. But, working for an internist, it wasn't top of mind during a normal day – not like she was working in one of the weight-loss clinics, certified or fly-by-night, that had sprung up around town like weeds in the past generation.

Sally clicked on the email and opened it.

"Hi GF" – the usual opening. "GF" was their shorthand for "girlfriend," and it was their greeting of many years' standing. "I'm really liking Westchester at this time of year. It's starting to get green, and it's not as humid as Atlanta…"

Sally read on, but it was a short and not very informative note. She thought about her reply – and the fact that Tina, er Suzy, hadn't visited Little Rock in more than five years. Another visit seemed unlikely for the foreseeable future. She clung to the fact that she and Suzy had a raft of memories that only they shared, and that Suzy – beautiful, clever Suzy – still chose to confide in her, to tell her things no one else would ever know.

Westchester County, NY

18.

It didn't take long: after a few unseasonably mild days in the 70s, Westchester was, in mid-April, being kissed by the warmth of spring. Alex made some mental notes as he drove to the office: the weeping willows were sweeping toward the ground in swaths of light green, and the maples were starting to send out frilly reddish buds. Forsythias were blooming in masses of brilliant yellow, almost as if they'd harnessed the sun.

He and the staff at the magazine were deep into writing and production of another issue. It was the monthly onus, and you could vary the timing here and there by a few days – until the final week, when the deadlines were practically set in cement. Oh, you could be a few days early, but the production house had its own schedules, and your magazine had its set hours on the press – so being early was no advantage.

While "recreational equipment" suggested a broad mandate, the magazine had historically steered clear of territory claimed by single-sport magazines devoted to skiing, tennis, golf and the like. Its niche – which made perfect sense to Alex – was more in the home gym or smaller-budget outdoor sports, especially those that were growing and had a good advertising base. Jet skis, or "personal watercraft," was a good example; so were all-terrain vehicles, though Alex had his reservations about the latter, both for safety and environmental reasons.

He had just finished an interview with a top dealer of kayaks for an upcoming feature, taking notes on the computer with the phone on speaker – gone were the days when he took notes in longhand and had to transpose them. The phone rang, and he saw it was Dean.

"Hi, Dad."

"Hi, Boyo. You busy?"

"After a fashion. What's up?"

"We'd like to take you guys to the club for dinner again. Friday night work?"

Alex rolled his eyes. "Probably. I need to check with Lisa and get back to you."

"Fine, let me know." There was a pause. "And there's something you could help me with. Actually, maybe you and Jason."

"What's that?"

"I want to clean out the garage. There are a bunch of boxes that need to be gone through. I've done some of it already, but I think I could use some help."

"Okay, I'm sure we could do that." He didn't want to sound hesitant, but he felt his reluctance might have come through. "Maybe Sunday. I have my usual ride on Saturday." The bike club had started its season the weekend before, traveling up the local roads to Katonah and back in a long string of sleek bicycles and Lycra-clad riders.

"Sounds fine. Let me know about that, and dinner."

"Sure thing. Bye."

Pulling up the Mini Cooper into Dean's complex, Alex saw that the garage door was wide open and the Mercedes was pulled out in the driveway. He parked at the curb, and he and Jason stepped out and walked toward the garage, where they could see Dean with his back to them, reaching toward some shelves. It was a gray day in the low 60s with low-slung clouds and occasional drizzle, and Alex was glad the job was indoors.

He looked at Jason, whose sullenness was palpable. He'll outgrow it, he thought, just as he would fill out; at almost 17, Jason had the long, gangly limbs of boys a couple of years younger. But he was no weakling, as Alex had found out several times in the past year when they worked together on moving heavy stuff around the house.

"Hi, Dad," Alex called out as they walked inside the garage.

"Oh, hey." Dean turned to them and smiled. "Good of you guys to come."

"It's our solemn and bounded duty," Alex replied, grinning. "What d'you need done?"

Dean, wearing a gray sweatshirt and tan corduroys, waved an arm up toward several high shelves at the back. "See those boxes?" Several large cardboard boxes sat on heavy molded plastic shelving; they were labeled, but Alex couldn't make out the wording from where he stood. "I'd like to get those down and get rid of most of what's in them. Most of it's mine; some is Suzy's." He stood with his hand on his hips. "But you'll need the ladder, and it will take both of you. The boxes are bulky."

"Okay." Alex looked up at the shelves again. "So, once we get them down, you'll go through them?"

"Yes, but" – Dean looked up as well. "A lot of what's in there are magazines, and those can go straight out. I don't really know why I kept them. See this big trash can?" He pointed to a big black plastic can. "You can dump them in there."

"Got it."

Jason spoke up. "Just the magazines, Granddy?"

Dean smiled at him. "Yep, just the magazines. If there are papers, I need to look at them."

"Alright."

It was a fairly simple job for the two of them, in theory, but the boxes were heavy and balancing on the ladder and holding a box in both hands wasn't easy; it didn't require Wallenda-level balance, but more than once Alex had to catch himself briefly before he could make it down a couple of steps and hand the box to Jason. There were just three boxes, but Alex understood why Dean had asked for his help – they were heavy, and trying to do it alone was simply inviting a trip to the emergency room.

Dean had gone back into the house, and Alex and Jason surveyed the boxes on the smooth-finished garage floor. Nothing unusual about them, but they were stuffed with paper material, most of it magazines.

"Bring over the big can, would you?" Alex said to Jason, who wheeled the empty can close to the boxes. "I'll take this one, you start on that," Alex said, pointing. "Remember, toss the magazines and keep any papers for him to look at."

Tedium set in. Alex pulled out the magazines, looking at them briefly before tossing them. Many, he saw, dated back five years or more. There were glossy issues of *Time, The New Yorker, Vanity Fair, Golf, Consumer Reports* – all things that he knew Dean had subscribed to over the years. Had he read them all? Doubtful. And perhaps it was too big an effort to cull them and throw out a selected few.

Jason wasn't working quite as fast, and Alex finished the first box and tackled the second. This had a good deal less in it, and he quickly concluded a lot of it was Suzy's – there were issues of *Good Housekeeping, People, Gourmet,* and *Southern Living,* among others. He looked at the label on one – it was made out to Suzy Rittenhouse at an Atlanta address.

It was down toward the bottom that he came across it. Sticking out of the back cover of a magazine was a yellowed scrap of newsprint; he opened the magazine and saw it was partially stuck to the back flap. Alex pulled it out and looked at it, and did a double-take. It was an obituary of a man named David Tallman, and the dateline was Clayton, Missouri. But it wasn't dated in any way; it was impossible to guess how old it was.

It wasn't long, probably five or six paragraphs. He glanced at Jason, who was still pulling out magazines, and slipped the obit into the back pocket of his jeans. This would be important reading, but not here.

Back home, alone in his study, Alex pulled out the obituary and read it with a growing sense of consternation. The headline was perfunctory: "David Tallman, 48; Clayton Man Headed Dealerships."

It went on:

> *"David Tallman, 48, died Tuesday of an apparent heart attack at his office in Clayton.*
>
> *"Tallman was the chief executive of the Tallman Group, an auto dealership consortium, headquartered in Clayton, with a dozen locations in the western St. Louis suburbs. He had*

inherited a small dealership from his father and built it into a regional operation, selling primarily Fords but branching into other brands, including Mazda, Hyundai and Subaru.

"Tallman was a leading figure in the Clayton business community and had served as board chairman of the Chamber of Commerce and chairman for several years of the local United Way. He was a major benefactor of the Boys and Girls Clubs and the YMCA, and was a member of Clayton Country Club.

"Raised in Clayton and a product of the local schools, he was a graduate of Washington University in St. Louis and was a major donor to the school's scholarship fund.

"Tallman is survived by his wife, Bettina, and a daughter, Alicia, as well as by a brother, Larry, and a sister, Nancy. Funeral arrangements are incomplete, but donations may be made in his honor to the Boys and Girls Clubs of Greater St. Louis."

Alex stared at the last paragraph and slowly shook his head. Bettina Tallman – the name the woman at the Ritz had used when she saw Suzy. And she had a daughter? There had never been any mention of an earlier marriage, let alone a child. He felt his scalp tingle.

He thought hard. He couldn't take this to Dean, not just yet. He had to know more. If this was Suzy, what else was she hiding?

19.

Alex ruminated hard on what to do with this apparent clue to Suzy's past, which had hit him like a two-by-four to the temple. Should he bring Lisa in on it? Sharing it would bring another head into the situation, and hers was a level-headed one, but could she avoid telegraphing her discomfort or suspicion in Suzy's presence? It would be hard enough for him. He concluded he could.

His mind swirled with questions and suspicions, as shapeless as an amoeba on a high school biology slide. Suzy, despite her vivaciousness and obvious people skills, was something of an enigma. Her past was an unknown, but until the last few weeks, it wasn't an issue. Now, like a dark, misshapen cloud on an otherwise tractless horizon, it was a full-blown concern.

That night, as they got into bed, he set down his glasses on the bedside table and turned to Lisa, who was plumping the pillows on her side.

"There's something I need to share with you – something I found at Dad's house today."

Her eyes widened in puzzlement – this was odd. "What is it?"

He reached into the top drawer in the table and pulled out the obituary. "This was stuck to a magazine in a box that had a bunch of Suzy's stuff. It's an obituary of a man from Missouri, and – you may find this hard to swallow – I have a strong feeling that he was married to Suzy many years ago."

"What?" She stared at him, the bedside lamp putting half her face in shadow.

"Here, read through it." He handed it to her gently, as if were made of glass. He had strong hands, with long fingers, and she took it from him like she was accepting a wafer at a church communion.

She read it silently and looked back at him. "And you think Bettina became Suzy?"

"I do. And, look – she had, and may still have – a daughter. Maybe other grandchildren."

"When is this from?"

He shook his head slowly. "I just don't know. If my hunch is right, it was shortly before she went to Atlanta and married Avery. They were married for more than 20 years."

Lisa squinted. "What ties Suzy to this Bettina?"

He sighed. "Well, I didn't tell you earlier, but Dad told me a story from their Christmas visit to the Ritz. He said a woman came up to Suzy at a restaurant and insisted she knew her, and said her name was Tina Tallman from Missouri. Suzy denied it, but Dad said it seemed to unnerve her a little."

"Wow." Lisa was quiet for some moments. "So – what do we do?" She bit her lip softly.

"I want to try to reach out to her step-children and see what they know."

"Okay, but do you know how to contact them?"

He shook his head. "No, and I don't want to alert Suzy at any cost. I need to do some research. And I think I can swing a trip there if need be – there's a conference coming up next month in Atlanta." He put his hand on hers gently. "But in the meantime, mum is definitely the word. Nothing to anyone – it has to be our secret."

It was a busy week coming up, but Alex's first thought when he came in to work on Monday morning was to see if he could find a phone number for Tom Rittenhouse in Atlanta. He didn't like working with the online White Pages – which often directed users to assemble profiles of a person, for a fee – but he decided that for such an unusual name, it probably might be a sufficiently narrow search to avoid such a trap.

Calling up the site for White Pages, he typed in "Thomas Rittenhouse" and, asked for a location, simply put in "Atlanta, GA." Two names came up – and identified them by age. One, aged 34, was clearly the one he wanted – but there was no phone number, and he was asked to join a "premium" membership for a phone number and assorted and sundry other information that the site would bring up: family, marriage history, court judgments, arrests, etc. Christ, couldn't he just get a phone number? Nope. But the site did provide an address.

So he picked up the phone and dialed 411 and chose "residential" listing. A female voice came on, asking, "What city and state, please?"

"Atlanta, please. Looking for a residential listing for Tom Rittenhouse on Toler Parkway."

There was a pause, then, "Hold for the number."

Alex dutifully wrote it down, opting not to connect just yet. It was mid-morning, and this was a home number - little or no chance Tom would be home. This was a call he'd have to make in the evening.

Just past 8 o'clock that night, sitting alone in his half-lit study, Alex stared a bit nervously at the phone and rehearsed what he planned to say. Then he lifted the handset and punched in the numbers.

On the third ring, a woman's voice said, "Hello?"

This was exactly what Alex had feared – Tom's wife would pick up and he'd have to explain who he was; she was a crucial gatekeeper.

"Hi, I'm calling for Tom."

"Okay, can I tell him who's calling?" She had a light Southern drawl, mellifluous and soothing.

"My name is Alex Perry. My Dad married Suzy, his step-mother. I – I just wanted to introduce myself and talk for a couple of minutes."

There was a brief silence. "Oh, hi, I guess. Um – let me get him."

"Thank you."

He could hear some voices in the background for a few seconds.

"Hello, this is Tom." The voice was a light tenor, mostly unaccented.

"Tom, this is Alex Perry. My Dad, Dean, married Suzy last year."

"Oh, of course. Remind me – where are you calling from?"

"Westchester County, just outside New York. We live just a few miles from them."

"Right, right. What, ah, what can I do for you?" Alex detected a note, no more than a light shading, really, of suspicion, which he had expected; this wasn't an ordinary phone call.

"I'm trying to learn more about Suzy, now that she's an important person in my life, and my family's. I don't expect we could do this over the phone, but I'm planning to be down in Atlanta in a couple of weeks for a conference. Is – is it possible we could meet for lunch?"

Silence. "I, I guess so. Is there a date you had in mind?"

"Probably May 2 or 3rd. Is that possible for you?"

"I think so. What kinds of things are you looking to find out?"

Alex paused; this was where things could get tricky. He wanted to keep things vague, general, and not raise any red flags. "Suzy doesn't talk at all about her past. There are just things I want to know about her, and her time with your family."

He heard a light snort. "I'm not surprised she doesn't talk about us. We've had some – well, issues, my sister and I. Would you want to talk to her, too? She lives not far away."

"If it works out, absolutely."

"Let me give you my work email – it's probably the best way to contact me. Though this number works, too, of course." He spelled out the email.

"Thanks, Tom." Alex's relief was almost palpable over the phone. "Nice talking to you, and I look forward to meeting you."

20.

Saturdays were busy days at malls across the country, thanks in part to millions of teenagers untethered from the demands of school. The Galleria in White Plains was no exception. Kids in all kinds of dress roamed the mall in small, mostly same-sex groups – Lisa noted a few in Goth attire and makeup, as well as some boys in shorts and t-shirts, even though it was barely nudging 60 outside. Many were staring at their phones or slowing to a shuffle to text their friends. It was the social curse that afflicted American teens of every demographic, and to Lisa, it was only getting worse.

Jennifer, in jeans and a blue turtleneck and a small black purse hung on a long strap over her shoulder, was by her side, mostly silent. They were walking next to Suzy, clad in a khaki pantsuit and a bright yellow patterned scarf at her neck. Their destination: Macy's, where Suzy had promised Jennifer she'd buy her a dress for the school's spring dance.

Jennifer, who'd rather be toting a lacrosse stick than shopping, had decidedly mixed feelings about this trip, but a part of her really did want to explore the more grown-up world of clothes shopping and get more comfortable with the notion of dressing up.

"Oh, these malls are endless," Suzy said. "But I can see the store ahead." They were moving steadily past the usual mix of stores with their floor-to-ceiling windows: athletic shoe stores, sportswear, electronics, casual clothes. The chain stores they passed were the usual suspects; they could have been in North Carolina or Northern California. Bland pop music sounded from speakers somewhere overhead.

Suzy's low heels clicked on the patterned tile floor. Her limp was obvious but not jarring; she had told the family it had resulted from a car accident when she was young. It was one obvious defect, if that was the right word, that sullied an image of otherwise near-perfection, like a blotch on the front of a snow-white dress.

Then they were in Macy's and confronting the bewildering array of women's clothing, assembled by designer and category and spreading over the floor in archipelagos of colors and patterns that almost defied understanding. They paused.

Suzy turned to Lisa. "Do you know this store?"

"Not really, though I've been here a few times."

"Well, I think we want to look for good dresses, but not formal wear- this isn't a prom, right?"

"No, it isn't," Jennifer spoke up.

"Okay, let's find a directory. There should be one around here." She looked diagonally to her left and saw one, near the escalator. "Over here."

Studying it, they saw a section marked "misses dresses." "I think that's what we want," Suzy said. "If it isn't, I guess we'll just have to explore a little more."

Passing the perfume counter, with its myriad of spray bottles and cosmetic jars arranged neatly on glass shelves, they soon found the section they were looking for. Lisa frowned slightly, but said nothing: her eye told her that many of the dresses were short, probably well above the knee. With some prodding, Jennifer and her mother started eying the racks, while Suzy was ahead of them, scouting.

A saleswoman, young and eager, approached them and said brightly, "Can I help you?" Lisa detected an accent that sounded Spanish.

Suzy spoke coolly. "Not now, thank you."

"Okay, just let me know." The smile never left her face, as if it had been ironed on. She spun quickly on her heels and walked off.

"Now, what do think of this, Jennifer?" Suzy held up a blue patterned dress with a slightly scooped neckline. Jennifer pursed her lips and mumbled, "I don't know."

Thirty minutes later, Jennifer and Lisa emerged from the dressing room with a dress they both liked: white with blue and black squiggles in something of a randomized pattern. To Lisa's comfort, it was about two inches above the knee, no more. It had broad shoulder straps and was tucked in somewhat at the waist.

Jennifer posed in front of Suzy, who had taken a padded armchair outside the fitting room and was reading. "What do you think?" Lisa asked. "We both like this a lot."

Lisa sensed that Suzy was struggling to show an appropriate level of enthusiasm. "Well, it looks nice on you. That's the important thing." Her smile looked genuine, but there was a guardedness in her eyes that suggested a distinct lack of enthusiasm.

"And it was on the 30 percent off rack, for what that's worth," Lisa said, smiling at her.

"Okay, mission accomplished." Suzy smiled back and rose from the chair, brushing her lap as if dust had settled on it. "Let's go find a cashier."

Two or three registers in that area were vacant, but they saw a couple of people waiting at one down in the sportswear section, and they walked over and waited.

Suzy had the dress on its hanger folded under one forearm. She tapped her feet and sighed, as if the wait were a major annoyance. And the customer ahead of them chose to open a charge account, which added a few more minutes to the process.

When it was finally their turn, she set the dress on the counter and stared at the saleswoman. "Will this be it today?" the woman asked cheerily.

"Yes, just this."

"This is a nice dress," the woman said sweetly and scanned the tag. "That will be $92.55."

Lisa spoke up. "That was the original price, but the rack said 30 percent off."

"Oh, well, it seems the computer isn't recognizing that. Are you sure it came off that rack?"

"Yes, I saw it clearly," Lisa replied.

The clerk looked at them imploringly. "I'm sorry, but I need someone to do a quick price check. It's store policy."

"I understand." Suzy's smile was gracious. "These things happen – we all know that."

Lisa looked at Jennifer, who was staring at the floor. This wasn't what they expected; Suzy was far from imperious – she was turning on a few watts of her charm. Within a few minutes, another clerk appeared and confirmed that the dress was on sale. Suzy dutifully produced her credit card and thanked the clerk when the transaction was complete.

Walking out of the store and back into the mall, Suzy offered a few words of explanation.

"You know, I worked in a department store when I was young, and had a few issues like this. I remember what it was like to be treated badly by customers." She pursed her lips. "It wasn't fun, and I carry that memory with me. The salespeople don't really have any power, so why make their lives miserable?"

"Thanks for sharing that, Suzy." Lisa meant it. "It's a good thought for all of us."

Atlanta, GA

21.

Descending through the pillowy clouds, the plane shook a few times, like a fish trying to throw a hook. Alex shuddered slightly – he didn't consider himself a nervous flyer, but turbulence always unsettled him. This quickly eased, however, and he saw the ground, still thousands of feet below, and made out the flash of pools in the backyards of a number of homes, glinting in the sun.

Arranging the trip to Atlanta had been easy. He had made a case to his publisher that the trade show, one of the year's largest, would be a great source of ideas and contacts. He was staying at the convention hotel downtown for three nights and had time to get acclimated before the show got underway the next day.

The jet taxied to the gate, and, like so many other passengers, Alex switched his phone off airplane mode and took a glance at his emails. Not much of any consequence, though there was a work-related one from Julie that he scanned through quickly – nothing important. He sighed and stretched. Getting off a plane was always confounding – why couldn't the airlines widen the aisles? He answered his own question: money. They packed in as many seats as they could, and they'd squeezed passengers like riders getting stuffed into a Tokyo subway.

Ten minutes later, he was wheeling his small blue suitcase down the corridor and following the signs for ground transportation; it was another five minutes before he was outside the glass doors and waiting at the taxi stand. He hadn't yet latched onto the merits of Uber or Lyft, especially when expense wasn't an issue. A cab would be just fine.

It was lunchtime, and traffic inched onto the I-75 headed north toward the city. Alex could make out the glass towers of downtown and quickly thought they could be from almost any large city in the country. Could he distinguish aerial photos of Atlanta, Houston or Minneapolis? He didn't think so. Iconic skylines like New York or Chicago, yes, but this? It was simply American megapolis, writ large, glass towers that often struck him as monuments to corporate vanity.

He glanced at his watch: 12:15. The conference started with a dinner that night, but he'd have plenty of time to get situated, have lunch and then walk around; he liked walking and getting something of a sense of a city, a bit like a blind person feeling a new face. It was sunny and mild, probably 15 degrees warmer than Westchester. He sat back and smiled.

After sitting through a couple of panel discussions the next morning – both lightened by good PowerPoint presentations – Alex felt no remorse about skipping the lunch and making his way out of the hotel and to his arranged lunch with Tom Rittenhouse. He didn't even need a cab – the restaurant was just five blocks away, and he wanted to stretch his legs.

The trees here were already in almost full leaf, putting large swaths of sidewalk in shadow. He carried his zippered case under his arm and walked briskly, dodging occasionally as pedestrians came at him in irregular intervals, many on their phones. He waited patiently at one intersection with a gaggle of others until the pedestrian signal turned green – so unlike Manhattan, he thought, where red signals meant nothing and people squeezed defiantly between cars and taxis trying to turn with the traffic signals.

They'd agreed to meet at a popular chophouse that Tom said was a few blocks from his office, just off Peachtree Road, Atlanta's throbbing aorta. Alex felt a pang in the pit of his stomach as he saw the restaurant sign; he'd been rehearsing his lines in his head, but he really had no idea how this meeting would go. Would Tom be open and frank, or would his suspicions get the better of him? It was a toss-up.

Passing the umbrellas on the small streetside patio and walking under the red awning above the stoop, Alex stepped inside. It was dark as twilight, and his eyes took a moment to adjust. A bar with its gleaming brass rail was to the left; the hostess station was just to his right, and he walked up and looked around. There was no one else waiting.

The hostess – young, blonde and good-looking in a snug black dress – smiled at him.

"I'm waiting for someone," Alex said simply. He had described himself to Tom and said he'd wait for him if they missed each other at the entrance.

"Okay, sure." The girl's smile never wavered. "Let me know when you're ready."

Alex took a seat at a curved wooden bench by the door and took his phone from his pocket. He checked – there were no messages. So, he went to his gmail account and looked at a couple of emails.

The door opened and a young man, fresh-faced and in a dark suit, walked in and looked around. "Are you Alex?" he asked.

"Sure am." Alex rose and extended his hand. "Glad to meet you, Tom – and thanks for taking the time to see me."

"Sure. And this gets me out of the office – no lunch at the desk today." He grinned, and Alex studied him quickly: he was over six feet, with close-cut brown hair, brown eyes under light brows, a small nose and thin lips. Alex recalled that he had none of Suzy's bloodlines.

They went to the hostess, who seated them in a booth with a black upholstered seat and back, unremarkable but comfortable and lit by a sconce on the wall. They made small talk about the weather and Alex's conference as they studied the menu, then talked for a few minutes about their children.

It was after they had ordered that Alex took the plunge. "Tom, I asked you here because I really want to know more about Suzy. Well, I told you that already, and you're probably wondering why I would take the trouble to do all this."

"Well, it has crossed my mind." Tom gave him a half-smile and studied Alex briefly. Alex's cobalt blue shirt and khakis rang absolutely true for someone attending a professional conference.

"I just know so little about her, apart from the social interactions we have," Alex said, leaning forward. "My father is crazy about her, but I think it's a little strange that she seems to have – from what I gather – minimal interest in her step-children and grand-children. Or that she left Atlanta not long after your father's death."

Tom looked at him intently for a moment. "Suzy can be a tough bird to figure out. She definitely marches to her own drummer." He went on to describe how she had come into his and his sister's lives after their father's divorce, a beautiful, sometimes mercurial presence who seemed to have sprung from nowhere, a new person in Avery's circle. She gave up working after they married, and she really didn't need to cook: Avery had long ago hired a cook, a middle-aged black woman who was an integral part of the family.

"What did she do? Did she have hobbies?"

"Well, she joined a bridge club and a book club, and spent quite a bit of time at those. And she painted – she had a room downstairs that was converted into something of a studio for her. She was in there practically every day."

"Really?" Alex couldn't hide his surprise. "She hasn't done any painting at my Dad's' house."

"Interesting." Tom put his chin in his hand. "Maybe it was something she outgrew."

"What kind of painting did she do?"

"Oh, they were abstract, lots of bright colors and geometric shapes. I actually thought some were pretty good, but it didn't seem like there was a lot of talent there, just a good sense of proportion. Several were hung around the house – Dad really thought they were terrific."

"If you don't mind my asking, what was she like as a mother?"

Tom paused. "Different. Not motherly, but certainly not a harpy, the nightmare step-mom. I – I always felt Suzy saw us kids as something she had to put up with – it was part of the deal, and she had to adjust to it. Our own mother moved to Florida and remarried, so she wasn't in our lives much."

They talked about Suzy's parenting, and her apparent devotion to Avery, for several more minutes before Alex asked, "Why do you think she left Atlanta?"

"Boy, that's a good question. It seemed to come very suddenly. We had a dinner a few months after Dad died, and she told me and Robin that she missed Dad so badly that a change of scene might be necessary – like she felt his presence in the house all the time."

"Huh." Alex was silent for a few moments. "Tom, do you know anything about her life before she met your Dad?" He took a bite out of his tuna sandwich.

"No. She never talked about it. I was curious about it now and then, but the time to talk about it might have been in the first few years. By the time we were adults, that would have been ancient history."

Alex cleared his throat. "Never any suggestion that she might have come from Missouri, and might have been married earlier?"

"Missouri?" Tom looked puzzled. "No, nothing of the kind." He looked at Alex closely. "Do you know anything to points to any of that?"

"It's very vague at this point, honestly. But it definitely sounds like you guys were never told anything."

"We certainly weren't. We were like mushrooms, kept in the dark." He paused and fiddled with his fork, something Alex caught himself doing now and then. "I think Dad wanted it that way, so that's the way it was."

Alex studied his hands. "Oh, yeah, there was one more thing I meant to ask. What was Suzy's maiden name, or whatever, when she married your Dad?"

"Walker. Suzy Walker. As kids, we thought it was kind of funny, because she wasn't fond of walking. And she does have that minor limp-"

Alex nodded slightly. "Yeah, I know. She told us about that – said it was the result of an old car accident."

"That's what we heard, too." Tom took a sip of his water. "Is it the real story? Who knows? Again, at this point, I don't know that it really matters."

Westchester County, NY

22.

A week later, when the magazine had gone to the printer, Alex allowed himself to think harder about what to do next. It seemed imperative that he run down the Bettina Tallman lead in Missouri, but the track would have grown cold. Still, if there was a daughter, as he was led to believe, she held the key to what could be a trove of more information. Where was she?

He leaned back in his office chair and pulled at his lip.

As good as the Internet was as a resource, he didn't see how it could provide the answers. Bettina would have changed her name before the Web was out of its infancy, and he didn't see how it could handle name changes. Searching under "Bettina Tallman" failed to bring up anyone who might have been Suzy.

He didn't have the time or the energy to go to St. Louis and start poking around old newspaper archives; the obituary was a tantalizing clue, like a wonderful aroma wafting from a kitchen, but little more. Alex really didn't like the idea of going to a private detective – he'd seen too many TV shows that portrayed them as incompetents or drunks nursing Old Fashioneds in seedy bars – but the more he thought about it, the fewer the options presented themselves.

He decided to search for "private detectives St. Louis," not having any great expectations. To his surprise, there were a number of websites listed, and a map giving locations. There was even a rating given to the three best – but he could learn more only if he joined Angie's List, the national service that rates contractors. Several agencies seemed to have fairly good sites that talked about the kinds of work they did and the years of experience put in by the partners.

Well and good – but this was something he'd have to talk over with Lisa. A job that ran into thousands of dollars was doable but unappealing, and he recalled all the hard-boiled PIs from TV and movies talking about a set fee per day "plus expenses." Wasn't that the way they'd done it in *"The Rockford Files?"* The expenses issue was the big unknown, obviously, but he assumed the work would be mostly local. He wasn't worried about confidentiality – without it, these people couldn't function.

It made sense to him to target a mid-sized agency, one that was clearly professional but wasn't geared to corporate clients or big-time litigation. That would take some study.

He felt confident that between email and telephone, he could negotiate a clearly defined job and set a general time frame; he was equally sure that he could convince the investigators of the legitimacy of the project without having to make a personal visit. That was unusual, probably, but they had to be able to work with customers from around the country, didn't they?

He decided to put a dollar cap on the job, but wanted to get Lisa's blessing as to just how much they could spend. As vital as this seemed to be, a blank check was out of the question.

Following another bedtime discussion, he and Lisa agreed to limit the search to $5,000. That probably meant that the agency might pad its expenses to reach that level, but Alex didn't feel he could do much about that – and the key was setting a ceiling.

The next morning at the office was the opening act of a gloomy day – rain was pelting down, and droplets spattered his windows. He closed his office door, a sign that he didn't want to be disturbed. Alex set about looking for an agency, returning to the search parameters he'd put in the day before.

He ruled out two companies right off the bat: they advertised corporate work and background investigations in court cases, not what he was looking for. Two other firms, however, seemed to strike a good middle ground and had professional sites that detailed their history and the partners' experience. Both apparently did video surveillance and sweeps for "bugs" - outside the realm of his interests, certainly – but also talked about personal cases like missing persons.

After an hour or so of intense study, Alex settled on the Maris Agency, with a roughly similar firm as a backup. He jotted a few notes down for a script, then dialed the toll-free number. As he expected, an office manager answered, on the second ring. When he said he was calling from out of state with a missing person's request, she politely told him to hold. Ten seconds later, a man answered, with a deep voice that immediately reminded him of Dr. Phil, the TV psychotherapist.

"This is Bob Insana. How can I help you?"

Alex took a deep breath. "Hello, my name is Alex Perry. I'm calling from Westchester County, New York, but I'm trying to trace a woman I believe used to live in the St. Louis area."

"I see." He paused. "Is this woman still alive?"

"Very much so. She's married to my father. But it appears that she had another life in Missouri, changed her name and remarried after she left."

"Uh-huh." Polite but noncommittal. "Do you suspect anything criminal on her part?"

"I don't think so, but I have a suspicion that she may have had a daughter and possibly grandchildren that no one in my family knows about – not even my father. Her past is a real mystery, and I want to know more about it."

"Okay. How long ago do she think she lived here?"

"At least 20 years ago. I came across an old obituary that seems to identify her as being married to a man in Clayton, Missouri. Her husband died of a heart attack, and she moved to Atlanta and changed her name – or so I believe."

Silence. "Well, we certainly handle these kinds of cases. It would be easy enough to find out if there was someone by that name living in Clayton back then, especially if you have an obituary that seems to confirm that. Driver's license records, Social Security – those could all be checked prior to any name change she might have done."

"That's really what I'm after, but I keep thinking that a photograph would be the clincher."

"Hmmm, that may be a challenge. Missouri didn't have a system of photo driver's licenses that long ago. But there may be other photos from newspapers or friends." He paused again. "Why don't you send me an email with her name and scan the obituary if you can – that would be especially helpful. I'll give you our email in a minute.

"Her husband's name and business would be important pieces of information. Then I can draw up a standard contract and email it to you. I'm assuming you're not planning to come out here."

"I was certainly hoping not to – it would be a big inconvenience, and I don't want to alert her in any way." Alex drummed his fingers on his desk. "Can you – can you give me an idea of your basic expense structure?"

"Sure. Three hundred dollars a day plus expenses. We don't ask you to pay for any meals, but most other things, and a lot of the research is covered in the daily fee."

"Well, Bob, would I be dealing with you personally?" Alex asked.

He heard him clear his throat. "I'd probably be ultimately responsible, but others would be doing most of the legwork. We would give you a full briefing over the phone, plus a written report, when we're done. I could also call with updates, if you'd like."

"That sounds good."

"Before we go any further, let me ask you if you had any monetary limit in mind. I need to be sure it's a job we would want to take on."

"I'm setting it at $5,000."

Alex almost detected a smile over the phone. "That would work. If it's all local, we might be able to wrap it up within a week – but no promises."

"That would be great, but we're certainly willing to wait as long as it takes."

"Good – Alex, is it? Look forward to your email. And thanks in advance for choosing us."

23.

To Dean, Suzy's financial independence was a mixed blessing. With Marjorie, all their accounts were under one roof, and all the statements went to Dean. Marjorie wasn't curious – she left the financial management to him, though there had been discussions earlier in their marriage about key events: buying a house, paying for the kids' private schools. She'd worked in real estate – dabbled, really, like so many suburban housewives - and Dean was clearly the breadwinner.

But Suzy had her own money, lots of it, apparently – how much, he really didn't know; she talked about in very general terms without mentioning a figure. But Avery had been very well off, a grandee of sorts in Atlanta, and had left most of his estate to her after providing for his children in significant trust funds – that much he knew. The money was being managed in Atlanta with a regional brokerage, and Suzy was writing checks from one of the accounts there when she needed to.

So, while Dean had no worries, her financial freedom and reluctance to share the details with him were a little troubling, like an itch that his fingers fumbled to scratch. Even before their marriage, she had confided in him that she wanted to keep their accounts separate, that she was bringing her own money into the union. Eager to please her, he had quickly acquiesced. He knew where she kept her records, but he persuaded himself to refrain from looking at them.

Still, when they sat down a couple of weeks after the wedding to talk about his will, he said he would be changing it to give half of his holdings to her – but no more. He wanted to provide for his children and grandchildren, and surely she could see the logic in that. Dean was relieved that she smiled graciously and said she completely understood; after all, she had plenty of resources of her own.

When they'd met with his attorney – a golf buddy from the club who specialized in trusts and estates – things had gone very smoothly. Suzy was a picture of composure, answering his questions with aplomb and patiently signing the documents with her rounded hand. All the documents were handed to them in a ring binder, which was duly placed in a cabinet in their den with other financial matters.

Even so, it surprised him when Suzy insisted on paying for their upcoming trip to Bermuda. He'd protested mildly, almost reflexively, but she said she wanted to treat him for his birthday, even though that date and the timing of the trip didn't coincide. It would be her gift to him.

It was mid-afternoon Thursday, three days after Alex had signed the contract with the Maris Agency, scanned it and emailed it back. He was in the midst of writing a brief for the front of the magazine when the phone on his desk rang. The Caller ID was explicit: the Maris Agency.

He picked up. "This is Alex."

"Hi Alex. This is Bob Insana in St. Louis. I have some news for you." There was that Dr. Phil voice again.

He caught his breath. "Really, so soon?"

"Well, it's not a whole lot, but… I'll give you some highlights over the phone and then we'll send you a written update by email, probably tomorrow."

"Sounds good."

He cleared his throat. "Okay, there was definitely a Bettina Tallman married to David, as the obituary claimed. And there was a daughter. But – here's where things get a little odd." A pause. "She moved out of town not long after the funeral, and the trail goes cold – no forwarding address, no contacts with friends. In essence, Bettina Tallman disappears."

Alex pulled at his lip. "That's what I thought – and then she goes to Atlanta as Suzy Walker."

"Well, we haven't run that one down yet. But what struck us – I should say, my two folks – as curious that when we asked around town, no one that knew her had any subsequent contact with her. None. She just cut all her ties to Clayton."

"That's not exactly normal, is it?" Alex asked.

"Not in my experience. No sir." He paused. "We haven't been able to find a good photo yet, but we're still looking. We found a group shot, but the detail is pretty poor – not good enough to really clinch any identity."

"Okay. What about the daughter?"

"Well, it appears that she's an art professor in LA, divorced, with two daughters. We haven't interviewed her yet. We could go out there, but that would run the bill up quite a bit."

Alex thought for a moment. "No need for that, I think. Could – could you give me her contact information? I think I'd like to approach her myself."

"We could do that. You're the boss."

"I'd like to look at your report and see what it suggests – but I would like to see if you can find anything more about Suzy Walker in Atlanta. I – I wonder how easy it is to change your name. It doesn't seem like a normal thing to do."

Insana chuckled lightly. "Well, no, it isn't normal – but it doesn't necessarily mean anything criminal. Some people think a new name gives them a new start. In some states, you can do it simply through usage – you start calling yourself Jimmy Doe. You don't have to go through a formal process. But it is a challenge when you want to change your passport, birth certificate, those kinds of things. There, you would need name-change documents certified by the necessary authorities."

"I guess I'd like to know if she did that."

"We'll see what we can find out. We know how to work those angles."

"This is great, Bob. Look forward to seeing your report." He hung up, leaned back in his chair and thought about calling the daughter. Now, that would be a phone call to prepare for.

St. Louis, MO

24.

Looking back, as she did now and then after decades had passed, Suzy recalled the wonderful early years with David. Their marriage was in full flower, and he was building a burgeoning business in the auto dealership network he had inherited from his father.

They'd met in quite a conventional way. Tina Squires was doing marketing programs for local companies and had been promoted to handle regional accounts that were doing television spots in the St. Louis market. When she drove to Tallman's to talk about the first commercial, she had immediately taken to David; there was just something about him.

He wasn't tall, just an inch or so taller than she was. But he was trim and handsome in a way that almost hinted at Hollywood; she likened him to Montgomery Clift, with an open, boyish face, magnetic eyes and dark hair that swirled beguilingly around his head. What's more, he carried himself with an exuberance that captivated her, a lightness combined with a sense of grace. And he dressed well, with neatly pressed shirts and slacks and bold ties that hinted at a spirit of adventure.

The TV spots were a big success. They didn't rely on gimmicks, like so many dealers in smaller markets who saddled up horses or bulls, dressed in nauseating plaids or smashed plate-glass windows with sledge hammers to get attention. David proved unfalteringly telegenic, and he sounded sober and responsible; he didn't shout about price, but talked about reliability and customer service. A series of seven or eight spots, most 15 or 30 seconds, ran for years.

They dated exclusively for eight months before David proposed, having a waiter bring Tina an engagement ring in a cobalt-blue box on a plate instead of her dessert. She was bowled over. This was only her second serious, long-term relationship as an adult, and it was blissful. David was generous, kind and playful enough to keep her guessing. And he was well off: he squired her around town in a Corvette, and they went to prime restaurants several times a week.

David was obviously smitten as well, and he made peace with her limp; if anything, it made him feel more protective toward her. True, she couldn't play tennis with him – and he played every weekend – but she could get around just fine, and he didn't see why she couldn't play golf if she wanted to.

The limp: she had been lying to everyone for years, telling them she'd had a serious car accident at age 16. It seemed reasonable, indisputable – the real fall on the rocks still burned in her memory like a bonfire now and then, but as the years passed, it became partially buried in layers of time and distance, like sediment settling in a riverbed.

Their wedding was a fairly fancy affair at the Clayton Country Club, with dozens of locals, mostly David's and his parents' friends. There was an ice swan looming over chilled champagne glasses, a bower of seasonal flowers, and lawn chairs set in tidy rows on the grass on a late summer afternoon. Tina was a gorgeous bride, in an ivory wedding dress with a tight-fitting lace bodice that showed off her figure and a spray of baby's breath in her hair.

Some of the guests did talk among themselves about the paucity of people there for the bride. In fact, there was only Sally Pritchard, her maid of honor, in the wedding party; the two other bridesmaids were David's sister and a close cousin about his age. A pair of women from her office had also come. The fact that her parents weren't present made for more than idle gossip: were they dead? Very few knew they hadn't been invited. Sally herself was there only because David paid for her trip.

Within five years, David and Tina had moved from a tidy brick ranch in a nice area to a large white colonial in one of the best neighborhoods, with broad lawns front and back and tall elms shading the entrance. Alicia had been born in the first year after they married, and she was thriving. Tina had quit her job to mother her daughter, but to her, that felt more like a duty than a joy. Black moods would steal over Tina now and again, but in the main, she was happy. True, she'd suffered a miscarriage a couple of years after Alicia was born, but they resolved they would try again.

Then, one cold January day when the icicles from the gutters glistened overhead, she felt a tremendous pain in her lower abdomen. It came in waves, and it wasn't abating. She lay in torment for a few hours before calling David, who heard her distress. He rushed back to the house and took her to the hospital, with her moaning in pain on the seat beside him while a woman from his office watched Alicia.

The doctors found an ovarian tumor that had grown to the size of a small lemon and was pressing on the nerves. What was worse – it proved to be malignant. Later the next day, she was wheeled into surgery and the tumor, a defiant ogre within her body, was summarily removed. She left the hospital two days later on David's arm, a bit woozy. There would be no more children.

Something about Tina changed after that. It never announced itself, but it settled on her like a film on a camera lens that couldn't be effaced. Most people weren't aware of it, but the family saw it; her cheeriness, her ability to laugh abated. She felt an outsized sense of victimhood – first her leg, now this. It wasn't fair. A chip lodged on her shoulder, and Sally sensed it in their phone calls. Tina realized it affected the way she interacted with her daughter, but she couldn't help herself.

As the years went by and Alicia was in school, Tina realized she needed to do more to fend off boredom. She'd learned how to play bridge from a colleague at the marketing firm, and she threw herself into a local bridge club composed of housewives like herself. And she joined a book club that met monthly; the overlap was such that several of the same women were, like herself, in both clubs. It was the kind of thing that nonworking suburban women did, apart from tennis and real estate; Suzy couldn't do the former and didn't care for the latter.

David's' dealership business kept growing and growing, assimilating several rivals and moving into other brands. When he'd started, it had been essentially a Ford dealership selling the full line, including trucks; by the early 1990s, it had added Mazda and Hyundai, then eventually

Subaru. Demand for the smaller and cheaper Japanese vehicles was considerable, and David was savvy enough to see that.

It was almost exactly at the point when one of those new brands came on, in the Normandy area, that Tina found out about the affair. Something nagged at her now and then when she called and David was unavailable in the middle of the day; he was "out of the office" or "driving to another dealership." This was in the era before cell phones, and Tina was like an explorer without a map. She just couldn't locate him, though he would often call an hour or two later, apologetic, saying he had just gotten her message.

The actual discovery was like something out of a film noir: she was ironing a couple of his oxford shirts one morning when she saw a smudge on the collar. Peering closely, she thought she saw lipstick. Bending still closer, she sniffed and caught a faint scent of cologne – no, it wasn't cologne. David didn't wear any. It was perfume.

She sniffed again and thought she recognized it – Guerlain. Very flowery. One of her co-workers once had used it liberally. She herself used only Chanel No. 5, and sparingly. She looked down at the collar again and felt her jaw set, firm. This seemed to have come from another woman – was there any other explanation?

Tina knew David was attractive to women – he was appealing to everyone. Their sex life was good, she mused, generally twice a week. He was an attentive and gentle lover most times, though he could be demanding now and then. She thought hard – was there something that she wasn't willing to do that another woman would?

Strong suspicion of his straying came a few days later. She drove to the office, unannounced, shortly after noon. David wasn't there, and his car was gone from the coveted space by the entrance. Another space nearby was also empty, and Tina knew it belonged to Brenda Newsome, the company bookkeeper. They'd chatted briefly at office parties, and she struck Tina as smart and competent and good-looking in a not quite put-together way, with long, dark hair that she wore loose and a big bust that strained at her tops.

She walked in and asked the receptionist if she knew when David was coming back.

"No, ma'am, I don't." The girl was young and polite to the point of being obsequious.

"And Ms. Newsome is gone as well?"

"Yes, she left a little after Mr. Tallman."

"Okay, thank you."

Driving back, she realized that if anything were going on, they would definitely not want to be seen coming and going together. She decided she would test Brenda by dropping into her office that afternoon. Tina could read people well – it was a skill she had honed over the years - and she sensed that if Brenda was indeed involved, she would have trouble meeting Tina's eyes.

Alicia was long out of the house, in college, and Tina had hours on her hands. She sat down with the novel she'd been reading for the book club, but found she couldn't concentrate on it; her mind kept coming back to her surprise visit. She watched part of an old black-and-white movie from the 1930s, when the men dressed in wide-lapel suits, flattened their hair with pomade and sported the quasi-English accent that Hollywood associated with the upper crust. She made herself wait until about 4 before leaving the house.

Her plan worked to perfection. She walked past the receptionist and down the short hall to Brenda's office, knocked, and stuck her head in and said hello.

"Oh, hi, Tina. This is a surprise." Brenda flushed and looked at her with her eyes hooded, then looked down at the desk. To Tina, she was as nervous as someone caught stealing off another's plate, and ordinarily she would have no reason to be. Moreover, Tina caught a faint whiff of Guerlain in the air.

Tina beamed at her as if everything was in its place. "I was in the office and just wanted to say hi. That's all. Didn't want to disturb you."

"Oh, no problem." The woman was still struggling to look at her.

"Bye now." Tina walked out with a look of grim determination that the receptionist, who looked up from buffing her bright pink nails with an emery board, failed to see.

25.

Two days later, after stewing over her morning coffee - strong and black, as she always had it - Tina came up with a plan. She picked up the jar of honey from the table, sealed tightly with a screw top, selected a spreader from the silverware drawer, and took them over to her purse. She went to the hall closet and took out her biggest straw hat, wide-brimmed, then went to the car in the garage and drove to the dealership.

She arrived at 9:30, as the dealership was in the midst of its morning grind, when most people brought their cars in for servicing. She parked some distance from the building and walked slowly over toward Brenda's car, parked in its usual space. She looked around carefully - nothing. There was a salesman, recognizable in his pale blue shirt, in the lot with a customer, but they were far away and had their backs to her. The parking space was around the corner of the building from the showroom windows and mostly out of sight for anyone inside.

Tina crouched down by the driver's side, feeling a slight creak in her right knee; she ignored it. Reaching into her purse, she took out the honey and the spreader and opened the jar. Then she daubed a glob of honey on the spreader and smeared it on the door handle, repeating the process three times. The silver handle gleamed as gold as an Egyptian amulet.

Satisfied, she crept around the back of the car and went to the passenger door, where she did the same. The whole process took less than two minutes. She walked slowly away and back to her car. Suzy got in and exhaled, then she smiled. What she'd done was insanely risky; if she'd been spotted and identified, she would have been caught red-handed. The wife of the owner pulling a cruel prank - the tongues would have been wagging incessantly. And what would David think?

It was a calculated risk, and she'd done it without a lot of forethought. But the scales came down on the side of action, and she acted. This woman wasn't going to get away unpunished.

When David came home that night, he set down his briefcase and kissed her on the cheek. He smelled lightly of sweat and aftershave.

"The weirdest thing happened at the office today," he said simply. "I still can't get over it."

"What was that?" She was the picture of innocent curiosity.

"Someone smeared honey on Brenda's car, on the door handles. It was a mess, and there were bees swarming all over it. She couldn't get in because they did the passenger door, too." He shook his head and smiled. "It was a nasty prank."

She leaned on the counter with her elbows and looked up at him. "That is nasty. So, did they get it off?"

"Well, we had to take it into the garage and use a pressurized hose and spray it off. It wasn't easy, and the bees weren't exactly happy."

She chuckled. "I bet they weren't."

"Brenda was pretty upset, understandably. She couldn't imagine why anyone would do that do her, and in broad daylight."

"It does seem weird. And that stuff is so sticky."

"It sure is. I had one of the guys wipe it down carefully to get it all off. That wasn't easy, believe me."

"No, I'm sure." She beamed at him. "Now, I bet the office will be buzzing -- oh, sorry about the pun -- for a while."

He laughed, his eyes crinkling. "Touche."

In some ways, the honey episode recalled what Tina had done many years earlier, after her breakup with Terry Jamison, her boyfriend of six months in Memphis. Terry, tall and handsome with a forelock of dark hair that fell casually over his forehead like spilled ink, was a business major at the college, a native of Nashville who had wanted to see a different part of the state.

Terry had charmed her. A top tennis player in high school in the city of Nashville, he was rangy, athletic and boyishly enthusiastic about everything from steaks to nice cars to long walks in the parks; he had brought Tina along on all of these interests. He drove a souped-up Mustang, cherry red with a black interior, that he doted on, washing it on weekends outside his apartment, waxing it like a jeweler polishing a stone.

Tina had rented a small apartment near the campus, a small-second floor flat with a nice view out the back of grass and graceful elms. But it was indeed small, barely more than a studio, and all she could afford. Terry, on the other hand, had a full one-bedroom a five-minute walk away that sat on a park and near tennis courts - cracked in places like the tracery of spider veins, but serviceable - where he often played on weekends.

After dating for about a month, Tina's reservations melted like chocolate on a hot day. They had sex, and then more sex, usually in his apartment. It was good; no, more than good. Terry was patient and warm. He like to hold her, and he insisted on long minutes of foreplay. She learned to love the feel of his fingers, his hands on her, caressing and probing; gradually, the teeth-clenching memories of her father's rough touch receded, as surely as the half-light of dawn gives way to morning.

They made love in the shower, on the black leather couch, and a couple of times – in the cover of darkness, on a quiet street draped with trees – in his car. It felt reckless, but she succumbed. He insisted on wearing protection at first, but then she went to the infirmary and got a prescription for the pill, and he put the condoms away.

Things went swimmingly for months, with only a few petty arguments over things that mattered little; in each case, one or the other of them was tired or frustrated by classwork. They often rendezoused for lunch at the school cafeteria, where they'd first met, and dinner was usually something on the fly: if they stayed home, perhaps as simple as grilled-cheese sandwiches and a salad, maybe pasta. If they went out, Terry liked steak or barbeque. He'd learned to love the Memphis dry rub, with its intoxicating yet subtle mix of flavors, and introduced Tina to it.

Their breakup came on gradually. The seed was a cold that Tina came down with in early April, a hacking cough combined with a chest cold that laid her low for a week; she barely made it to class and suffered through long nights where the cough purloined her sleep like a legion of buzzing mosquitoes. On her insistence, but also being practical, Terry mostly stayed away.

When she recovered, something had gone from their romance, almost like tarnish starting to spread on a silver spoon. The ardor of the earlier infatuation was gone; they both recognized it. It was a mature phase of their relationship, where things became more routine. Tina would sense it later, in her marriages, but in this first instance, it troubled her; she looked for a spark to reignite the flame, but it stayed hidden from her.

Terry started to pull away gradually, citing tennis commitments or the need to study; final exams for the year were on the horizon. She accepted his rationale, but something nagged at her. Their lovemaking dwindled to a few times a week and seemed to her more perfunctory – still satisfying, certainly, but without the zeal they'd once had.

Then, one mild night in early May – a Thursday, she remembered – she drove to a nearby strip mall, to one of the casual restaurants they'd found that served good comfort food: stews, heavy soups, grits and Southern specialties like fried okra or plantains. Terry had begged off, saying he had a group study session on the campus. The restaurant had a long white formica counter where she could order alone and not feel uncomfortable.

Just as she approached the door, she heard a familiar laugh and spun her head to the right. Two doors down, emerging from another restaurant, was Terry. He had his back to her, but there was no mistaking him; he wore the blue-and-white striped Oxford shirt that was an essential cog of his wardrobe. He was leaning over and whispering to a woman, a brunette with hair that cascaded down her back, and he had his hand around her waist.

She watched in stunned silence as they sauntered down the sidewalk, lost in each other. Further down, she made out the front of Terry's Mustang. Her mouth open in astonishment, she watched as he went around the car and opened the door for her. She caught a glimpse of the woman as she got in – pretty, with an olive complexion; Tina didn't recognize her.

Anger hit her like heat rising off a summer sidewalk. Tina clenched her fists and watched as the car pulled out and disappeared into traffic. Then she strode into the restaurant, went to the counter, and sat down quickly. There was only one other patron at the counter, a middle-aged guy who was hunched over his meal almost protectively. He paid no attention to her, and she picked up the menu and started to study it when she realized, as quickly as a finger snapping, that she just wasn't hungry.

Around eight the next morning, after a hard night in which her mind raced and sleep was long in coming, Tina called Terry at his apartment. She knew his schedule: it was Friday, and he only had a couple of classes starting late in the morning.

"Hi." He answered a bit groggily, it seemed to her.

"I saw you last night." She practically bit off the words.

"You saw me what?" His voice was all surprise.

"Walking out of the restaurant with some girl. You seemed pretty fond of her. Then you got in the car and drove off."

There was a long silence. "Well, I can't deny it, Tina." Then he sounded a note that wavered between contrition and defiance. "Look, it's not as if we're married. I – I think we should be free to see other people, to make sure what we have is what we both want for the long term."

"Huh." Her voice went cold. "I'm not seeing anyone else. Should I be?"

"I'm not saying you should, no," he said slowly. "But if I can, you can – the rules should be equal."

"I see," she replied icily. "Well, it's something I have to think about."

"Do that." He sounded conciliatory. "You caught me – I can't pretend it didn't happen. Both of us need to think seriously about where we're headed, and the summer is coming up." Each of them had lined up summer internships in the area, though his was a substantial distance away.

"I'm sorry if I hurt you," he said. Hearing no response, he went on, "I'll call you later today after my classes."

But then he didn't, and the weekend went by, and she hadn't heard from him. She stewed, she cursed him under her breath; she couldn't bring her mind to concentrate on anything but the simplest tasks. Was it truly over – had this blissful thing they had just melted away?

Tina disliked confrontation, but she had to have it out with him. On Tuesday, late in the afternoon after classes, she drove to his apartment, where the Mustang was parked at the curb. The air was soft and sweet with the fragrance of something she couldn't quite place. She walked slowly toward the front door, then stopped short when she heard voices through an open window. Stopping abruptly, she sank into a crouch, then stole over the grass toward the window, his kitchen window, her heart racing.

She lifted her eyes above the small trimmed privet hedge and looked in through the screen. Terry and the girl from the other day were sitting at the kitchen table; he had what looked like a glass of bourbon, while she was holding a glass of white wine. He said something softly, looking at her with a smile, and reached over and touched her arm, and stroked it. She smiled and murmured something back.

Tina had seen enough. Her blood boiling, she stalked back to her car and drove home, faster than she ordinarily would. She barely stopped at the stop signs, as if they merely read, "slow." Back in her apartment, she fixated on only one thing: his betrayal, and what kind of payback was needed. She poured herself a big glass of white wine, sat down at the white wooden table and mulled over what she could do.

The next night, after dark, she drove over to his apartment. The Mustang was in its usual spot. It was a quiet neighborhood, and the streetlamps by the park didn't cast much light on the street itself; moths were circling under the lamps like little dervishes. The only issue might be a car driving by.

Tina wore black for the occasion, a black cotton top and black jeans; somehow it seemed fitting. She parked a half-block away and walked up the sidewalk; it was a warm and cloudy night, and she had to swat at a few mosquitoes that buzzed by her head. Reaching into the bag she'd brought with her, she brought out the box cutter and slunk up to his car.

Kneeling down, Tina slashed the right rear tire, cutting directly across the treads with enough force to feel the blade sink in, like a knife cutting into a tart apple. Then she stole around the front and went to the left front tire and did the same. She moved back quickly toward the sidewalk when she saw the headlights of a car approaching from behind the Mustang, but the car flashed by and was gone.

She liked the idea of symmetry – not slashing all four tires, but one on each end. Four seemed like overkill.

Then Tina applied what she considered the *coup de grace*. She reached into the canvas bag and brought out the paper bag she had laboriously filled several hours earlier, the detritus from thoughtless or careless dog owners who failed to pick up after their pets. Picking some of it up was easy, but scraping other, softer turds out of the grass was a chore. She spent 15 minutes or so collecting at least a dozen specimens – ranging widely in size, not surprisingly – and dumping them in a brown shopping bag. It all smelled terrible, of course, and she wrinkled her nose any number of times.

Now, at the car, she really wanted to overturn the bag inside, on the seats, but she suspected the car was locked. She looked around, then moved to the driver's door and tried the handle. Locked. So, she went to Plan B. She dumped about half of the contents of the bag slowly on the windshield, watching the turds slide down to the windshield wipers. She moved around the car to the other side of the windshield and deposited the rest, then she smiled. Even in the dim light, it looked awful.

Looking around, she still saw nothing. She rolled up the paper bag, put it in the satchel, and walked back to her car as though she hadn't a care in the world.

The next morning, when Terry called her, his usual insouciance turned on its head, he accused her. She feigned innocence, and even sounded a note of sympathy. But she knew it was over between them, and he'd been the instrument; she'd simply asserted her right to hit back – not, as some women would have done, face to face. Her anger was channeled into more devious ways – things that couldn't be proven, only surmised. She was clever, and using her wits to avoid detection just felt right.

Westchester County, NY

26.

Alex stared at the email from Insana again. It listed Alicia Tallman, living at an address in Pasadena, with a phone number. Alex realized he hadn't thought to do a search for that name on the Internet – he'd somehow assumed that when she had married, she had changed her name. Her position at Cal State Northridge was also listed, along with an office number.

This would be another call that gave him real trepidation. If she cooperated, Alicia could be a key to unlocking much of the mystery surrounding Suzy. If she didn't, he gained nothing. Once again, he decided to call the home number – it was more likely to get a response.

He sat on the information for a day, electing to talk with Lisa that night about how to approach Alicia. They agreed he needed to be humble, eager for help – there could be nothing officious, nothing remotely heavy-handed.

So here it was, 10:30 p.m. on a warm, muggy Wednesday night in early June, when California was three hours behind East Coast time. Alex picked up the receiver on the home phone in the den and punched in the numbers, then blew out a breath, hard.

The phone rang, and rang. On the fifth ring, it went to voicemail. A woman's voice, distinct, said, "You've reached the Tallman household. We can't take your call at the moment, but please leave a message at the beep."

He had half expected this – so many people had Caller ID and simply didn't answer calls they didn't recognize. When he heard the beep, he decided to plunge on.

"Hi, I'm calling for Alicia. You don't know me. My name is Alex Perry. I'm calling from Westchester County, New York, and I'm trying to find out any information about Bettina Tallman, who I understand is your mother. She changed her name and is now married to my father--"

He heard a click on the other end. "Hello? My God." Silence for several seconds. "I can't believe – how do you know this is my mother?"

"I hired a private detective in St. Louis to look into her background, and I found an obituary of your father, David."

"My goodness." The voice was strained. "Wow. This is a phone call I wasn't sure I would ever get. You – you say she's married to your father?" The voice was low and a bit husky.

"Yes, since last year. She had come from Atlanta, where she had changed her name and was married for 20 years until her husband died."

"Wow again. What – what did she change her name to?"

"Suzy Walker when she went to Atlanta. Suzy Rittenhouse when she married there."

Alex could almost sense her confusion over the phone. "This – this is just hard to process. I haven't heard a word from my mother in more than 20 years. She vanished from my life."

"That's what I'd been led to believe."

"All I can tell you about her is at least 20 years old. And I have two daughters here – can we possibly talk when I'm in my office during the day? I need to collect my thoughts, too."

"Of course."

"Tell me your name again."

"Alex. Alex Perry."

"Okay, Alex. Can you call me tomorrow at 11 am my time? I'm between classes then – I'm a college professor."

"I know. My private detective collected that information, along with your office number. Let me read it to you and make sure I have it right." He did that, and she agreed it was correct.

"Well, Alex. I'm looking forward to our call."

"So am I, Alicia. Thank you so much for your willingness to help me out."

"Oh, it's more than just cooperation. My curiosity level about her is pretty high – you can probably imagine."

"I can. Thanks, Alicia, and talk to you tomorrow."

27.

"Hi, this is Professor Tallman." The voice was different somehow – brisk and efficient.

"Alicia, this is Alex Perry, calling as we had discussed."

"Oh, of course." A pause. "This is a good time for me, but I don't know how to begin. Maybe you should ask questions and I'll try to answer them."

"Okay. Let's start with you and your parents – I take it there was never another sibling?"

"That's right. It's something they never talked about, but I ended up as an only child."

"Were your parents close?"

"Oh, very. They seemed to be very much in love, as far as marriage goes – and I know what that means. They – they even held hands in public fairly often. My father doted on her. He loved me, but not, I would say, as much as he did her."

Alex thought for a second. "And how did she act toward you?"

"Fairly distant for a mother, at least in comparison to other mothers I met through friends. I – I really don't know what to tell you. There was never much anger at all, but no real warmth, either – and I was a top student who checked most of the boxes you'd want as a parent – no drugs, no seedy boyfriends."

"I heard second-hand that your mother was in a bridge club there."

"That's right. She played every week with the same group of women at the country club."

"Well, she did the same thing in Atlanta," Alex said.

"Hmmm. I can't say I'm surprised. She was very good, and it meant a lot to her."

"It seems a shame that you lost your father so young."

"It was incomprehensible to me at the time. My Dad was active and very healthy – he had no issues that I ever knew of. Dying suddenly of a heart attack was a complete shock."

"After he died, what was your contact with her?"

"Well, we had a good cry at the funeral, and then I went back to my studies at UCLA. That's when things really changed. I had this cryptic phone call with her when she told me she was selling the house and leaving town – and she wouldn't tell me where she was going."

"And then she disappeared…" Alex drew out the last syllable.

"Absolutely. It was almost inconceivable. We never had a bitter falling out, and then – poof! – she's gone."

"Did you ever try to find her?"

Alicia spoke for several minutes about her belief that Tina had abandoned her and didn't want to reconnect – a belief cemented by the decades that had passed since. She had considered and dismissed hiring a detective, she told him, and every year that passed put her mother further behind her. That had made his call a jolt to her system.

"Why do you think she might have changed her name, and why go to Atlanta?"

"Your guess is as good as mine. I have no idea."

"Where did she come from, originally?"

"Little Rock. She grew up there and moved to St. Louis after getting a degree in marketing. That's where she met Dad." He heard a door on her end, and some muffled words.

"Sorry, had to shoo someone from my office." She paused. "She had an old childhood friend in Little Rock that she corresponded with all the time."

"Do you remember this friend's name?" Alex asked.

"Um - Sally something. Sorry – that's all I remember."

"And what was your mother's maiden name?"

"Squires, Bettina Squires."

"What were they like, her parents – your grandparents?"

"I, um, really can't tell you a thing. I never even knew their names. My mother had cut them out of her life even before she met Dad. They were ciphers to me."

"You're kidding!"

"No, and it always seemed sad to me. Whenever I asked about them growing up, she would badmouth them – she said they were drunks who had abused her and she wanted no part of them and didn't want me to see them."

"Alicia, do you have a good photo of your mother?"

He heard her sigh. "I do. It's old, of course, but it's a good closeup of her with Dad, taken a few years before he died."

"Would you be able to scan it or take a good photo of it and send it to me? I'll give you my email address."

"Of course, but it's at home, so I couldn't send it for a while."

"That would be fantastic. You know, everything we have at this point, you could say, is circumstantial. But a good likeness could be the final piece in the puzzle."

"I hope so, for your sake. Please call me and let me know. But meanwhile, I need to hang up and start my office hours."

"Okay. Here's my work email," he said, spelling it out. "Many thanks, Alicia. We'll talk soon."

28.

That night, Alex and Lisa had another long conversation where he updated her on the call to Alicia. Sometimes he felt like he almost had to whisper, as if the walls had been wired with bugs; neither of them had been involved in anything so secretive before. She absorbed it all, wide-eyed, with only a few questions.

"So, we just really need the photo to be sure, don't we?" she asked. They were in bed, propped up on the pillows; a thunderstorm rumbled outside, tormenting the windows and hurling flashes of bright light into the mostly darkened room.

"Looks that way," Alex said. "I'd be shocked if it isn't her."

"Will you call me and let me know?"

"Of course."

"But – but what do we tell your Dad?"

He sighed. "Nothing for right now. I still have the Maris people on the case to see if there is anything suspicious about her name change and the move to Atlanta."

"And if there is?"

He looked at her for a few seconds. "Christ, I don't know. We'll just have to play that one by ear."

It was practically unthinkable for them to share any of this with Jason and Jennifer. They would understand some things, certainly, but Alex and Lisa agreed they would try to shield them as much as possible. True, it was summer, and the kids didn't have the distractions of schoolwork, but both had part-time jobs – things meant to stretch them, to nudge them toward the adult world of work. They had enough on their plates.

Lisa was pensive for a moment. "Do you think we – I guess you – should talk to Debra about any of this? She is a family therapist."

Alex pursed his lips. "Maybe. She might have some insights about Suzy's behavior. But – well, I really don't know that I want to get her very involved. And I definitely don't want her talking to Dad."

"She can keep a secret, can't she?"

He sighed. "Yeah, but I'd want to tread carefully. And I don't like the way she's drinking and what not – loose lips sink ships, as they say."

"I guess they do." Lisa looked at him, hard, for a moment. "I'll leave that up to you, honey, but I do think she might be helpful."

Lisa had thought hard for several weeks about the situation they were in, lost in thought at times in her office. Having to keep secrets from everyone was something new. All her life, she'd been a straight arrow – the oldest daughter, the upright, obedient one. Alex had recognized those virtues when he was dating her. She wasn't nervous, excitable, unprepared – but the drip-drip accumulation of information about Suzy had upset her equilibrium like a tree bent by a freshening wind.

Still, she trusted Alex, and she knew he would make her part of all the decision-making. It was the way they worked together, the way they ran the household and raised the children. They were in it together, and if she was uneasy, she knew he was, too.

Sally reached into the shoebox of old letters that sat at the bottom of the lowest drawer of the white desk in their den. It held most of the letters that Suzy had sent her over many years, ending when they joined the rest of the world on email. Actually, there had been as many phone calls as letters, but it was in the letters that Suzy revealed more of herself, provided details that she rarely shared on the phone.

She reached toward the back and pulled one out at started to read. It was dated March 23, 1979, and it had Suzy's somewhat florid hand, written in black ink.

"Dear Sal:

Things are busy up here! David's dealerships keep spreading — he just added another that he had been eyeing for a few years now. That makes eight locations, so many that I think he's spread kinda thin. Hard to be too many places at once! But it's hard to complain: we're certainly doing well financially.

I still feel a little restless — it's been years since I was working. (That must sound weird to you.) Every now and then, I get involved in reviewing some of the marketing stuff that David does. But other than that, I'm pretty much on the sidelines.

I do play a good deal of bridge at the country club with a bunch of other women, and I really enjoy it. And I'm good at it. It's nice to feel really competent at something, and something that requires a brain. God knows, I'll never be able to do anything difficult physically, as you know all too well.

I'm also starting to get involved with some fundraisers for things like the local library — things that can be tied to David's business. It certainly never hurts when a business can be seen as giving back to the community. We did one recently for the YMCA that was really successful. They needed money to refurbish the pool and update their gym, and we raised something like $400,000. Great stuff!

My biggest concern is Alicia. She's seven now, and in second grade. She's a very bright girl, and very well-behaved. She should be the least of my concerns, but I find it hard to bring myself to spend lots of time with her, to read to her, play with her. Sometimes I look at her and get a little irritated; she reminds me that the hysterectomy robbed me of a chance to have another child. I want to cherish her, and I should, but I can't. I know you don't have any such problems with your kids. This is all on me.

I hope I may be able to swing down to Little Rock this summer, after school lets out. Maybe in June — I'll give you plenty of warning. I always wish we weren't so far apart, but that's life, isn't it?

Best to Harold and the kids—
Love, Tina

Sally sat back and sighed, still holding the letter. She barely remembered it, but she put in context: She and Harold were dealing with three young children at home then, and between their activities and issues and her nursing job, there wasn't much time for reflection.

She put the letter back into roughly the same area and took out another, more recent missive. This one was in an odd ink, a relatively light blue. Sally leaned back, unfolded it, and read:

September 6, 1988

Hi Sal:

Another summer down! It was a good one for us. We took a trip to the Rockies last month, driving through Colorado and down into New Mexico before heading home. We were gone about two weeks – it's hard for David to go any longer than that before worrying about the business. You know how it is with these business owners! We stayed mostly in hotels, but we took Alicia to a working dude ranch for a couple of days. She had a ball riding horses – not for me (or David).

Alicia started school yesterday – she's 16 and is starting her junior year at St. Louis Country Day. She's already learning about things you and I never heard about. It's an excellent school and she's a top student, as I've probably told you too often. But it is a source of pride for me and David. I think she'll be playing soccer again this fall. How are your oldest boys doing? I know you told me Richard was going to community college this year.

I do appreciate your periodic updates about my parents. I know that sounds odd, since I never communicate with them, but some part of me wants to hear about them now and then. It's strange when the people who brought you into the world are no longer part of your life, but in my case, I know you understand. There's more than just water under that bridge.

I appreciate your keeping any details of my life away from Tommy. You've said he's called you a few times and asked questions. I'm not surprised to learn that he became a mechanic – he was always good with his hands, but never *had any ambition. And he's still a drummer in a band? You'd think he'd be getting a little old for that!*

We're planning to add on to our house – a large family room with a fireplace, and a new office area for David. This would be the first change since we bought it. We've been working with an architect and an interior designer, and it's pretty exciting. The work will probably start in a couple of weeks – I'll try to send you some photos when it's done.

You know I haven't kept up with the high school crowd, but I'm curious to hear what's happened to Bo Thompson – he was always one of my favorites. Do let me know what he's up to – though, come to think of it, he may have moved out years ago. I always thought he was headed for good things.

Okay, gotta run –

Love, Tina

Sally closed her eyes. She looked at the clock – 5:03. The kids were in their rooms. Harold would be on his way home, and she had to start thinking about dinner.

29.

It was well after dark in Plano when the phone rang in the condo, housed in one of many cookie-cutter brick buildings in a development now just three years old. Nancy set down her book and looked over to the table to see the caller ID, then picked up.

"Hi, honey. What's going on?"

"Hi, Mom. I'd ask about the weather, but I know it's been cold there."

"You're right about that. We had an ice storm two nights ago. I just stayed home – the roads were frightful."

"We had an ice storm last week, but it doesn't sound like it was as bad. Anyway, I had a question for you, Mom."

"Sure, Baxter. What is it?"

"This may start sounding a little crazy. I just took on a client – actually a couple of clients. The husband was a rich insurance executive, a CEO, but it's his wife who really grabbed my attention. I really don't remember Tina all that well, but this woman was a spitting image of what I do remember of her. And she even has a limp."

"My God." Nancy caught herself, startled. "That would be amazing, after all these years. And you say she's in Atlanta now?"

"And she goes by Suzy. Suzy Rittenhouse is her married name."

Nancy thought hard for a moment. "This would be an incredible coincidence, Baxter. What – what do you think I could help with?"

"You have some good family photos that I remember have her in it. I need to compare a photo with the real person to be sure."

"Well, of course. I'm sure I can find those somewhere. When your Dad died, I put a lot of the old family scrapbooks away, but I took them with me here." She had moved to the Dallas area three years earlier after Jack Dennison, her husband of 40 years, developed lymphoma and died in the space of a few months. Kathy, her oldest daughter, lived nearby with her family.

She went on, "I can mail something to you. Don't ask me to put it in a computer or anything." She glanced at her watch: only 7:23.

"Mail would be fine, Mom."

She thought for a moment, "Baxter, d'you think there's any chance she could recognize you?"

"Not likely. As I remember it, I was a teenager, just going to college, when she left. We didn't see her that often, and, of course, she knew me as Will." It is in his junior year at Emory that Baxter chose to go by his middle name; he always disliked Wilbur, the name his father had insisted on in honor of the Wright Brothers. Baxter had forever rejoiced internally that his middle name wasn't Orville.

He liked the sound of W. Baxter Dennison; more importantly, it seemed to him to convey a sense of sophistication, of wealth – things that could be shiny assets in the world of money management that he'd chosen as a career.

"I can probably mail something out to you tomorrow," Nancy said. "Is that okay?"

"Fine, Mom," Baxter replied. "There's no big rush, really."

The conversation moved briefly to Kathy and her family, and then the call ended with the obligatory "love you's." It was a signature closure for calls with his mother; it would never have happened with his father.

Nancy sat back and was lost in thought. If this was Suzy, it was incredible. People do move and change their names, she realized, but few, she imagined, would have done it so abruptly and so completely – and left their past behind like it had been merely an unhappy dream.

The pub had started to fill up with brightly clad couples, many of the men in Bermuda shorts and knee socks, and some in Navy blazers. Smiles and laughter erupted all around them. Why not? Hamilton,

Bermuda, was for many just this side of paradise, with its quaintness, dearth of cars and semi-tropical breezes.

Dean had loved Bermuda since his parents had taken him and his brother there when Dean was just 14. The island tickled the budding Anglophile in him; even the formality of dress, so unlike the slide toward unkemptness that was happening all around him in the '60s, was appealing here. It was almost a fantasy, a land of pastel houses out of a children's book and brilliantly clear water lapping at the sand.

Now, he and Suzy were studying the menu while the clip-clop of horse-drawn carriages reached their ears from the street outside. She looks great, he thought, in a simple turquoise shift that showed off her shoulders and the graceful lines of her neck, just now showing the predictable creases of age. She wore a necklace of light blue glass beads and earrings to match. I'll bet I'm the envy of many of these codgers, he smiled to himself.

Suzy had ordered a glass of champagne, while Dean treated himself to a summer favorite, Tanqueray gin with tonic, on the rocks.

Dean looked at her over his reading glasses. "I know we just had fish yesterday, but I'm going to go with the snapper with beurre blanc. I'll bet it's top-notch."

She studied the menu for a while, then looked up. "I think I'll do the scampi."

"Well, my goodness, if it isn't Suzy." The voice came from her left, and she looked over with a start. It was Richard Washburn, one of Avery's golf buddies, smiling at her like a Cheshire Cat.

She struggled to focus for a moment, then smiled, as if she were an actor just given her cue. "Oh, hi Richard. This is a surprise. What brings you here?"

"Golf – no surprise there, right?" He was lean and tanned, medium height, his skin the color of light walnut stain against a white polo shirt. "We're here to play at few rounds at Port Royal and Mid-Ocean." He glanced at Dean and extended his hand. "Hi, I'm Richard Washburn, from Atlanta. I was an old friend of her husband Avery's."

Dean shook his hand, without much conviction; Washburn's appearance had taken him by surprise, too.

"Hi, I'm Dean Perry. Suzy and I married last year."

Washburn's face clouded slightly before he caught himself and smiled again. "Well, well. That's great."

Suzy had recovered her wits enough to sound gracious. "Dean and I live in Rye, New York. We met after I moved there. We – we're celebrating his birthday here with a short trip."

"Sounds great." His smile was as steady as if it had been quick-frozen. "Well, I don't want to intrude. I just had to say hello. Avery and I played golf for 30 years together, and I miss him. I knew his health wasn't the best, but a heart attack shocked me."

He straightened up. "We played with a cardiologist buddy of ours, and he told me he had a hard time believing Avery went out that way. Anyway… Suzy, you look terrific, as always. Atlanta misses you."

She smiled broadly at Washburn. "Thanks so much, Richard. It's great to see you – thanks for coming over." She looked around him at the tables beyond. "Is Mary Lou here with you?"

"Nope." He grinned. "Boys' trip. She's givin' me a hall pass, as they say."

Dean and Suzy chuckled. "Well, she's a forgiving soul, isn't she?" Suzy said.

"She certainly is." He grinned again. "Nice to meet you, Dean, and Suzy, if you're ever back in Atlanta, give us a call." He walked slowly away with a wave that was as quick as it was reflexive.

Westchester County, NY

30.

Scrolling through his emails in the office, Alex saw the usual mix of promotional chaff from PR agencies touting their clients' products, as well as interoffice and intercompany memos – the latter would require more of his attention, certainly.

Then he saw it: the header read, *atallman@csun.edu*. And there was an attachment.

He clicked on it, holding his breath. The message was brief and succinct:

> "Dear Alex: Here's the photo of my mother that you asked for. Remember that it's almost 25 years old. Please let me know if she is indeed your new mother-in-law. Best, Alicia."

He clicked on the attachment and gasped. It was a black and white close-up, a formal studio shot, no doubt. The woman was younger and even more striking, but the smile and the hair were unmistakable. It was Suzy.

It was only a matter of seconds before he was dialing Lisa in her office. She picked up on the third ring.

"Hon, I just got the photo from Alicia." He let the sentence linger in the air.

"And?" She blurted.

"It's Suzy, in spades. Unmistakable. I can forward you the email."

"Great. Well, well. I – I think we knew this was the case."

"Certainly seemed that way. Now we know."

There was a long silence. "What now, hubby?" This was a term of endearment she used now and then.

"Hmmmm. We want to hear more from Insana and his people about the name change and what she did in Atlanta. That should come pretty quickly. Then we'll see where we go from there."

The next day, a bright, hot day with thunderstorms in the offing, the phone rang in Alex's office. He glanced at the screen: it was the Maris agency again. He picked up.

"Hi, this is Alex."

"Alex, Bob Insana here. I have some more news for you."

"Okay, shoot."

"Well," he paused. "It seems that Bettina Tallman had a legitimate name change when she moved to Atlanta. Those records are on file with the state, and were made with the local court."

"So it was completely legit?"

"It seems that way."

"And was she working before she married Avery?"

"Yes. I know it was a marketing agency – I don't recall the name offhand," Insana said. "She left that job almost 20 years ago, it seems, about the time she married Avery." He paused and coughed. "My guy tells me that the agency did a lot of work coordinating events with charities."

"Interesting. I wonder if that's how she met Avery. He was big in charity circles, or so I understand."

"Could have been."

He cleared his throat. "Bob, I have news for you – I got a photo from the daughter. Tina Tallman is unquestionably Suzy."

"Aha. Well, that's been our supposition all along."

"It has. Tell me, Bob, how are we doing on our fee limit?"

"Oh, we're a ways under it, certainly."

"I'd be interested in finding out the time frame between when she arrives in Atlanta and when she married Avery."

"Okay." Insana sounded a little dubious. "But I'm not sure how that information really helps you."

"Well, I have a theory. Suzy apparently isn't a believer in long courtships."

Insana chuckled. "That may be true. But we probably can't find out when she met Avery without a lot of digging."

"Hmmm, you're right about that," Alex said slowly. "You know, her children might know, but they were quite young. I may try calling them again."

"Okay."

"Bob, I don't know if you checked, but has there been anything at all you've come across that would be on someone's record – traffic accidents, non-payment of rent, whatever?"

"Not that we've seen so far. Do you want to look at both Missouri and Atlanta?"

"I guess so, but I would concentrate on Atlanta."

"All right, I'll have them check some Georgia databases in both names, Walker and Rittenhouse."

"Great."

"Alex, do you have any suspicions you can share?" Alex detected a note of anxiety in his voice.

He made a clucking sound. "No, not really. Call it a journalist's hunch."

"All right then. We'll keep checking on the databases. Hopefully, we can get that done quickly."

"Sounds good. Thanks, Bob. Call me if there's anything significant."

"Will do. Bye now."

31.

It was almost by accident that Tina found out about Carolina jasmine. She was visiting Sally during one of her regular, almost annual sojourns back to her hometown. Sally lived in the western part of town, several miles from there they had grown up; it was a similar neighborhood, established but a bit run-down, of small ranch and split-level houses crowded on narrow lots, with mature trees offering welcome shade in the summer.

Her parents were still in their family home, but Tina had cut off communication with them not long after she left Little Rock. They knew nothing of their daughter's life in Clayton, or their granddaughter; they were as oblivious to her whereabouts as if she lived in a distant galaxy. The pain of the estrangement was permanently etched in their faces, perhaps more so as the long years passed. When strangers asked her parents about their children, they told them they had only one child, a son.

Sally was still in her powder-blue nurse's uniform, and they were talking in the kitchen before Harold came home. They were snacking on some Ritz crackers and cheese spread before Sally changed and started cooking; a little white wine flowed, and they sat at the small table in the kitchen, decked in a bright floral tablecloth.

Sally was talking about a strange case that had come in the day before – a young boy, about 12, was experiencing nausea and dizziness, and when his mother brought him into the doctor's office, he was close to being unconscious. The doctor did vigorous CPR – pumping his chest and breathing into his mouth – and he began to revive, then rolled to one side and vomited profusely. Sally called for an ambulance, and the boy and his mother were soon speeding to the hospital.

"It was serious, and I feared that boy was gonna die," she told Tina.

"Did he eat something bad?" Tina asked.

"Well, that's the thing," Sally said, taking another sip of wine. "The mother called today, and she said he'd eaten some leaves from a vine growing near their house. When he got home, that's when he started feeling terrible."

"You mean like nightshade, or something?" Tina was familiar with the plant, related to the tomato, with its small white star-shaped flowers; she'd been told by her mother to steer clear of it.

"No. Dr. Roberts told me it's something called 'Carolina jasmine.' It's a vine with pretty flowers, and it's pretty common – but very poisonous. He said that virtually every part of the plant is poisonous, and that it acts a lot like strychnine."

Tina looked puzzled. "So why would a boy be chewing on something like that?"

"The mother thought one of his friends told him it would get him high. Well, not quite. It almost got him dead." She shook her head.

"Did the boy survive?"

"He did, but it was apparently a near thing. He was lucky."

Four days later, back in Clayton, Tina drove to the library and did some research. She took down a tome on American trees and plants, and looked up Carolina jasmine. What she found intrigued her.

She discovered that the plant, *Gelsenium sempervirens*, was found widely in the Southeast. It was a handsome, evergreen vine with fragrant, funnel-shaped yellow flowers; it was even grown as an ornamental. Most often, she read, poisonings occurred as part of a misguided herbal preparation. Symptoms included dry mouth, headaches and dizziness and difficulty speaking. In sufficient doses and without proper treatment, ingestion could be fatal.

She studied a photo of the plant: it had a lovely yellow flower and leaves shaped much like a rhododendron. It certainly looked innocent enough.

Reading further, she learned that *Gelsenium* poisoning, in addition to the symptoms listed, presented itself, more than anything, as a heart attack. She stared at the page for a few long moments. Then she reached into her purse, pulled out a small notebook and jotted down the Latin name. Then she left the book at the end of the stack, to be reshelved, and walked back out the entrance.

32.

He was underwater, looking up to see pale sunlight washing into the sky-blue water. He kicked upward, and his head broke the waves – but now the sun was enveloped in shroud of fog. Treading water and struggling to keep his mouth clear, he looked around him and saw nothing – only a narrow scrim of light on the horizon that could have come from anywhere. He was completely alone.

Alex woke up with a start – bad dreams were rare for him. He glanced over at the clock and saw it read 5:40. Dawn had trickled under the shades, and Lisa was still asleep – he could hear regular breathing.

He shook his head to clear it and sat up on the edge of the bed, rubbing his knees.

This dream had nothing to do with Suzy and the investigation, he thought – or did it? He wasn't into the analysis of dreams, which struck him as nonsensical as reading tea leaves or the clouds in a coffee cup. But his choice not to involve Dean did make him feel at times as if he were a solitary swimmer struggling against a strong current. Thank God for Lisa. He looked over again; she had yet to stir. He swung his legs off the bed and moved to the bathroom.

Alex had just gotten off the phone after an interview, and was staring at the screen where he'd taken his notes. The phone rang, and he glanced at the screen and saw it was Maris. He picked up.

"Hi, Bob."

"Hi, Alex. We turned up something interesting in our research in Missouri that I wanted to let you know about."

"Really."

"Yep. It seems that David Tallman's older brother, Larry, filed a motion challenging the official cause of death. In effect, he accused the medical examiner of missing something."

"What?" Alex sat up in his seat.

"It happened a month or so after David died. Larry was convinced, apparently, that there's no way David could have died of a heart attack, but he had nothing concrete to base that on."

"So, what happened?"

Insana paused. "He actually asked that the body be disinterred and more analysis done. But that didn't happen – Bettina blocked it."

"Ah." That was all that escaped from his mouth. Alex felt his scalp tingle.

"From what we could gather," Insana said, "she responded that digging him up was a sacrilege, that he should be allowed to rest in peace. As the spouse, she has the right to block another autopsy unless there is a material case for it. And the medical examiner's office had no basis for going against her."

Alex thought hard. "Bob, does that sound suspicious to you?"

"Honestly, not so much. Families tend to be very protective of remains. They've suffered a tremendous loss, and they don't want to compound it by having the loved one dug up again."

"But if she had something to hide—"

"That's a little far-fetched, Alex – but if she did, sure. She wouldn't want any part of a thorough autopsy."

"Is this brother still alive?"

"I don't know. He would be quite elderly, but it's certainly possible."

"If he is, I'd love to know if he had any theories or suspicions."

"Do you want us to check that out?"

"Absolutely. Sounds like it would be a phone call, really, not much more."

"Okay, we'll look into it and let you know."

"Thanks."

33.

Suzy's life in Atlanta prior to meeting Avery wasn't proving fruitful for the Maris investigators, and Alex got an email to that effect. Apart from her name change, there wasn't anything unusual they could turn up. Her employer, the Corcoran Group, had folded a decade or so earlier, and Insana said he didn't see much point in trying to chat up any of the old partners to try to learn anything more.

And the lead on Larry Tallman went nowhere as well. Insana wrote that he had died 9 years earlier of pancreatic cancer, at 69. But one of the Maris investigators spoke to Larry's wife, June, about the now-generations-old challenge over David's death - and turned up something interesting. She said it had been common knowledge in the family that David had taken out a $1.5 million life insurance policy only about three months before he died – at Tina's behest.

While the timing might seem suspicious, Insana wrote, David had built the dealership into a major operation, and a policy of that size for a wealthy man wasn't that unusual. His net worth was almost certainly several times that size.

It was late afternoon when Alex called St. Louis and asked to speak to Insana. He thought it was paramount to ask if there were any avenues worth pursuing before they wrapped things up. He wasn't in and Alex left a message.

An hour or so later, Insana called back and Alex picked up quickly.

"Bob, is there anything else we should be looking at, in your opinion?"

Insana sighed. "Well, I'm not sure there is, honestly. We've pretty much covered the bases in those two locations."

"So, in your professional opinion, we've basically reached a dead end," Alex said.

"Yeah, I think so. And you're almost at your limit. I don't want to run up the bill chasing down rabbit holes."

"So," Alex stroked his chin. "We have a woman who abandoned her parents and her daughter and was widowed twice in what could be seen as tragic, but normal, events. She changes her name. She emerges as a very wealthy widow who has virtually no contact with her stepchildren, whom she lived with for many years. Doesn't that sound more than a little odd?"

Insana clicked his tongue. "You could look at it that way. Certainly, she isn't a candidate for mother of the year. Oh – sorry. I don't mean to be flip. But is there anything criminal to look at? Not at this point. Her daughter, for instance, was well into her 20s when Suzy – er, Tina - broke things off. That's very odd, but it isn't child abandonment."

Alex thought for a moment. "Well then, Bob, I guess I'm prepared to write you a check. Send me an invoice. And – and I have to thank you for all the work you guys have done. We know a lot more about Suzy than we did, and I've got to say it hasn't been reassuring."

"No, I can imagine it hasn't."

Debra picked up on the fourth ring. After some idle chit-chat about their families – Debra had a daughter at the University of Oregon and a son who was headed into his senior year at high school – Alex took her into his confidence.

He spent long minutes filling her in about the private investigation and what it had turned up, interrupted only a couple of times by questions from Debra. She sounded sober, he thought – either that, or her drinking was having less and less effect on her faculties. Her voice was relatively high-pitched, and she spoke quickly, sometimes in sudden torrents of words.

"Whew!" She exclaimed. "I had no idea about any of this. Does Dad know? How could he?"

"I haven't told him yet – all of this has been playing out in the past few weeks. He's crazy about her. I think I'll have to go to him, though, at least to tell him things she obviously hasn't." He paused. "And I have to swear you to secrecy at least until then."

"That's okay with me. I don't talk to him that often, anyway – you know that."

"I do. Now – now I'm gonna ask you to put on your therapist hat. Obviously, her behavior isn't normal. What do you make of it?"

There was silence for several moments. "Honestly, Alex, from what you've just told me, I think she has some pronounced sociopathic tendencies. Burning your bridges to your family, your past – those are abnormal things. And there may be a high level of narcissism – she sees herself as better-looking, and more clever, than those around her. Such a person isn't above scheming to better her lot in life."

Alex thought for a moment. "Sociopath, narcissist - those aren't positive terms, in my mind."

"Nor mine. I've seen examples in my practice, both men and women. And the families were always the losers." She paused for a few moments, and he pictured her gulping more of a drink. "Sociopaths are scheming, but they can often be easily frustrated. And they often have a distinct lack of empathy for others around them."

Alex thought immediately of Jennifer's field hockey injury and Suzy's cold-blooded reaction to it. "We've already seen an instance of that. I won't bore you with the details."

"What you really need to worry about are psychopaths," Debra said. "That's a misused term, of course, but it's the most dangerous type – the potential serial killers. While sociopaths are impulsive, psychopaths are often very detail-oriented, careful planners."

"Uh-huh. Bad actors, for sure."

"Alex, I haven't been around Suzy much, of course. Have you seen anything about her that seems impulsive?"

He thought hard. "No, not really. But then I only see her in social settings."

"I wondered. Well, of course, those would be situations where a sociopath might be best – where he or she gets to act, and usually only in their best interests."

He blew out a breath. "I will say that she seems to be a good actor – she comes across as genuine most of the time. But I wonder every now and then if she's faking it. She can be opaque."

They chatted for a couple of more minutes before Alex wished her a good night and hung up. He sat for several minutes, deep in thought, before he rose and walked into the hall.

Cape Cod

34.

The fog hung heavy in the air, turning the morning landscape into a dim gray facsimile of itself. Suzy stared out the window from the bedroom and half-turned as she heard Dean stirring in bed. Fog was a common morning event on Cape Cod and would probably burn off by late morning, but it just dampened her spirits.

She and Dean were on a long weekend trip to Chatham, nestled at the crook of the Cape's elbow; they had booked a bed and breakfast that he found on the Internet. It was cozy and inviting in a not-so-nauseating nautical way, and the beach beckoned from across the road – but even the road was no more than a dark shape in the grip of the fog. She walked softly to the bathroom, closed the door and started her morning makeup ritual. It was only a month after their marriage, but Dean was already accustomed to her routine.

After a hearty breakfast with an omelet and blueberry pancakes that they shared, Dean and Suzy drove up toward Truro and passed the high dunes sculpted by the breezes whipping off the ocean. They were headed to Provincetown, a tourist town par excellence, with its charming Victorian ambience and raft of gift shops artfully stuffed with nautical-themed souvenirs: lighthouses on pillows and trays, brass clocks and lamps and all sorts of whale-related paraphernalia – stuffed animals and mini-blackboards everywhere. And then there were the ubiquitous wooden signs with cute messages, the most common seemingly "Life's a Beach," decorated with an umbrella or flip-flops, or both.

The sun was brightening in the gray-blue sky as they strolled along Bradford Street, the main avenue, and ducked into a handful of shops;

to the employees who asked brightly if they could help, they simply mumbled something about "browsing." And they certainly weren't looking for anything in particular. It was what you did in such towns when you had time on your hands and weren't on the beach; even young families did it.

It was in perhaps the third or fourth shop that Suzy nudged Dean and pointed to an embroidered pillow, ivory-colored, that featured a clam shell outlined in pale blue. It was small but charming.

"I like this for the chair in the bedroom," she said to him, hefting it as she checked the price: $39.95.

"Yeah, I like that too," he said, smiling. "Wanna get it?"

"Sure." She picked it up and after a few more minutes, went to the register and pulled out her wallet and selected a Visa card. The salesgirl smiled at her and said, "Could you show an ID as well? Maybe a driver's license?"

Suzy stared at her. "Really, do you need that?"

The girl pointed to a sign by the register and said, "I'm sorry, but it's just store policy."

Suzy looked at the sign and shrugged. "Okay." She pulled out her New York driver's license and handed it to the girl. Suzy's photo, her mouth curled in the hint of a smile, stared out from the card. She had needed to get another card after she married Dean and took his name, and she preferred her likeness on the old card better. *I wish I had another chance to take that photo*, she thought quickly to herself.

With the pillow tucked away in a bright blue plastic bag, they walked back to the Mercedes, parked in a crowded pay lot that would be virtually vacant in a few months except for the herring gulls idling about, avoiding the worst of the winter winds. Suzy put the bag in the trunk, and they walked back to the crowded main drag and looked for a spot to have lunch. Dean zeroed in on a seafood restaurant at the end of a long block, a low-slung white-framed building with a blue-and-white-striped awning facing the street.

"I'm in the mood for fried clams," he said, squeezing her hand. "I rarely get to eat them anymore."

Her mouth worked into a frown. "Really?" She had never had them, and wasn't about to start. "Well, dear, that's your thing. But I'm sure I can find something else."

He chuckled. "I'm sure you can."

After waiting for 15 minutes in the crowded lobby, they were taken to a table by a window, featuring a miniature ship's wheel atop a bin holding the condiments and paper placemats showing clipper ships under full sail. Service was slow and it was noisy, with the peals of kids' laughter everywhere. While Dean professed to love his fried clams, the fish and chips were too heavily battered for Suzy. But she soldiered on, eating most of it.

Dean excused himself and went to the men's room. Thank God his prostate is under control, she thought – he was able to go hours without a toilet stop. Avery had suffered from urinary issues, occasioning frequent bathroom visits wherever they were in his later years; she got accustomed to his "sorry, Dear's" and "you know's."

Suzy and Avery had been to the ocean many times, but most of those visits were to much swankier surroundings, often Hilton Head and Sea Island, where taste ruled and the few gift shops were selling far pricier fare. She found she liked the smell of salt air – though not so much at low tide – and the cooling sea breezes, so welcoming in the damp humidity of the Southeast coast, but the voracious mosquitoes that swarmed at dusk were little short of awful.

In fact, she and Avery had rented a townhouse in Hilton Head several times, something he had arranged through the company. It was a lovely spot, hard by the shore of the Harbor River, and Suzy had always felt relaxed there, with nothing more to fret about than where they would go for dinner and what she'd wear. The kids were grown by then, and had other plans to attend to.

As the waitress cleared the table, Suzy checked her phone, and there it was – the predictable email from Baxter.

> *"I've deducted the $10k, per our arrangement. Nothing has changed; our deal is still in place, as you know. My silence is assured.*
>
> *All my best, Baxter*

Damn him, she thought. Blackmail was never pretty, and here she was, as helpless as a butterfly fluttering in a net. Baxter had been shocked by the sudden death of Avery, one of his biggest clients, and from Baxter's sister, who was married to a cardiologist, he'd gathered information that gradually led him to believe that the death was anything but natural, even if that wasn't reflected on the death certificate. That Suzy had complained to him about Avery's aging – mostly in offhand comments - also raised his suspicions about her love for her husband.

It was over a lunch near his office that he broached the subject to Suzy on a blustery winter day, a week after the funeral. Baxter, boyishly handsome with his black hair carefully combed back and his red tie as bright as a holly berry, started the conversation with consoling words about Avery's death, and how he had been such a force in the community. He didn't need to point out how much money Avery had thrown his way, a great deal of which was now hers.

After they ordered, he sat back against the red leather in the booth and smiled as he laid out a proposal for her. I believe you killed Avery, he told her, and I think an exhumation would prove it. He went on, almost casually, as she stared at him wide-eyed, to say he planned to make a series of withdrawals from her accounts every quarter to maintain his silence. Otherwise, he would take his suspicions to Tom and Robin and suggest an exhumation.

"And that's not all," he said, looking at her hard. "I think you were Tina Tallman, and you probably murdered my uncle, David."

"Whaaa?" Her head spun. She fixated on his face but saw nothing she recognized. "Who are you?"

"You knew me as Will Dennison. I'm Jack and Nancy's son."

She gasped. Words wouldn't come out.

"I changed my name in college. I never liked Wilbur." He smiled at her mischievously. "Quite the coincidence, right? Your past rises up to strike you."

Suzy looked down at the table and back up again, trying to frame words into a sentence. "And you think I'm, who - Tina?"

Baxter folded his elbows on the table and looked hard at her. "I probably couldn't prove it without a lot of trouble, and without some help from you. But I'm pretty sure. Family photos don't lie, and then there's your limp, which is exactly as I remembered it. For a long time after meeting you, I couldn't put my finger on it – you seemed familiar. But it came to me one day. So... Aunt Tina, in the flesh."

She cast her eyes about like a trapped animal. "And you want me to buy your silence? Well, this is something I have to think about," she told him hesitantly.

His mouth had hardened. "There's nothing to think about. I've been thinking about it a good deal, and this is what I propose: I take a payment out of your account at regular intervals. That's the price for my silence, and I will be silent." He licked his lips. "Money talks, but I won't." His eyes smiled. He'd clearly calculated the effect this blackmail could have on their relationship, but he didn't care, and if he was right, and she accepted the proposition he was about to make to her, she had all the more reason to keep money with him.

Suzy had stared at him. "What are we talking about?"

He'd spread his hands on the table. "Well, I think a quarterly payment of ten thousand would be sufficient. You have a great deal, as you know – you wouldn't miss that."

She had gaped at him. "And – and how long would this go on?" Her face, so often a model of poise, had gone slack; her lips quivered.

He had shrugged slightly. "Indefinitely – or as long as this thing about his death goes undetected. Hopefully, it will never be discovered, and the same with David. And, to guarantee that this arrangement comes off as specified, I've already drafted a sealed note and given it to my lawyer. It says that if anything happens to me – anything – that the police should suspect you."

She'd swallowed hard, and the rest of the lunch was a blur in her memory, like a video taken from a whirling carousel. But she had tacitly agreed – how could she do otherwise? The withdrawals had started the following month, and now it had been well over a year, a slow and steady seepage. It was true that she didn't really miss the money, but the process was frightening; Baxter was like the ghost of Christmas past, forever reminding her of her sins.

St. Louis, MO

35.

David's affair had rocked their marriage like a small earthquake that leaves aftershocks in its wake and knocks glass jars off store shelves. There was a mess on the floor, and Tina made sure she rubbed his nose in it.

He was apologetic, remorseful, seemingly contrite – but more than anything, he was ashamed of being caught. He loved Tina, but in a domestic sort of way that had been dulled by long years of habit. By contrast, Brenda was fresh, vibrant and exciting; there was a spontaneity to their sex, with him literally tearing at her clothes, that was intoxicating. He didn't want it to end, but now it had to.

Tina wasn't the forgiving sort, and she saw herself in many ways as David's equal; she was a woman wronged, and she wasn't about to let the issue simply melt away. The first few days after her visit to the office were filled with her icy recriminations and his apologies. He couldn't really explain why he had done it, but the reasons were clear in her mind: an alluring mix of availability, reciprocal interest and the excitement of the new.

She could have added middle-aged angst – David was 47 and privy to the anxiety so many men feel as their vitality starts to diminish. In some ways, Tina would have preferred that he had gone to prostitutes. Dalliance with a younger woman in the office was like a time bomb waiting to detonate in too many marriages, in movies and real life, where executives married their secretaries or assistants and cast the first wife aside like a used napkin. That wasn't going to happen to her.

It took weeks for her anger to cool, for the annealing process to play out. David went out of his way to be solicitous, to be home early, to show her small acts of kindness, replaying in his head the way he had acted in the first years of their union. He touched her more often, her hands and her shoulders, and stroked her hair when they were on the couch together. Her resistance began to melt like a roadside snowbank in a January thaw; it was gradual, and noticeable only over time.

Apart from that, nothing really changed in their lives. Tina was still busy with her bridge and book clubs, though she started to work out two mornings a week at a health club. It wasn't rigorous, certainly, but she lifted small weights, walked on a treadmill, and stretched on a rubber mat. This had been triggered by her sense that without regular exercise, she was losing muscle tone and her clothes were starting to feel a big snug.

When the betrayal recurred, fourteen months later, it was like a pistol going off by her ear. David was a prominent member of the Rotary Club, and was a regular at their monthly meetings. It was October, a bright, breezy day with a north wind tossing the branches overhead. The microwave door in their kitchen had suddenly jammed, and Tina called the restaurant where the Rotary met to get David's thoughts on what to do. But he wasn't there – the girl answering the phone said she hadn't seen him.

Her suspicions immediately kicked into high gear. She called the office – he wasn't there, either. She grabbed her car keys and stalked into the garage before driving to the office to do what was, by any other name, surveillance.

She parked at a safe distance in the lot, where her car would be hard to spot, and waited. About 15 minutes later, David pulled in to his space and got out, adjusting his tie as he walked back in. She waited. Five minutes later, Brenda's car swung into the lot. Brenda got out slowly, and in Tina's mind, literally sauntered into the office. She wore a cream-colored top, unadorned, but to Tina it was emblazoned with a scarlet "A."

Tina stewed for hours, her anger like hot lava, bubbling and burning. That evening, when David got home, she greeted him stonily and accused him of resuming the affair. At first, he denied it, but when she told him what she'd seen – and that he hadn't been at the lunch – he paled. He started apologizing profusely, saying he knew this was hurting her, but he had trouble controlling himself. He – he would have to fire Brenda. The temptation with her in the office was unmanageable.

As she lay awake in the guest bedroom that night - their first night apart, at her insistence – she knew what she had to do. She would find a gardening outlet and order Carolina jasmine. A couple of plants would do. It was a pretty flower, and the vine would look good on their wooden palisade fence in back beside the trailing roses. By next summer, it would be grown. David had brought this on himself, and he would need to pay.

Atlanta, GA

36.

Baxter Dennison glanced impatiently at his Rolex: 9:10. He'd agreed to meet Childers at this diner at 9, and he had a client meeting at 10 – there wouldn't be much time to talk, have breakfast and make it back to the office in time.

The diner wasn't the New Jersey variety, the venerable aluminum-sided numbers with menus so large that it felt like you'd been given a phone book to read. This was Atlanta, and the exterior was red brick; the place had less of the glass and metal that prevailed up north, more plaster and wooden accents. Baxter sipped his coffee and started to look at his watch again when Childers strolled up and took a seat with little more than, "Mornin'. Sorry I'm late." He extended a beefy hand in greeting.

While Childers looked over the menu, Baxter studied him closely. He could have fit a dictionary definition of "grizzled," he thought, with a heavily lined face, a bristly mustache and hair cut military-style, the kind of buzz cut they administered to recruits in boot camp. I bet he's always worn it this way, Baxter thought, and he's probably been heavy like this since he made it to adulthood. His arms practically popped out of his white short-sleeved cotton shirt, and gray chest hairs peeked from inside the front of the collar.

Ray Childers was a detective sergeant of long standing with the Atlanta Police Department, and their paths probably never would have crossed except for one thing: the sudden death of Avery Rittenhouse. It was a day after the funeral when Baxter, nursing his suspicions, called the police and asked if anyone felt it worth investigating the death, which the medical examiner had deemed natural. He'd been directed to Childers, who listened carefully when Baxter laid out his theory about a possible poisoning or overdose of some kind.

From the first, Childers had taken Baxter's suspicions seriously. "Really?" he asked in a gravelly voice that suggested a heavy smoker. "What makes you think that?"

Baxter talked about the discussion he'd had with his sister, whose husband had a friend in the medical examiner's office who had raised suspicions about the cause of death. Avery was my client, and a very rich one, Baxter had told him – and his widow stood to inherit a great deal of money.

Childers had replied that he would talk to the medical examiner's office, but as it was, there wasn't much to go on. The ME had signed off on the death certificate, and there was no evidence whatsoever of a crime.

"Who found the body?" he asked.

"The cook, I believe. The wife was at a bridge game at her country club."

Childers was silent for a few moments. "Sounds like a pretty good alibi to me, if she needed one."

"I guess," Baxter replied evenly. "But my thinking is that she administered something long before, and her absence was deliberate."

"Uh-huh. Well, as I say, let me talk to the ME's office. But it sounds kinda pro forma. I'll let you know what I hear."

Childers had called him back two days later to say that the matter was closed, and that it would require a petition to exhume Avery's body. That would have to come from his children or from Suzy herself, he added, since the family – barring a directive from law enforcement - would need to make the request. Even then, there would need to be good cause presented to do it; exhumations weren't everyday events.

It was shortly after that when Baxter decided to launch his blackmail scheme, which had gone swimmingly. Suzy obviously wouldn't want an exhumation, but the children might – and that could conceivably stop the gravy train. He thought about Childers: could he derail any investigation?

He sounded Childers out in a phone call. If there was an investigation, he asked, what role would Childers be expected to have? The detective said that wasn't clear, but as a senior guy in the department, he would certainly be likely to be involved.

Baxter made it clear that he'd changed his mind and that an investigation, in his view, wasn't in anyone's best interest. Avery had been a prominent member of the community, he said, and any scandal would be horrible for the family and for the charities he so heavily endowed – and there could be major complications to settling the estate.

Childers ruminated on this for a few moments. "What are you saying? That if there is evidence that he was poisoned, we should ignore it?"

"Well, not ignore it, but soft-pedal it, suggest there could be other ways he could have died. String it out."

Childers snorted. "Why would we do that?"

Baxter had to play his card and see what happened. "I could make it worth your while."

Another long silence. "What are we talking about?"

"Well, how about $5,000, for starters? And more if there is an autopsy that suggests something criminal."

"Bribing a police officer? That's not a good career move," Childers replied stiffly.

"Relax, Sergeant," Baxter responded smoothly. "I haven't given you anything – nothing has changed hands. I'm merely suggesting a business arrangement." He paused. "Think about it. You have my number. If I haven't heard from you in a week, I'll assume you're not interested."

Three days later, Childers phoned back. The connection was scratchy, and Baxter assumed he was on a cell phone, well away from his office. I'll do it, he told the broker, but nothing can be in writing. And no check – the money has to be in cash. Baxter had agreed, and they set up a meeting at a diner in two days to make the transaction.

He beamed as he set down the phone. Things were progressing nicely. He was in treacherous waters, he realized, but he was a strong swimmer; things would work out, even if he had to figure them out on the fly. He was like a migratory bird that winged its way through storms but always made it safely to land.

At the diner, he told Childers he had a tight time window and needed to be on his way soon. They ordered, an egg and English muffin for Baxter and ham and eggs, with grits, for Childers.

After they handed their menus back to the waitress, Childers leaned over conspiratorially and asked in a half-whisper, "You have the money?"

"I do. Want me to hand it to you under the table?" Baxter grinned at his joke.

Childers gave him a wry smile. "That's probably not a bad idea" - his drawl transformed the word to "ah-dee-yah." He added quickly, "I like the symbolism."

"Okay." Baxter reached into his briefcase for the brown office envelope and brought it under the table; he felt Childers reach for it and take it.

"Count it if you like," Baxter said.

Childers slid the envelope into a folder he had set beside him on the seat and shook his head. He pursed his lips, his mustache twitching. "No, I trust you." Then he grinned. "Oh, I will count it. Not just here."

"Remember, there may be more where that came from, depending on circumstances."

Childers stared at him. "I remember." To him, Baxter seemed like a classic country-clubber, smooth and handsome and insincere – a type he instinctively disliked. But this guy was putting his neck on the line, and if Childers was somehow implicated, he had his own position and reputation to fall back on. The money wouldn't be traceable. In the end, it seemed like a windfall he'd be stupid to pass up.

"Oh, and this breakfast is on me," Baxter said.

"I was figuring that." Childers smiled, and Baxter saw an uneven row of nicotine-stained teeth. But the smile was genuine.

Many months later, following the exhumation and the subsequent finding of the *Gelsenium*, Baxter was conflicted: He was proud that his suspicions had proved true, but realized the evidence of the crime would throw the inexorable machinery of law enforcement into motion. A warrant would be issued and a freeze, vise-like, would almost certainly be put on her accounts.

He learned about the poisoning discovery from Childers, who'd been alerted by the ME's office. Childers said another detective had been made lead investigator, and while Childers would be involved as a supervisor, he would not be hands-on in any way.

Baxter had sensed that he had to put the offer out there again. "I'd be willing to offer another $5,000 if it would help delay things, as we discussed."

Silence. Then, "You know, I appreciate the offer. I could use the money. But this thing could get pretty hot. I think that my poo-pooing any suspicion of murder isn't gonna be a good thing for me. I'm afraid I'm out. And, you know," he paused slightly, "if the first payment gets discovered, I could be in a world of shit. Taking a second one is only gonna make it worse."

"I see," Baxter replied evenly. "Well, I understand your position."

"Glad you do. And -- you know, you were certainly right about what happened to Avery."

"Lot of good it does me. There's going to be a freeze put on her accounts, right?"

"I s'pose. I don't have much experience along those lines, but I think so."

Baxter blew out a breath. "Well, I'll probably hear about it from my boss when it happens. In the meantime, if you hear anything specific about Suzy - like where she turns up - please call me."

"I will," Childers promised, but there was a note in his voice that suggested that was unlikely.

Baxter looked out his office window and averted his eyes from the late morning glare. A thought struck him, and he swiveled to his computer and dove into Suzy's accounts, making a few quick keystrokes to highlight the various subaccounts. He stared when he brought up her cash account, which had been set up for $400,000. She'd made a few small withdrawals in the past year, but here was evidence of two checks written in the past two weeks. She'd essentially drained it - there was less than $10,000 left.

Wow, he thought. She clearly foresaw the day when her access to her accounts could end. She wouldn't be rich, but she'd be just fine. Could she be frugal? He wondered.

He'd long ago come up with an explanation for the $10,000 withdrawals, if some sharp-eyed forensic accountant poring over her accounts discovered them. Baxter would say that Suzy had authorized him to make payments to selected charities in Atlanta, and to do them with appreciated stock to take advantage of the tax deductions.

No, there was no written instruction - it was a verbal request she'd made. If there were further questions about where that money had gone - which he doubted - he'd have to get inventive. He'd cross that bridge when the time came.

St. Louis, MO

37.

The day of David's funeral was overcast and then showery, with a fickle southwest wind that snapped the flags around Clayton like an unseen banshee. Tina had found a simple but elegant black dress for the occasion, and she wore a pearl choker and pearl earrings. Alicia, red-eyed and quiet, had arrived the day before from Los Angeles and had brought a long-sleeved navy dress with a belt cinched at the waist. She didn't look well; she was pale, and her hair was unkempt, as if she'd just awakened.

Inside the funeral home, the speakers played an array of classical music that Tina had picked out – some Bach preludes, Mozart's *Einkleine Nachtmusik*, and the haunting Albinoni adagio. Flowers were everywhere, in vases short and tall, arranged in something of a semicircle around the closed casket. Before the service, the funeral director – too unctuous, in Tina's opinion - had allowed the immediate family to view the body. Alicia had knelt beside it and wept quietly; David's brother and sister sniffled and rubbed at their eyes. The shock of his sudden passing had rendered them speechless, as if Medusa had turned their tongues to stone.

Sally and her husband, Harold, were there – Sally in a charcoal dress that did nothing to conceal her plumpness, Harold in an ill-fitting brown suit that seemed at least a size too small. They stood awkwardly to one side, watching silently until Tina came up, smiling, and hugged Sally for long seconds. They seemed to melt into one figure, and Tina felt Sally's tears on her neck.

The actual service was quite short, and featured remarks by Bill Savery, David's long-time colleague and the vice-president at the dealership. He spoke movingly of David's intellect, his skill at building the business, his many friends and his charity work in the community. Tina moved around the room, getting hugs and shaking hands; everyone was so surprised and so, so sorry. The hypocrisy on Tina's part was galling, but she played her part like a maestro.

Alicia stood with David's brother, Larry, whom she had always liked, her hands held together just above her knees, and watched her mother accept condolences from couples and small knots of people, some of who she recognized from her childhood. They were older now. Grayer.

When it was over, the music was still playing softly and the guests filed slowly out of the funeral home and walked to the parking lot in a light drizzle, the wind playing at the hems of the women's skirts. Tina thanked the funeral director and, with Alicia, took the bound book where people attending the service had signed in. When she counted the names that night, she was surprised – the count was 153. David had made his mark.

The next night, Alicia had returned to UCLA and Tina was alone, watching TV in the living room when the phone rang. She picked up on the third ring.

"Hi, is this Tina?" She didn't recognize the voice.

"Yes, it is."

"This is your brother, Tommy. Long time, no see."

Her heart sank, and then she collected herself. "Well, I guess you found me."

"I did, but it wasn't easy. Nope." There was that Little Rock twang in his voice. "I know Harold Pritchard from the Elks Lodge, and he told me he and Sally were going to your husband's funeral and that it was in Missouri. I made him tell me the name of the town."

"Okay. I was sure you didn't hear about it from Sally."

"Sure didn't. That gal seems sworn to secrecy."

"She sure is. She's the best friend I've ever had."

"Look, Tina, I know you don't want me in your life – that's pretty clear." He sounded a bit subdued. "But what about Mom and Dad? They don't know anything about you. They don't even know you're alive."

Tina's mind worked for a few moments. "Well, you can assume that's the way I want it. Things happened to me in that house that I won't talk about. Things that made me want to get away and turn my back completely on the past. I don't expect you to understand."

"Well, you're right. I don't. What – what could be that bad?"

"I said I won't talk about it."

"You know – you know I could tell them where you are and how to contact you."

This was a nightmare. "I guess I would plead with you not to."

"Well, there is something." There it was – cryptic. The sentence hung in the air.

She rubbed at her forehead. Here it comes, she thought.

"I understand your husband was a rich man. So, I think there's something you could help me with—"

"You want me to buy your silence?"

"I s'pose you could look at it that way. Don't worry, I won't ask for the moon."

"So, it won't be the moon – great." She couldn't keep the sarcasm out of her voice. "What is it?"

"You don't know, 'less Sally has told you, but I'm a mechanic and I got child support to pay. It's always a stretch. But I play drums in a band – you remember how much music meant to me."

"I do."

"So, we play around Little Rock every weekend – mostly 60s and 70s rock. We're pretty good. But I need a new drum set – mine is on its last legs."

"So, you want me to chip in—"

"No, I'd like you to pay for the whole kit and kaboodle. Kind of a long-delayed payment for you walking out on your family."

Tina sighed. "How much are we talking about?"

"Not that much – three grand."

"And if I do that, you'll leave me alone and keep my location from our parents?"

"I will, I promise."

"Why should I trust you? You were never the most honest guy I've been around."

"Well, I guess you just have to. You don't have a lot of choice. My word is important to me, sis. Mom and Dad are doing okay, considering. Getting rejected again by you would be worse than what they're dealin' with now."

"Alright, Tommy. Give me your address. You've given me your word, and so you'll get your money."

"Great."

"Oh, and Sally tells me a little about you now and then. I knew you were a mechanic, and you've been divorced. How many kids do you have?"

"Two, Amy and Sam. They're ten and fifteen. Their mother--"

She cut him off like an iron gate closing. "I don't need to know any more. And Tommy, please don't call me again. Our lives are very different now. We don't have much to talk about. I think you understand. Take care of yourself."

She set the phone down in its cradle, exhaled and leaned back. Then she stood up and walked to the window. Outside, the stars and the clouds were dancing in and out and the moon, a pale sliver, hung above the treetops like an inverted streetlamp. The rain had ended, and a cold front would soon be sweeping in.

Westchester County, NY

38.

Suzy had taken the bridge club at Oak Hills by storm. Most of the women there, roughly her age and older, had known each other for decades – so well, they could practically finish each other's sentences. Now, this newcomer had burst onto the scene and started tongues wagging, if only discreetly.

She was attractive and chic, certainly, but it was her skill that they admired most. She knew all the conventions, and she rarely lost – and then, usually when her partner messed up. Her style was cool, regal and brisk; she rarely waited for more than a few seconds to play her cards. She bid audaciously, but it usually worked. She was like a tennis doubles champ whom they all wanted to play with – but really wanted to play against and beat.

The club met twice a month, in late morning, in the ladies' lounge, with walls and chairs in soothing shades of teal and white. Classical music played lightly from speakers near the ceiling. There were usually three or four tables, and they rotated partners in a pre-designed manner, usually playing four rubbers before lunch. A few of the older women, some over 80, would nurse glasses of sherry or white wine, but Suzy drank only tea or water.

A feeling of superiority washed over Suzy like a warm towel every time she played. These women were solidly upper crust, some with boarding school pedigrees from places like Foxcroft or Miss Porter's – new names to her - and degrees from schools like Smith and Vassar. Many hadn't worked a day in their lives. And here she was, an erstwhile redneck from Arkansas, handing them their lunch at the tables month after month. She read their body language and sensed their envy; God, it was satisfying.

Actually, her pedigree, such as it was, had come up early. At the buffet table one day, a couple of women asked casually where she had gone to school, hanging on every word. She told them she'd graduated from Washington University in St. Louis – it was David's alma mater and was well-known around the country as an excellent small liberal arts college. Their heads bobbed up and down in approval. Suzy knew she'd never be called on it – none of these women's circles extended beyond a small bevy of elite Northeastern schools.

There was one woman who she clearly seemed unable to charm, a longtime club member named Bitsy Granger. She wasn't tall, and she always wore flats, but she was attractive and well-turned out, with a youthful face that spoke either of good genes or excellent plastic surgery. Her gray hair, cut just to the nape, was always nicely coiffed and her hands well-manicured. She wasn't chatty at the tables, as many were; she played intently, and in all probably was second only to Suzy in terms of skill.

One day, before play started, one of the younger club members took her aside.

"You probably won't get much warmth from Bitsy," the woman said, looking at her almost conspiratorially. "She and Dean were an item for some time until you came along."

Suzy's eyebrows went up. "Really?"

"That's right. Her husband died of cancer a few years ago, and a while after Dean's wife died, they started seeing each other."

"Well, that does explain some of her frostiness."

The woman went on. "Dean actually invited her to your wedding, but she declined."

"Ah." Suzy didn't know what to add.

"I just wanted you to know." The woman, Janet Engvahl, smiled slightly.

"Thanks so much, Janet." Suzy was sincere; this was useful information indeed. "Now I know where she's coming from."

Her bridge club had been different in Atlanta, where most of the women, if not local, were Southern and were more like her: they didn't all come from money, though they had it now, chiefly because their husbands were highly paid professionals of some stripe. Suzy had made up a saying about the difference between Atlanta and Rye that brought on a little giggle: the closest association the Atlanta women had to the Mayflower was the moving company by that name.

By now, in Rye, it was near the end of June, and late in the season: the club suspended play in July and August and resumed after Labor Day. It was a schedule that clung closely to the school calendar – a relic of an earlier generation, when more families went somewhere for long periods in the summer: Nantucket, Martha's Vineyard, the Cape, Maine, the Adirondacks. Still, no one saw any reason to change.

It was when Suzy left for the latest session that Alex drove over to the condo and broke the news of what he had found to Dean. He had checked to make certain Suzy was out of the house, and the two of them could be alone. He had been dreading this, but it was time.

They sat in the living room, quiet except for the ticking of a clock, and Alex began. As he spun out the story, Dean grew increasingly agitated. His face reddened, his mouth worked, but most of his reaction came in exclamations of surprise and incredulity, as well as anger.

"You hired a private eye?" he gasped at one point. "Unbelievable."

As Alex went on, detailing Suzy's prior life in Missouri, her daughter in California, and her name change on reaching Atlanta, Dean felt himself besieged by a welter of emotions: shock, dismay, and a growing sense of something close to regret. What had he really known about her? She didn't tell him, and he was so smitten he didn't ask. He'd always assumed that Avery had been her only husband, that she'd married late.

"Dad, you know I'm not doing this to upset you." Alex sounded suddenly sheepish. "I want to protect you, and by extension, our family. This is a very different kind of woman from Mom."

Dean was silent for several long seconds, and he looked hard at Alex. "I really need to confront her and find out why she never told me any of this." He glanced at his watch. "She should be home in an hour.

I – I just can't sit on this. I'll have to have it out." He looked down. "Oh, Jesus. This is bad."

Alex leaned forward and tried to give him his most comforting look. "I can't tell you what to say. Only you know that." His eyes behind his glasses were almost downcast.

The moment was close to excruciating for both of them. Dean nodded. "I guess so."

Alex rose slowly to leave. "It will be alright. Let me know what happens," he said soothingly.

He could see the pain in his father's eyes. "I will," Dean said simply. "I will."

39.

Things were moving fast. Alex sent Tom Rittenhouse an email asking if he could call him that night and get Robin on the line as well; he said he had a lot of information about Suzy that they'd want to hear. Tom replied after a while that he could do a call around 8 that night, and he would conference Robin in.

Alex and Lisa sat by the phone in their study for a few minutes before Alex picked up the handset and dialed Tom's number. He picked up on the third ring.

"Hi, Alex?"

"Yeah, good evening. I'm here with my wife, Lisa. She's been privy to all this."

"Great. Hello from Atlanta."

"Thanks," Lisa said. "I look forward to meeting you one of these days."

"Me, too," he said, rather perfunctorally. "Let me patch Robin in." After a few seconds, there was an audible click and a woman's voice came on.

"Hi, this is Robin." Her voice was soft and carried a trace of a drawl. "Nice to hear from you. Alex, sorry we didn't get to meet while you were down here."

"Next time, I hope," he replied. "Now, let me get to the point of his call." He spent long minutes detailing what he knew about Suzy's prior life, including her growing up in Little Rock, her marriage to David, his sudden death, her cutting off ties to her parents and her daughter. The two in Atlanta said nothing until he was finished.

"My God," Tom exclaimed. "I can't say I'm totally surprised, but this is pretty damning in some ways. To cut off ties to her parents and even her daughter... I mean, I guess when we were old enough, we assumed her parents were dead."

"Shocking," said Robin.

"You say you talked to her daughter?" Tom asked.

"At length. And she sent me a photo from many years ago, from that first marriage. It was Suzy, no question whatsoever."

"And the daughter has daughters of her own?"

"Two teenagers."

"Huh." Tom paused. "Do you think Suzy is aware of them at all?"

"I don't know how she could be. Alicia, the daughter, hasn't had any contact with her for over 20 years."

"Wow," Robin said softly. "The things you don't know about somebody."

"So, let me get this straight," Tom said. "Her first husband dies suddenly, and then she abruptly leaves town and comes to Atlanta and changes her name. Sounds like she had something to hide."

"On the surface, yes," Alex replied. "But I had a private detective agency in St. Louis do a lot of checking on her, and they couldn't find any smoking gun – just a lot of things that might look odd. And changing your name is apparently something that's done more often than we might think – often as a way of making a fresh start."

Tom snorted. "It was certainly that."

Robin spoke up. "Tom probably told you that we really never learned about her prior life. We always assumed she came from Atlanta, and certainly never knew she'd been married before."

"I told Alex that she played things close to the vest," Tom said. He went on, a bit haltingly: "You know, the news that her first husband died suddenly at a young age really disturbs me. I've heard from some of Dad's old buddies, including a cardiologist, that his death shocked them. He'd had a thorough physical with an EKG only two months earlier, and everything checked out."

"So, you suspect something?" Alex asked.

"I don't know, I don't know." Alex could almost see him shaking his head. "But I wonder if we, as the family, can ask for an autopsy. What was done after his death was pretty casual, as I understand it – he was an older man, and quite overweight."

"Wait, Tom, are you saying"—Robin interjected. "You mean, dig up the body?" Avery had been laid to rest near his parents, with a large marble headstone in a shady church plot.

"I think I am. You know, Alex, Suzy wanted him cremated, but Robin and I told her that Dad's legal instructions were that he would be buried. She didn't like it, but she went along."

"Really?" Alex spoke up. "Well, that's interesting, and probably makes things more suspicious. But you know, exhumation will almost certainly require Suzy's permission. Exactly the same thing happened in Missouri, and she quashed it."

"What?" Tom almost shouted.

Alex told them about David's brother's request for an exhumation, which had been turned down after Tina objected.

"Whew, this is something," Tom muttered. "What do you think, sis?"

"Maybe we should do it," Robin said softly. "We owe it to Dad, now that we've heard all this." She paused. "Now that she's remarried, there isn't anything she could do to stop it, is there?"

"Hmm. I think you're right on that," Alex said slowly. "What do you think they might find? Evidence of sedatives, or something?"

"Maybe," Tom replied. "Or something else – maybe even poison."

40.

It was a typical bridge club outing – Suzy had racked up the most wins, though attendance was down to two tables, which dampened some of her elation. She gathered her purse to leave and turned to find Bitsy staring at her.

"Well done, as usual," Bitsy said without a smile. She wore a gray and white linen dress with a smart black broche in the shape of a triangle. She was several inches shorter, enough so that Suzy sensed she was looking up at her.

"Well, thanks," Suzy said, and forced a smile. "The cards went my way today."

"They usually do, from what I've seen," Bitsy said. "You're really very good. Where did you learn to play so well?" Her dark eyes were alert and as cold as obsidian, and seemed to bore into Suzy.

Suzy felt herself measuring her reply. "In Atlanta. I belonged to a club down there, and a really good player there took me under her wing. I learned a lot from her."

"Obviously." Bitsy cocked her head. "You clearly do other things well, too. You may have heard that Dean and I were seeing each other until you came on the scene."

"Um, I did hear that." Where is she going? Suzy wondered. "I'm sorry if my being here makes you uncomfortable."

Bitsy gave her a sardonic smile. "I'm a big girl. I can roll with the punches. I'm telling you this because Dean is a special man, very special to me, even if we did part ways. Our families were close for many years. My husband died five years ago, and Dean helped me deal with that."

"I'm sure he did." Suzy did her best to sound soothing. "He's good at things like that."

Bitsy pursed her lips. "Yes, he is." She looked directly at Suzy for several long seconds. "I just want to make sure he doesn't get hurt."

Suzy started, as if she'd been slapped lightly on the cheek. "Okay," she said, drawing out the word slowly. "I certainly don't want to hurt him. He's my husband, and I love him."

Bitsy offered up that wry smile again. "Oh, I'm sure that's what anyone in your position would say. But just know – know – that I'm watching." She smiled, showing her teeth, and pivoted away. "Please tell Dean," she said, calling over her shoulder, "that Bitsy sends him her very best."

Opening her email that night, Suzy saw a message from Sally and the header, "bad news." She clicked and opened it and read the first paragraph quickly.

> "Hi GF: I know you told me you hadn't heard anything from your brother Tommy in many years. Well, Harold told me today that Tommy's come down with esophageal (I looked up the spelling!) cancer, stage 4. He's terminal. Thought you'd want to know.

Suzy turned her face away from the screen and licked her lips. Tommy wasn't part of her life – he was an inextricable part of the past she had done her best to bury. Yet – and yet – there was something about the news that gnawed at her. Apart from her mother, feeble and doddering (so she'd heard), he was the only part of her unhappy family still upright and breathing. And now he was dying.

If she' been sentimental, or even a woman with the normal range of emotions, this would have been like a thunderclap, or a sudden blow to the solar plexus. With her, however, it was just cause for a few moments of reflection and mulling over what she would do. She wouldn't go to the funeral, of course; her mother would be there, swaddled in grief. Suzy couldn't abide that.

And while she could easily pay for the funeral, and make sure it was done to her own high standards, that just wasn't feasible. Even doing it anonymously, she mused, would have been a tacit admission of some kind of guilt. But she could send a bouquet, a beautiful cornucopia of lilies and orchids that would outmatch all the other flowers. That could be done anonymously, of course.

She might tell Sally her plan when the time came. Or she might not. There'd be time to make a decision: he hadn't died yet.

Headed West

41.

She hated being on the run. It was nothing she had ever known – she'd always been the one in control, the one looking at the chessboard and knowing her moves well in advance. But this was different.

Suzy had taken the Mercedes from the garage, pulled out of the driveway and headed west. She knew the local roads well enough to know that she needed to work her way from Rye to I-95 and take it west over the George Washington Bridge and onto Route 80. From there, things were hazy. She input "Little Rock" into the car GPS and saw a spider web of routing south and west, mostly on the interstates.

She knew people would eventually be looking for the car – though she probably had at least a day's grace. Dean was getting a ride back from his golf game and would be surprised and concerned that she'd left without a note, but hours would probably go by before he'd be frantic – likely not until dinnertime.

Even then, she would be no more than a missing person; she wasn't being sought in connection with a crime, so it seemed unlikely there would be any dragnet. She had switched off her cell phone and the Bluetooth in the car: surely he would be calling her, perplexed and concerned. Dean – loving, trusting Dean – had confronted her two days ago with information about her past, details she thought he would never know.

Dean had found about her daughter and grand-daughters in California, about her early marriage to David. She couldn't deny them, wish them away like a bad dream, but neither could she explain why she hadn't told him about them. How did he get that information?

That was her first reaction, and her skin grew cold when he confessed that Alex had gone behind his back and hired a private detective to delve into her past.

Her instinct was to immediately go on the defensive, throw up smoke screens. A private detective? What was she, a criminal? Her emotional, choking response had its desired effect: Dean was apologetic, subdued. Alex was only looking out for him, he said. But the transgressions lay between them like a set of soiled linens – her burying of her past, and her abandonment of her daughter, was to him unimaginable.

It got worse for Suzy. She checked Dean's email when he was out the next day and saw something that made her gasp: Alex had written to him that authorities in Atlanta were considering exhuming Avery's body to look for anything suspicious. Suzy's knowledge of such testing was minimal, but she sensed that her worst fears – the nightmare she thought would never materialize – might be coming true.

That forensic process could take weeks, or even months, but how could she live with the strain? She'd be under suspicion, as circumscribed as a parolee with an ankle monitor. Better to run, to live by her wits. Sally would help her, at least for a while, until she could get her head straight, devise a plan that would take her to a new identity and her next life.

She thought she might go to Texas – Dallas or San Antonio, maybe; Houston was too humid, too swampy, like the worst of Florida. She'd heard it had mosquitoes the size of hummingbirds. Texas had a reputation as a deeply red state that enforced privacy laws, and it had scads of new residents arriving every year. Easier to start anew in a place like that, where no one knows your face and acceptance is almost assured.

Suzy checked out of the hotel in Nashville and soon saw a sign for Waffle House, a postcard from her past; her family used to go there after church on Sundays, she in a white Oxford shirt, tartan plaid skirt and Mary Janes, the epitome of a churchgoing childhood. But Suzy had put the Baptist church behind her when she left Little Rock; it was an emotional link to her parents, and especially to her father, that she needed to sever.

Walking in the door, she quickly sensed that Waffle House hadn't changed much, apart from the prices. The aromas of coffee and batter wafted over her and comforted her. She was dressed in old bermudas, beige sandals and a soft white cotton top with cap sleeves, and no one seemed to be paying any attention to her. In this environment, that was just fine.

She sipped her coffee and was soon lost in thought. How could she access her money, the millions in Atlanta that Baxter oversaw? Suzy Perry had to disappear, but with that sleight of hand the access to her accounts would surely go with it. Well, she could still write checks on close to a half-million in a money market account for now, but how long could that continue?

Suzy couldn't see how she find a route to her money under a new name without calling attention to herself. More than likely, the money would be frozen – particularly if an autopsy of Avery did indeed turn up the *Gelsenium*. Everything she had worked and planned for – damn Alex, for digging into her past. What had tipped him off, anyway?

The sky outside had turned an ugly shade of gray, like an old bruise. Suzy dropped a couple of singles on the counter and walked her bill to the cashier, a young girl in a dark brown ponytail who smiled at her robotically and wished her a good day. Walking back out to the Focus, she sat for a few long moments and watched as the traffic, turtle-slow, inched along the Lebanon Pike. She could be in Little Rock that afternoon. She picked up her phone and dialed Sally's cell – she would probably be just arriving at work.

Sally sounded surprised and as delighted as a five-year-old just handed an ice cream cone. Suzy apologized for the short notice, but didn't explain further, and said she'd probably be staying for a couple of days.

She steered the car onto I-40 where it joined with I-24 and turned on the cruise control for 70. Hundreds of miles of boring interstate highway loomed. The first drops spotted her windshield in a soft mist as she passed her first semi of the day, a Wal-Mart logo splashed along its side. Arkansas, here I come, she thought with a faint smile. Her mother was still alive; Sally had reminded her of that the other week. But Suzy wouldn't be dropping by. Some things were just left better off the way they were.

Westchester County, NY

42.

Dean couldn't sit still; he shuttled back and forth on the light gray carpet like a puppy searching for a toy. It was Thursday evening, long hours after Suzy had taken off, and he didn't even know when she'd left. He'd been picked up by John Sessions, one of his regular golf buddies, about 8. When he got back at 2, after a nice lunch at the club grill – a chicken salad sandwich and a beer – he found no one home. He'd called her name and went back to the bedroom, but Suzy wasn't there. He went to the garage, and saw the Mercedes was gone.

He immediately called her cell, but it went straight to voicemail. He shook his head as if to clear it and called Alex, who was still in the office. Alex immediately heard the note in his father's voice: fear, almost panic.

"She's gone, and she didn't leave any kind of note. I just can't understand it. I called, but there's no answer."

"Oh, wow." Alex sought to be reassuring. "Well, maybe she just went shopping for a while, or something."

"But she'd always call me or leave a note."

"Alright. I'll be home by six. If she hasn't come home, call me."

"Okay."

Three hours later, he and Lisa were in Dean's condo. They had rushed over after Dean called, leaving the kids to share a frozen pizza, emergency rations stored in the freezer.

It was an awkward grouping: the two of them sat on the living room couch, leaning forward, their hands folded in front of them, while Dean stood up and paced, sat down in an armchair, then paced again. Alex hadn't seen him like this since his mother was dying.

"It's my fault. I confronted her, and I was a little angry," Dean said ruefully. "I hurt her."

"Come on, Dad," Alex replied. "You did what any husband would do when he learned something unsavory about his wife's past, things she hadn't told him. You told me yourself you couldn't just sit on this. Nobody could."

"I agree," Lisa spoke up. "For her not to tell you about her previous marriage, and her daughter" – she grimaced. "It's practically unforgiveable."

"I know, I know," Dean said with more than a little agitation. "But I can't think of where she would go to. She doesn't know that many people here, apart from her bridge club gals. And I can't see her going to one of them."

"Maybe she's just buying some time, getting away from the house to think things through a little," Lisa said.

"I keep waiting to hear the garage door open," Dean said. "It's driving me a little crazy." He looked at them in turn. "What do I do if she doesn't come back tonight? Call the police?" He paused again. "You know, there could be another explanation, though I think it's unlikely – she might have had an accident."

"I suppose that's possible," Alex said slowly. "But it's hard to imagine."

"Dean, can I make you something to eat?" Lisa asked, starting to get up. "What would you like?"

"I'm really not hungry," he said, pursing his lips. "There is some cold chicken in the fridge if I do want something. So, thanks, Lisa, but I'm okay."

She nodded. "Alright." It was clear to her she shouldn't press the issue.

Alex stood up as well. "We'll go home. Obviously, call us if she comes back."

"Will do."

They said goodnight and left him, a figure now as still as a Rodin statue. It was twilight, and as they walked to the Volvo, small bats darted overhead as crazily as if they were being chased by goblins.

Promptly at six the next morning, the phone rang. It was Dean.

"She hasn't come home, and the calls keep going to voicemail," he said simply. "I've left three messages, and I probably sound pretty desperate. Nothing. I'm going to call the police. I guess I have to call it a missing person."

"Right." Alex had hoped the news would be different. "They need to look for the Mercedes. Hopefully, she's with it. And they would certainly check the hospitals."

"Uh-huh." Dean thought hard. "You know, they might be able to trace the car through the GPS. Can't they do that now, with all the technology they have with Mercedes?" It had a top-of-the-line navigation system that commanded the center of the dashboard.

"I think so," Alex said slowly. "Certainly, I would ask the cops that. Or they might be able to use the GPS in her iPhone." He sipped on some cold coffee from the day before. "You know, Dad, I'm going to take some time off work and help you with this. Things are slow, and we have a double issue coming up, which pushes back our deadlines. It's no big sacrifice."

"You're sure? I'd really appreciate that, Alex."

"Done. I'll be over in an hour or so. Wait for me and we'll call the cops together."

"Okay, thanks."

They put through the call, not knowing what to expect. The police dispatcher passed them on to a duty officer, who walked them through a missing person's form, getting a description of Suzy and the car. At one point, Dean was asked if she had any "distinguishing marks." He thought for a moment, then said, "Not really, but she does walk with a limp. Her left leg is weak."

"Okay, that's helpful." The officer sounded bored, and he probably was, Alex thought.

They were told the GPS could serve as a locator, if it were switched on. First, Dean had to produce a VIN number, which he retrieved from a dog-eared manila folder in the study; it took several tries to relay the lengthy sequence correctly. He also gave them Suzy's cell number to see if a GPS signal was active there; Alex told him he'd heard of the technology but had never had reason to use it.

"Well, Mr. Perry, we'll call around to all the hospitals and clinics, and we'll try to put in a trace through the GPS," the officer said. "It would also be helpful if we have a good photo of your wife. Do you have something on your phone or computer you could send us?"

Dean immediately thought of a good closeup that had been taken months earlier in Naples. "I do. Where should it go to?"

"You can email it to us at this address," he replied, spelling it out.

"Got it."

"Okay then," the officer said. "Someone will get back to you later in the day. Hopefully, something will turn up."

"I really appreciate it."

Dean hung up and leaned back slowly in the chair. "Well, that much is done."

Alex gave him a quick smile. "And now we wait."

Waiting was almost physically painful for Dean. He had stopped pacing, and he tried to read, first *The New York Times* and then a magazine, but he couldn't concentrate. Alex, who was also reading, looked up from time to time and sensed his father's consternation.

They had agreed there wasn't much point in heading off in the Mini Cooper – to where? Suzy could be anyplace. "No sense in us acting like chickens with their heads cut off," Alex said to him, and Dean reluctantly nodded.

They ate lunch, Black Forest ham and Swiss sandwiches on marble rye, at the kitchen island, washed down with iced tea. Alex had made a quick call to Lisa and told her there was nothing to report except boredom and anxiety. Alex turned on the Golf Channel, and they watched some of a PGA tournament being played in the Washington,

D.C., area, where it was predictably warm and muggy – several of the players' shirts were stained dark with sweat.

The golf coverage, with its droning announcers, was a nice distraction, but the tension in the condo was palpable. Dean was clenching and unclenching his fists, seemingly unconsciously.

About 2, the house phone rang, and Dean pounced on it.

"Mr. Perry?"

"Speaking."

"This is Officer Bigliotti of the Rye Police. We have some news for you. A check of the hospitals turned up nothing. And we've located the car, but not your wife."

"Really?" Dean stared at the ceiling. "Where was it?" He put the phone on speaker so Alex could hear.

"Parked at a rental car facility in New Jersey – Parsippany. It's been there since yesterday. They called us, wondering why a woman from Rye left it there."

"What?"

Bigliotti spoke calmly and patiently. "It appears from talking to the manager there that your wife just left the Mercedes against a fence there, went in, and rented a smaller Ford. He said she rented it for a week, and told them she would drop it off in Dallas."

"Dallas?" Dean sounded incredulous. "I don't know that she knows anyone there."

"Okay. I – I have to say that we can rule out any foul play. It seems she deliberately changed cars and left for parts unknown."

Dean was silent, thinking furiously, and Alex spoke up. "This is his son. Was it clear from the manager that it was my mother-in-law?"

"Oh, yes. She used a credit card, and we texted him the photo you sent us. He confirmed it with his agent."

Alex asked, "What happens now in terms of tracing that car?"

"Well, procedurally, there's not a lot we can do at this point," Bigliotti said. "She's committed no crime we're aware of, so there's no cause to issue a bulletin to law enforcement around the country." He paused. "Mr. Perry, can I ask you if this stems from some kind of domestic dispute"-

"Yes, yes it does." He was clenching his teeth. "I'd rather not get into the details, but we haven't been married long, and I found out about some things in her past she'd never told me, upsetting things. I confronted her, and now it seems she took it even more badly than I'd thought."

"I see. Is – is there family that she would go to?"

Dean turned toward Alex as he spoke. "No, not really. That may sound strange, but it's true. I won't bore you with the details."

"Alright then." Bigliotti sounded subdued. "Well, we can try to run a credit card trace to see if she has charged meals or rooms somewhere. But we would need the card information to do that."

"Uh-huh. Phew, I do have statements somewhere for her Visa card. We have the same Amex account, so I don't think she'd use that. I'd have to dig the other up and call you back."

"Okay, whenever you're ready. Just ask for Bigliotti."

"Thank you, officer. I'll get back to you soon."

As he hung up, he looked at Alex like a tired bloodhound, his jaw sagging. His eyebrows seemed to have whitened more overnight, and the skin under his eyelids was puffy. "Can you believe this? I'm having a hard time, that's for sure. Jesus."

"Not really. She's acting very guilty, I'll say that." He scratched at his arm. "Is there any way she could have learned about the new autopsy request on Avery?"

Dean stared at him. "Not from me."

"Well, I don't really know where this leaves us. Do – do you to want me to stay here overnight?"

Dean exhaled. "Um, that would be great. Maybe just tonight - I need to get my wits about me. This is just such a shock."

"I'll call Lisa. Meanwhile, let's get the credit card stuff and call it over to them."

"Right." He turned slowly, and from behind, he seemed to have slumped; his head looked like it was resting not on his neck but uneasily on his shoulders. Alex sighed and followed him out of the room.

Little Rock, AR

43.

Suzy left I-40 at Route 365 and worked her way south, across the wide and still river toward Sally's house. It had been an uneventful drive, apart from being tailgated briefly by what she assumed was some young punk in Memphis. When he had a chance, his black Dodge Charger flew by her with the muffler blasting. She stared hard as he went by, but the tinted windows revealed nothing; within a minute, he was virtually out of sight.

She was headed for the old neighborhood of Capital View/Stiffton's Station, which Sally and Harold had moved to a few years after they married. It was near the capitol and south of the river, and while it had bona fide historic roots dating back to the early 1920s, most of the housing stock was modest and old; the same, in some ways, could be said of the residents.

Turning into the driveway, Suzy sensed that Sally must have already pulled into the one-car garage; Harold's pickup was nowhere to be seen, so he was probably still at work at the lumberyard. The house looked clean and tidy from the outside, just as she remembered it, with small swatches of annuals – zinnias and marigolds, mostly - in neat beds gracing the front on either side of the walk. She parked to one side of the drive and got out, walking to the trunk and pulling out her blue suitcase and wheeling it behind her up the flagstone walk.

Sally greeted her with a warm hug and led her back to the guest bedroom, all chintz and floral patterns; it was the very essence of feminine. The small bath with its combined shower and tub, hidden by a boldly striped shower curtain, was across the hall. Soon they were seated in the kitchen with a glass of white wine while Suzy told her about her trip, at least the parts she wanted her best friend to hear about.

Harold had learned of the visit only when Sally called to prepare him. Otherwise, he would have been nonplussed to see the white Focus with New Jersey plates in the driveway. He was as yet a little confused, somehow thinking Suzy was still in Atlanta, but then he remembered Sally telling him about her move to New York.

He walked into the kitchen, still feeling the sweat from the day in his armpits, and smiled. "Well, Suzy, this is a surprise."

"Hi, Harold." She stood up and they shared a quick and awkward hug, with Harold's beefy arms encircling her like the front claws of a crab. "How's it going?"

He flushed. "Oh, the usual. Busy summer shaping up." He looked at her, seeking some kind of validation; Suzy was still a striking woman, and looked a decade younger than Sally. With her, he was like a high school nerd trying to make small talk with the homecoming queen, expecting rejection and experiencing small jolts of pleasure when he sensed her approval.

Harold changed out of his work clothes, and Suzy insisted on taking them out for dinner. Sally's choice was Applebee's – Suzy cringed inwardly, wondering why she couldn't be more inventive – but cheerfully agreed. They climbed into Harold's truck, the three of them packed in the vinyl bench front seat like teenagers. Rush hour was over, and traffic had eased considerably, almost as if every third car had been abducted by beneficent aliens.

The restaurant was loud and busy, mostly with families, and utterly predictable. Most of the wait staff appeared to be high school or college kids working a summer job, and the service was a little slow and haphazard. They'd been at the table for almost five minutes before a young guy rushed up with a tray and passed out water glasses. This is what you get with chain restaurants, Suzy mused to herself: corporate overseers forever ratcheting down budgets, high turnover.

They chatted amiably about Harold and Sally's children and grandchildren, and briefly about Suzy's own step-grandkids in Atlanta.

To Sally's questions, Suzy also talked about her great life with Dean, their condo in Rye, and their trip to Bermuda a few weeks earlier. Sally drunk it in like champagne; Harold said little as he picked through his plate of baby back ribs.

Then he said, almost in spite of himself, "I hope you can stay a while. Sally looks forward to your visits so much."

Suzy's face clouded ever so slightly. "Well, I think it's only going to be a couple of days. But I'm really happy to be here. Brings back old memories, always does."

"So then you'll be drivin' back to New York?" He was wiping his lips with the napkin.

"Uh-huh," she said for his benefit, after a moment's hesitation. She'd divulge her real plan to Sally.

"Great," he said. "Sal, you can take a bit of time off, can't you?"

Sally smiled. "Oh, I think so. Thursday can be pretty slow, and we get half of Friday off. So we should have some time to hang around, won't we?" She looked at Suzy almost imploringly.

"Absolutely." Suzy wowed them with her best smile. "We will do that."

The two friends were chatting over their morning coffee. Harold had left hurriedly just before 8; the yard was doing a monthly inventory, he said, and he had to be there early.

"I hear your momma's not doin' so good," Sally said. "Mrs. Robbins told me she has congestive heart failure now, and she's still dealing with Parkinson's."

"Well, she is plenty old," Suzy said simply. "She's what, 92?"

"Yep, I reckon so. She was a year older than my momma." Sally's mother had died a decade earlier after an agonizing siege of breast cancer, and while Sally accepted Suzy's estrangement from her family, and especially her father, she never truly understood it. It went hard against her grain to shunt family aside. And she knew better than to ask about Alicia, whom she had met when the latter was a child – she didn't even know where she lived, marriage, children. The things a mother knows like the back of her hand and usually needs the barest of openings to talk about.

Indeed, the whole process of transforming Tina into Suzy had baffled her. Why would anyone change their name? She still wanted to call her Tina – "Suzy" was like a foreign word on her lips, even after all these years. But Suzy was like royalty; her life was far more grand, with fancy houses and cars (she'd shared photos over the years) and trips to places Sally wouldn't be able to find on a map.

Sally was going to work only a short shift that day, from 9 to 12. They agreed they'd go out for lunch, then have dinner in; Sally would have Harold grill some chicken thighs and vegetables. But the afternoon was an open book.

"Anything you want to do this afternoon?" Sally ran her hand back through her gray hair, cut medium short, and looked expectantly at her friend. She hadn't applied any makeup yet, and there was a fine tracery of lines on her cheeks that Suzy saw more sharply in the morning light. Her oval face had filled out over the years, and she had noticeable jowls.

"Oh, I don't know. Is there anything new to look at?"

"Well…" Sally thought. "There is an art exhibit at the museum, 20th century art. Harold would never go. It's really quite close – you probably remember."

"I do. Sure, that sounds like fun."

"Okay, we can have lunch over in that direction. There are plenty of places."

"Sounds like a plan, girlfriend."

The exhibit at the Arkansas Art Museum was small but well put together, featuring lesser works from 20th Century European masters like Klee, Kandinsky and Ernst. Suzy moved more quickly through it, pausing briefly before each painting and reading the notes before moving on. Sally followed, usually two or three paintings behind. At several points, they came upon art students who were seated on the padded benches, sketching, in front of one of the works.

After that, they went through much of the permanent collection, some of which Sally remembered from a prior visit years earlier. Clotted groups of children, some with green or blue day camp tee shirts, comprised most of the other visitors; now and then a few would dart about or grab a friend's arm, drawing a whispered scolding from one of the adult supervisors.

They elected to have a late lunch in the museum cafeteria, and like many museum spaces, it was a bright, esthetically pleasing spot with nicely prepared plates, along with sandwiches and salads. Only a few other tables were occupied; this clearly wasn't a venue for the kids' groups. The two friends chatted about what they'd seen and about what was happening in Little Rock from Sally's perspective.

Suzy was near the bottom of her salad when Sally asked, "So, when do you think you'll be leaving?"

"Probably tomorrow." Seeing Sally's frown, she decided at the moment to get it over with, to unburden herself. "The truth is, I'm kind of on the run."

"You're what?"

Suzy sighed. "There's a lot I haven't told you. Dean and I have been doing really well, but a few days ago he found out about my marriage to David and about Alicia. I had tried to hide those from him. And he was plenty mad."

"You'd never told him?"

"No. You know me, I never like to talk about the past. And he never asked me, to tell you the truth."

Sally leaned on her elbows and looked across at her. "So you just took off to let things cool down a bit?"

"Well, that's one way of looking at it." Suzy picked at the silver bracelet on her wrist. "But the truth is, Sal, I'm in a spot."

"What d'you mean?"

Suzy leaned back and looked at her, and something like a sneer crossed her lips. "Dean's son actually hired a private eye to look into my past, and talked to my step-kids in Atlanta. It seems that they are preparing to exhume Avery's body for an autopsy."

Sally looked stunned. "I don't understand."

"Do you remember that incident many years ago with the kid in your office swallowing Carolina jasmine leaves?"

Sally screwed up her face. "Yeah, I do, but what"—

"I gave some to Avery, just as I'd given it to David."

Sally blanched, and felt a tingling, like tiny pinpricks, wash across her chest. "You mean"—

"I killed them both. In each case, the poison made it look like a heart attack. I'd ordered the plant for my garden in St. Louis and Atlanta."

Sally felt odd, almost dizzy. Finally, she croaked, "But why?"

To her, Suzy looked composed, almost defiant. "I caught David cheating on me, not once, but twice. And Avery was getting old and tired. Getting rid of them let me make a new start." She paused, and a twisted smile played on her face. "And, let's face it, it made me pretty rich."

Sally was speechless, and her eyes were fixed on her plate. She couldn't look at Suzy.

"So now you know," Suzy said almost casually. "Now, what I need your help with, is renting another car and heading further west. I need to rent it in your name – don't worry, it won't be a problem. You can always say I forced you to do it."

Sally felt nauseated. She held up her hand, stood up and ran to the bathroom, which she'd spotted on their way to the food line. She pushed open the door and lunged quickly into the first stall, but before she could reach the toilet, she retched, violently, three times on the floor.

Westchester County, NY

44.

It was Friday morning, and Suzy had been gone for two long days. Alex had ferried Dean to Parsippany the day before to pick up the Mercedes, which still sat forlornly against the chain link fence at the rental agency. Only the seat position offered any clue that Suzy had been driving. The car had been locked and standing in the sun, and it was almost as toasty as a sauna when Dean got in and pushed the ignition and they started home.

Alex had agreed to stay until late afternoon, but it wasn't clear what they would learn by then, if anything. Down in Atlanta, the authorities had agreed to hear Tom and Robin's petition to exhume their father's body; the request had gotten speedy attention after Suzy's flight. The actual hearing was scheduled for the following Tuesday.

Yet Suzy was still classified only as a missing person – no crime had been committed. Evidence was mounting, like a rogue wave building in mid-ocean, but no one could be sure that it wouldn't peter out before landfall.

They heard from Officer Bigliotti in late morning. He called to say that a credit card trace had turned up nothing beyond the original car rental.

"That seems odd," Alex said. "Does that suggest anything to you?"

"Well, unless there's a credit card we don't know about, it means she's been using cash. Mr. Perry, have you looked at your checking account to see if there have been some big ATM withdrawals?"

Dean stared at the phone. "No, no I haven't."

"I think it's worth checking," Bigliotti said. "Do you have computer access to that account?"

"Yes, but I almost never look at it."

Alex spoke up. "I'll help him check it out. But - aren't you limited to a set amount each day, like $300 or $400?"

"It varies," Bigliotti replied. "At some banks like Chase, if you have a certain high-level account, you can withdraw as much as $3,000 a day."

Alex grunted. "I didn't know that. Well, that's who they've been banking with. We'll take a look. Thanks."

"Any further thoughts on where she might have gone?" Bigliotti sounded solicitous.

"No, not really." Dean sounded disconsolate. "She could be anywhere. I know she has friends in Atlanta, but that would be the first place we would look. It's harder to be inconspicuous there."

"Nothing to that Dallas destination, then?"

"Honestly, no. It sounds more and more like a ruse," Dean said.

Ten minutes after hanging up with Bigliotti, Alex sat at the laptop in the office and used his father's user name and password to access the Chase account system. He clicked on the checking link and waited for the screen to populate. There it was – two withdrawals, one the day before and one the day she disappeared, for $2,000 each. Dean sat beside him, and they stared at the screen mutely.

"I'll be damned," Dean said finally. "Just unbelievable."

"You know, Dad, they have cameras at these ATMs. We could ask the cops to check the tapes—"

"What's the point?" He looked agonized. "Who else could it be?" He licked his lips. "And, you know, she has check-writing privileges on a brokerage account she's kept in Atlanta. She has access to lots of money."

"Um, I didn't know that," Alex responded. "But I'm not surprised."

They turned on the TV and started watching more golf, but Dean was clearly distracted. His new wife, his pride and joy, wasn't who he'd thought she was. And now she was in the wind.

It was just after 7 pm when the phone in Debra's kitchen rang. She saw it was Alex, and she picked up.

"Hi. This a good time?"

"Sure," she said brightly. "I'm alone – Rachel is still taking classes down in Eugene and Zack is off on a fishing trip with two of his buddies. What's up?"

"Well, I need to catch you up on what's been going on." He paused. "Suzy has disappeared, and apparently quite deliberately."

"Oh, God. When did this happen?"

"Wednesday morning. She took his car and drove to New Jersey, rented another car, and vanished. We have no idea where she may be – none."

"Wow." A long pause. "How is Dad taking all this?"

"About what you'd expect, I guess – badly. You see – he blames himself for precipitating it. He argued with her after I laid out things she had never told him – the things we talked about last time."

"So, he confronted her with all that stuff?"

"Yeah. And things quickly went south – she pulled some money from the ATM account and took off. It's just fucking unbelievable."

"My God." She blew out a breath and took a sip from her glass of wine. "You know, all this is starting to fit into the sociopath profile we were talking about."

"That's what I've been thinking," Alex said. "And it may get worse – Avery's kids in Atlanta, as well as his friends, have been suspicious about his death. Now they've petitioned to do a full autopsy."

"You mean—"

"I mean that there is now suspicion that he might have been given something, perhaps even a poison. The official cause of death was listed as a heart attack." He paused. "Now, get this. The first husband also died of a heart attack, and his brother had asked for an exhumation way back then. Suzy blocked it."

"Whoa," she replied. "This just keeps getting more interesting."

"I don't know, Deb. She hasn't broken any laws that we know of, it's all circumstantial. So, there's no dragnet out there. I – I was wondering if you had any theories about who someone like that might turn to."

She was silent for a few moments. "I think she'd turn to an old friend, someone she can trust – and manipulate. At least for a while, until she can think things through. Does – does she know about this autopsy request?"

"I don't think so," he said slowly. "But she may suspect it. It would certainly explain her flying the coop."

"What do you know about her past? Her childhood?"

"Very little. She seems to have cut off the people in Missouri completely. Her daughter told me she grew up in Little Rock and had a childhood friend she was very close to. But she didn't have a name – well, only a first name."

"Well, I think that's as good a place as any to look. But that may require some real digging."

Alex sighed. "It sounds that way. But that's a great idea. Let me work on it. Thanks."

Little Rock, AR

45.

Saturday morning dawned with a heavy haze and humidity that seemed as thick as churned butter. Sally had suffered through a terrible night, with hours spent staring at the ceiling and her mind turning this way and that. Suzy's confession had shocked her to her core, and now she was like a rock climber clinging to a precarious handhold on a vertical face.

She didn't really want to share any of this with Harold – he wouldn't understand – but she knew she had to, at least some of it. It was too much for anyone to keep to themselves, unbidden. She couldn't comprehend what Suzy said she had done; it was beyond understanding. Sally knew Suzy had carried a long and merciless grudge against her father, but she had no idea Suzy's animus seemed to go much deeper, against men she had claimed to love.

She was sitting in the kitchen in her striped pajamas, nursing a coffee, when Suzy walked in. Harold had to put in a Saturday morning shift at the yard and had already left. Suzy had applied fresh makeup and mascara and was plainly ready for the day. She looked at Sally, who kept her eyes fixed on the table. My God, Suzy thought, she looks like she's aged five years since yesterday.

"Sally, honey," she said. "I know all this has to be pretty upsetting. I've told you so many things, but these are my deepest, darkest secrets."

"I guess so," Sally mumbled.

"But this is when I need your help more than ever. Remember, I talked about renting another car in your name?"

"Yeah." Her voice was all but inaudible.

"I want to do that this morning. Then I'll be on my way. I'll drop it off in a day or two, and no one should be any the wiser."

Sally looked up at her. "Where are you going?"

Suzy offered a half-smile. "I'm not sure – and I'm telling you the truth. Probably Texas. I'll certainly let you know once I'm there."

Sally spread her hands on the table. "Are they looking for you?"

Suzy shrugged. "I don't think so, not in any major way. Even if there is an autopsy in Atlanta, it will be weeks before the results come back, as I understand it. I'll be long gone."

Sally's hands worked around the coffee cup in small circles before she spoke. "What will you do?"

"Well, I guess I have to reinvent myself with a new name." Suzy's eyes seemed especially bright. "I've done it before. I can do it again."

Sally had been especially sullen during the rental car process, Suzy thought, but at least she didn't balk. Sally rented the Chrysler 200 from Dollar for a week, and Suzy declined to list herself as a second driver – that would require turning over her driver's license. If she were stopped, it could certainly be a problem – she'd have to think that one through. She gave her destination for the rental return as Dallas.

They parted in the agency parking lot as Suzy took the keys and the rental papers from Sally and prepared to drive off. Suzy went to hug her, but Sally didn't reciprocate; her arms drooped at her sides, like a six-year-old being told her favorite rag doll had been lost. It was an awkward parting, and Suzy realized she simply had to get in the car and go. Sally's world had turned upside down, and Suzy knew she was the reason.

As she turned the key and adjusted the mirrors, she looked back at Sally, who hadn't moved. She seemed as lost as a child waiting for a parent who had forgotten to pick her up at day camp.

Suzy followed the signs for I-30 that took her to the east before swinging to the southwest. The sun was breaking through the haze, and she set the cruise control for 70, headed for Texarkana. Traffic seemed relatively light, and after she left the Little Rock metro area, it petered out to almost nothing. She looked at her watch: 10:40. She'd be across the state line in a couple of hours.

Westchester County, NY

46.

Ordinarily, Alex would be riding with his bike group on a fine Saturday morning. But this wasn't a normal Saturday, and he had realized the night before that he needed to give Alicia another call.

He called at 11:30, thinking she would probably be an early riser and it wouldn't be too early in LA. He retrieved her number and dialed it on the land line. There was an answer on the third ring – a girl's voice.

"Hi, can I speak to your mom?"

"Can I tell her who's calling?"

"Please tell her this is Alex Perry calling from New York. We've spoken a couple of times."

"Okay." She sounded hesitant. "Let me go ask her."

Some 20 seconds later, Alicia picked up. "Hi, Alex."

"Good morning, Alicia. I have some news for you." He paused. "Suzy was confronted by my Dad about a number of things, including you and your daughters – he only learned about that from me. They had a bit of a spat, I guess, and now she's taken off – we don't know where."

"Really," she exclaimed. "Did this just happen?"

"She took off on Wednesday. Took Dad's car, dropped it at a rental agency, rented a car and left for parts unknown."

"Sheesh." Alicia let out a breath. "Well, I wish I could help you find her, but as you know, she's like a cipher to me now."

"I know, I know. I – I was talking to my sister, who's a family therapist. She suggested that a good bet would be an old friend, like the one in Little Rock you told me about."

"Oh, right, Sally. Sally something."

"Is there anything you might have somewhere in the house that would have her last name?"

Silence. "I'm not sure," she said slowly. "I don't think so, but I'll look. If I do find something, how do I reach you?"

"Let me give you my cell," he said, and gave her the number. "Call me anytime at all."

"Okay, will do."

Two hours later, he and Lisa were driving back home after dropping Jennifer at a friend's house when his cell rang. It was Alicia. The phone was set on Bluetooth and he kept both hands on the wheel.

"Alex, I finally remembered the name. I kind of worked through the alphabet, and it came to me. Sally Pritchard."

"Great. Is that spelled with a t-c-h?"

"Yes." She confirmed the spelling.

"Wonderful. Thanks so much. We'll see if this takes us somewhere."

He looked over at Lisa. "So now we have a name to work with. I think I'm going to call Insana and see if they can follow up on this, find her and even talk to her."

Belted beside him in the passenger seat, Lisa half-turned to him and nodded. "This is hopeful."

When they got home, he dialed the Maris Agency number and got the expected voicemail message: the office was closed. But he wanted to leave a message, and he expected Insana or others to check on the mailbox over the weekend. This would be a second job for them, and he was sure they could take it on.

It was just before 6:30, and Alex was carrying out a platter of chicken breasts to the grill on the back patio when his cellphone in his shorts pocket went off. He set down the platter on the low rock wall and answered.

"Hi, Bob Insana here. I heard your message."

"Great. Would you be willing to run down this lead? I'm thinking someone would have to go to Little Rock and try to interview her. It's even possible Suzy could still be there, if that's where she went."

"Of course. You realize that we couldn't start on this until Monday…"

"I understand, sure."

"But we'd be happy to take it on," Insana said. "Let me work up an estimate for you, but I think one man day here sends about right. This woman is Suzy's age, isn't she?"

"Yes, they were school classmates, as I understand it."

"Well, that should certainly narrow it down. Um, I will call you Monday morning, if that's okay, to let you know what we're doing."

"Great. Have a good weekend, and thanks again."

It was about 8:30 on a warm summer night, with the sun still an orange ball suspended above the horizon, when the phone rang. Dean saw it was his daughter and picked up.

"Hi, Deb. To what do I owe this call?"

"Hi, Dad. Well, I'm worried about you. Alex has told me about Suzy's disappearance. I think I know what she meant to you. I wanted to know if you wanted to talk about it at all."

Dean sighed and sensed where she was going. "Not really, honey. Particularly if you want to come at this from some kind of psychological standpoint—"

"You got me there," Debra said almost apologetically. "I guess I can't help myself. Her behavior just seems so hard to understand." She paused, and Dean pictured her reaching for a cocktail. "I promise not to be too nosy."

"Well, I'm tired, and it's not like I have any answers."

"Okay, I'll keep this short – for me." She chuckled. "Did you have any inkling, any warning signs of all these secrets?"

"No, none. When Alex came to me with the stuff from the private investigator, it was like I got walloped on the head."

"I'm picturing her as a classic narcissist, the kind who wants to be the center of attention, who solicits compliments, who doesn't seem to care much about other's feelings."

"Well, I can't say I saw much of that. Okay, she did take special attention in her appearance, and she could come off as arrogant at times. But what man doesn't want a woman who looks good and cares about herself?"

"You've got me there. That has to be a big item for most men." She paused. "How did she respond when you confronted her with this stuff? Was she angry, or more quietly defensive?"

He sighed; it was a dark memory that he had respooled over and over again in his head. "A little of both, I guess. Her first reaction seemed to be very taken aback, and then it became anger – seemingly that I didn't trust her. She stalked out of the room, and things were pretty chilly the rest of the day. She took off the following day."

"Without any word of regret, or apology?"

"Not really. She told me over breakfast that I'd hurt her, and that I'd never done anything like that to her before," Dean said. "I think she expected me to apologize, but I certainly didn't. I thought the apology needed to come from her… well, it never did. And that was the last conversation we had."

"Oy." Deb clicked her tongue. "I kind of hate to ask this, but – do you think she's coming back? I mean, you guys are married, and there are legal issues at stake, property, you know."

"Oh, I hope so, honey, but I really don't know. She won't return my calls, and she turned off the GPS on her phone. I don't know where she is, and apparently she wants it that way." He sighed. "I feel like I'm in that old movie, 'Dazed and Confused.' That's where I am at this point."

"Well, Dad, you know I'd pray for you if I were religious. But I am keeping my fingers crossed for you."

"I appreciate it, honey. And thanks for the call."

On the Road

47.

The miles rolled by, and Suzy passed the green hills of the Ozarks rising in waves on the right. Traffic grew more knotted, with a number of cars and trucks towing boats or jet skis. Big, multi-armed reservoirs, bluer than the sky, were tucked in those hills, but they weren't visible from the road.

She enjoyed highway driving, despite having done relatively little of it in her life; the men usually drove, especially on longer trips - after all, that was a man's job, she thought. She fiddled with the radio now and then, alternating between stations playing pop and country music. When one starting gurgling with static, she would move the dial to another.

Going close to 75, Suzy passed a long cavalcade of single trucks, picking them off one by one in the left-hand lane and then moving right as she went by. Other cars presented a mixed bag: some were doing under 70, others over 80. Taking note of the plates, she saw that cars from California and New Mexico generally seemed to be going faster than anyone else. The slowest of all were RVs, often towing cars. They were like whales with dolphins riding in their wake.

Crossing the Texas border, she pulled off at Texarkana and looked for fast food restaurants, and she was upon a raft of them almost before she knew it. She settled for a Wendy's and waited patiently in a short line, entertaining herself by trying to guess which people were locals and which were fellow travelers.

The men in Stetsons and trucker's caps she pegged for locals, but the rest could be almost anything – apart from a few well-dressed women, in skirts and nice sandals, who were probably nearby office workers. Many of the younger customers were in t-shirts, shorts, and flip-flops, the current state of hot-weather attire in America.

Getting back in the car, she checked the map and saw she could be in greater Dallas in a couple of hours. It was a hot, sticky day, the way of summer in East Texas, and when she turned the engine on, she saw the temperature was already 96. A haze hung over the western horizon like a light blanket.

Suzy had already used one of her tablet apps to scout out a good motel location, and she chose a La Quinta in Garland, just off I-30 and only a few miles west of Lake Ray Hubbard, a huge impoundment that straddled the highway like a blue dragon with its head skewed to the south. As she drove across it, the lake was glassy and reflected the cumulus clouds overhead like balls of coarse cotton.

Check-in at the motel was easy, with a pleasant girl in a uniform shirt – college age, she guessed – handing her a form. She filled in Sally's name and address and prepaid in cash. Compared to her motel in Nashville, her first-floor room was modern and better appointed, but it offered nothing distinctive or memorable: the view of the parking lot out the window was, to say the least, uninspiring.

Unpacking, Suzy took her toiletries to the bathroom and unloaded them on the counter. The next morning, she decided, she needed to visit the local library and do some online research on name-change procedures in Texas. She was assuming they would be simple – as easy as Georgia, certainly – but she had to be sure. She could bring up the information on her phone, she realized, but it would be difficult to read on a small screen.

She sat on the bed, dangling her legs, and turned on her phone. There had been no messages from Dean in the past two days; he'd clearly realized that she was on the lam and had given up trying to talk to her. And there was nothing from Sally, either. No surprise there.

Her unburdening to Sally had been a little traumatic, and the upshot even more so. Sally would never see her the same way, never be the trusting, unsuspecting confidante, the woman locked in her shadow who always looked up to her. Suzy was now almost like a family dog that had turned and, as abruptly and shockingly as a snake, bitten its master.

Back in Little Rock, Sally sat blankly on her couch. The trust, the anticipation of hearing from her, Suzy's approval – all gone. Sally had never really seen her best friend's dark side, the narcissism; she had never looked for it, and for much of the time it had been carefully cloaked. More than anything, Sally thought she'd been used. Her hands clenched as her mouth hardened: Sally was a stranger to indignation, but she felt it now.

Indeed, Suzy sensed that Sally had progressed through shock and denial to something far more grave: anger. Betrayal can do that, like a suppurating sore that refuses to close, as she knew all too well. Suzy shrugged her shoulders, set the open suitcase on the second queen bed and lay down, slipping off her sandals and adjusting the pillow. The lights outside the window were relatively bright, but she had pulled the curtains over and blotted them out. Sleep never came easily to her unless a room was dark.

Finding the library was easy enough. After a mundane breakfast at a high-top table in the motel dining area, she went to the desk and asked the girl on duty for an address, which she produced after a minute or two on a scrap of motel stationery. Suzy thanked her and walked back through the long, beige-carpeted corridor to her room.

She was already packed, and she input the library address into the car's GPS. It appeared to be several miles away. She checked her watch: 8:30. It would probably open at 9 or 9:30, she guessed, so there wasn't much point in leaving now and cooling her heels in the parking lot. So, she flipped on the TV and watched CNN for a while, though it was more background noise than anything while she thought through her next moves. She did check the Weather Channel app on her phone and saw that the predicted high in Dallas was 102. Ugh.

T-shirts had never appealed to Suzy, and she always disliked the idea of anything too revealing. She wore a pair of plain navy shorts, gold-trimmed sandals, and a light pink sleeveless blouse with a scoop neckline – an outfit she felt made her polished but hardly conspicuous.

Not long after nine, she left the room, dropped the key card off at the desk and walked out to her car, which was bracketed by two pickups; one, with a jacked-up suspension, towered over the Chrysler.

Popping open the trunk and loading her suitcase, she was soon backing out and following the voice commands on the GPS. Traffic on the surface streets was moderately heavy, but she pulled into the well-marked library lot by 9:20.

Clearly, the building hadn't yet opened: four or five people, teenagers and adults, loitered by the door, obviously waiting. It was a low, dark brick edifice with a metal roof that looked relatively new. Several minutes later, the knot of people broke up as the doors opened and they filtered in; she followed.

Suzy walked to the information desk and asked the woman on duty about using the Internet.

"Sure," she said brightly. The woman was tall and almost skeletally thin, a stork in human form, wearing very little makeup but holding her reading glasses on a chain, the cliched librarian look. She pointed to an area in the middle of the room where Suzy saw several rows of terminals. "You'll find them right there. You'll need to use your credit card to access the Web."

"Yes, I thought so," Suzy said.

"Let me give you the access code to get in," the woman said, bending down to scribble a note, which she handed to Suzy with a smile. "If you have any trouble, let us know."

Suzy walked to the far terminal on the left in the first row and sat down. She turned the computer on and moved the mouse to the dialog box on the screen and typed in the code she'd been given. Up came the fee schedule: five dollars for an hour looked to be about right. She clicked on the box, swiped her credit card through the card-reader slot and waited for the Internet link to come up.

Soon she was on Google Chrome. She typed "Texas name-change requirements" into the search bar and watched as several links came up; she chose the first link that offered a PDF spelling out the legal steps needed.

Scrolling through it, her face clouded. It looked to entail a lot of work, and when she got to step 5, she muttered to herself: it talked about having fingerprints taken by local law enforcement and stapling those to the official change petition. Fingerprints? No way, she thought to herself. Texas was starting to look more than a little inhospitable, and that surprised her.

Well, what about New Mexico, she thought. She closed the link and went back to search mode, this time typing in name-change rules for New Mexico. Again, several links popped up quickly, and she chose the one from LegalZoom that promised a full overview.

As she read through it, her mood brightened: New Mexico didn't require any fingerprinting, and the one unusual request was to place a classified ad in a local newspaper once a week for two weeks "alerting the public" that you want to change your name. As she read on, one needed to file a comprehensive form including items like current name and address and a few other things that she might have to fudge a bit: birthplace and date, previous names and addresses, addresses of parents. It also had to be notarized, then taken to a court where a judge would certify it if no objections had been raised.

Straightforward enough. She stared into space and thought hard. She and Avery had been to Santa Fe years ago, and she'd loved the quaintness and the Spanish overlay – and the cultural efflorescence, with the renowned slew of galleries featuring painting, jewelry and sculpture. A few works she'd seen had even inspired her own painting efforts.

Suzy had sensed the city's bonhomie and open-mindedness, and they stuck in her memory. That's where I'll go, she thought to herself. The winters would be relatively cold, but the air was clean and the sun blazed in a blue sky most days in the year. She nodded to herself: this could be the place. Maybe I'll even start painting again.

But she'd have to rent an apartment before she could apply for a name change. That would take some doing, yet it had to be done quickly: if there was an autopsy on Avery, it could be coming before long; if it showed the *Gelsenium*, her status would change overnight. Alarm bells would sound, and she'd no longer be a woman who'd walked out on her husband; she'd almost certainly be a murder suspect.

She closed out the screen and sat for another minute, reviewing what she had learned. As she got up, a middle-aged woman sat down at the terminal next to her and smiled at her, the reflexive goodwill gesture of a stranger. Suzy gave her a quick smile back and walked back out to the car. She checked her watch: 9:50. Time was wasting.

Sally had rarely seen Harold so angry; he was a stolid, no-nonsense man, good at fixing most things with his beefy hands: plumbing, electrical, you name it. He rarely showed flashes of temper, but when he heard that Sally had accompanied Suzy to a rental agency and rented a car for Suzy in her name, he was practically dumbstruck; he thought of the cost, first and foremost.

"What were you thinking? How long is this rental for?" His broad face reddened.

"She said it would be just for a day or two. And she insisted she'd be paying for it, and if there was any hassle, she would send me a check."

"Oh, alright." He seemed mollified for a moment. "But why did she have to do it in your name?" He stared at her quizzically.

Sally looked down at her hands. "She's running from her husband."

"What? Why?"

She sighed and decided she would shave the truth and keep the worst from him. "They had a fight, and she was very upset. She doesn't want him to find her, not least right away."

Harold was silent for a moment and clenched his fist and brought it to his chin. "So, she ran to you, her best friend in the world, knowin' you would take care of her."

"Something like that." Sally tried to smile, but it was more of a grimace.

"This is unbelievable." He shook his head slowly, and his jowls quivered. "Where d'you think she's goin'?"

"Well, she said probably Texas, but she wasn't sure. Said she'd let me know once she got there."

"Some friend she is. I don't care if you guys have been tight forever – friends don't act like that."

Sally pursed her lips. "No, I don't suppose they do."

"You know, Sal, by my lights, she's not welcome here anymore." He leaned toward her slightly as he spoke.

"I hear you. And somehow, I don't think that will be a problem. I don't think she'll be here again."

"Good. We understand each other." As he turned and reached for the refrigerator door, Sally felt like her face was on fire.

Into Colorado

48.

Driving on I-70 west towards Denver, Suzy let herself be taken by the beauty of the Front Range, where the Rockies thrust up sharply from the brown plain, so flat and monotonous. Patches of snow on the highest peaks flashed now and then in the sun, like semaphores. She'd only been to Denver once for a brief visit, and she had no plans to stay there, but there was something about the contrast between the flatness and the jaggedness of the Rockies that captivated her.

As she swung north and approached the airport, she was struck by the sight of its huge white canopies, like sails billowing in the wind; she'd seen photos of it, but it was more imposing now, rising sharply from level ground. She braked as she saw signs for the rental car return and followed them to the off-site lot. Pulling up to the spaces marked for Dollar, she pulled the rental agreement out of the glove compartment and waited until the attendant finished with the car ahead, a black Dodge.

Suzy smiled as the attendant approached, and she lowered the window.

"Hi, how are you?"

The attendant, a slim young man in a light blue uniform shirt, smiled back. "Good, how are you? Any problems with the vehicle?" He looks Middle Eastern, she thought, with straight black hair and a thin tracing of stubble on his chin; the voice held a hint of an accent.

"None at all." She opened the door and handed him the agreement, and he walked slowly around the car to check for damage before getting into the front seat and checking the odometer. Then he got out and punched some buttons on his hand-held device, which clicked for a few moments before spitting out a paper receipt.

"Thank you, Mrs. Pritchard," he said, handing her the receipt.

"You're welcome," she said reflexively. "Um – is there a shuttle from the airport to downtown?" She had done some research on the Web and realized she needed to go into the city to catch a bus.

"Yes. It's with the rest of the ground transportation choices," he said. "The best one is really a rail link – it goes right downtown to Union Station."

"Thank you," she said, and retrieved her bag from the trunk and wheeled it behind her to the rental car building where she'd catch a shuttle to the airport. She looked at the receipt in her hand and made a mental note that she needed to send Sally a check for that amount to cover the cost of the rental. Suzy decided to send it from Denver before she left, so that would be the postmark that any investigators might find; she had several stamps in her purse and realized she could probably drop an envelope in the hotel lobby.

The sun was high in the sky, and the pavement was warm under her feet. She was completely alone, but she was at peace; her plan was working, and the past was receding with every step she took.

Dean rubbed his eyes and swung his legs out of the bed. He had long ago accepted the absence of another form on the other side of the bed, but now and again he would look over there wistfully.

After a long shower, he dressed slowly in khaki shorts and a red polo shirt and walked to the kitchen to fix breakfast. He made a cup of coffee with the Keurig machine that Suzy had given him for his birthday, then fried an egg and popped a couple of slices of whole wheat bread into the toaster. He ate slowly, like a condemned man savoring one of his last meals.

An hour later, in the study, he picked up the phone and called Alex, who was in his office. It was a Thursday, but Dean had a hard time remembering – or really, caring – what day of the week it was.

At his desk, Alex saw that it was his father calling. "Hi, Dad."

"Good morning – well, as good as it's going to get."

Alex paused for a moment. Dean was in the dumps, and he was constantly making others aware of it, like he was waving a white flag of surrender. "So, what's up?"

"Well, I was wondering if there's anything more we might be able to do to find her." He sighed audibly. "You know, maybe she's using one of her credit cards now. It's been over a week."

"Well, I guess I could ask Bigliotti if he could broadcast that information and see if anything turns up," Alex said. "But it could be quite a while before she works through the cash withdrawal."

"You know…" Dean said, drawing out the last word. "Can we cancel the Visa card? Then she'd have to apply for another, and the credit check might give us a pretty good clue."

Alex mulled that over. "Maybe. But I'm not sure we can cancel it – that request may have to come from her. And – and if we did, we wouldn't be able to trace any activity on it."

"Ah, you're right. May not be such a good idea."

"Let me run it by Insana and see what he thinks," Alex said.

"Would you?"

"Sure." Alex made a note on his pad. "And what about lunch later?"

"Actually, I'm supposed to go the club and meet a couple of the guys. They're trying to cheer me up."

"Good." Alex approved of the idea of Dean reaching out to his buddies. "Maybe next week."

"Sure. Okay, son. Talk soon."

49.

Using the rail link proved every bit as easy as Suzy had hoped, and it was mid-afternoon when she descended onto the platform at the train station. She'd done some research online, and opted for one of the older, cheaper hotels not far away. Union Station appeared to be a short cab ride away from the Denver Bus Center, according to Google Maps; she decided she'd simply spend the night and get on a bus the next morning for the trip to Santa Fe.

She smiled to herself: who would suspect Suzy Perry of riding a bus with the *hoi polloi*? It was part of her overarching strategy for her flight – steer clear of the finer lodging and transportation that would be the first places that anyone looking for her might check out. Not quite like the queen masquerading as a peasant, but the analogy had a ring of truth. She still had no inkling if a serious search for her was underway, but she assumed that Dean would spare no effort to find her.

The hotel, a sturdy stone edifice that looked like it had been around since before she'd been born, was nicer inside than she'd imagined, with a high vaulted ceiling and a vast skylight that let the sun cast long shadows on the marble lobby floor. She wheeled her suitcase to the reception desk and waited for a few moments before a bright-faced young woman got off the phone and attended to her.

"Hi." Suzy summoned up one of her best smiles. "I'd like to check in for one night. Would it be possible for me to prepay in cash?" She quickly studied the girl, dressed in a gray pants suit with a nametag that said "Kerri."

Kerri, a petite dark-eyed brunette, smiled and nodded. "Of course, ma'am. You'd just need to drop your room key in the box over here when you leave," she said, pointing to a large wooden box with a slot for keycards.

"Fine," Suzy said. "And can I get a room on a high floor? I've never been to Denver before, and I'd like to admire the view." That was a lie – she had been to the city years ago with Avery for one of his board meetings – but who cared? More than ever, lying was going to be second nature for her; this fib felt inconsequential, a trifle barely worth acknowledging.

"Certainly, let me see what I have." She stared at her computer screen for a few moments. "I have a room on the 23rd floor, number 2318. How would that be?"

"That sounds good," Suzy said.

"Perfect," Kerri said brightly. "Is one keycard enough?"

"Yes, one is all I need."

Kerri swiped the card through a reader and put in a small envelope and handed it to Suzy. "There you are. The elevators are to your left," she said, waving her arm that direction. "Enjoy your stay with us."

Suzy ate in one of the hotel's restaurants that night; no need to be out and about any more than she had to be. The meal, a chicken paillard with wild rice and summer squash presented with a sprig of parsley, was perfectly adequate, as was the Chardonnay she chose to go with it, but she wasn't really hungry; she left half of the food on her plate.

The other diners seemed to be caught up in their own business. Most were older couples or single business people, the latter focused on their phones or tablets as if the messages in front of them were the last they would ever see; while it was near the height of the summer tourist season, the room was less than half full. Most families wouldn't be staying downtown, she thought to herself. They'd be out by the airport or in a newer property off one of the expressway exits.

She glanced again, to her right, and did a quick double-take. A solitary man sat at a table against the wall and seemed to be staring at her. She hadn't noticed him before, but something about him was disconcerting. He was lanky and bald, with a long, narrow face and protruding ears. She met his glance briefly, then looked down at her plate.

He hadn't smiled, and his stare sent a quick shiver through her. Maybe he was harmless, but being on the run raised her suspicions and, in an unhappy alchemy, turned the ordinary into something more sinister. A minute later, she looked over at him and saw he was busy eating.

Ten minutes later, after paying her bill, she stood up and walked unhurriedly out of the restaurant. When she reached the elevator bays, she looked back. He was nowhere to be seen.

The two main elevators from the lobby absorbed all the guest traffic and were crowded and predictably glacial; it took what seemed minutes to get up to her floor. Getting off, the remaining guests on the car had dwindled to her and an older couple still headed for a higher floor; she ambled down the long hallway toward her room, seeing a few trays on the floor that had been left out by guests ordering room service. She shook her head slightly. Here was a tray with food and plates askew – would people leave a mess like that at home?

Back in her room, she pulled out a paperback she'd bought at the airport – a romance by Anne Rivers Siddons. She'd enjoyed a number of other Siddons books before and found the Southern charm that infused them very soothing. But as she settled in, her mind suddenly went to Baxter. He would certainly realize it when she drained her cash account, as she intended – and if her accounts were frozen, there might be an investigation… and his blackmail could surface.

Serves him right, she thought, smiling thinly. Play with fire and you may just get burned.

Suzy sat on the first queen bed, set the book down beside her and bowed her head, thinking. The episode with the ugly man in the dining room had triggered her self-preservation instincts and the notion that some kind of disguise might be needed. But what? Her hair, she thought, was her most recognizable feature, the thing that most announced her to the world. And here she needed to leave the next morning, too early to find anything as exotic as a wig; besides, that kind of purchase might be traceable if investigators picked up her trail - what woman with gorgeous hair needs a wig?

A head scarf? She couldn't pass for a Muslim in a cave, and that, too, might draw unwarranted attention. She'd never dyed her hair, her pride and joy, but the more she pondered on it, the more that seemed like the best option. Nothing too extreme - not black or red, but maybe a medium brown, the color of the muskrats she used to see swimming languidly at Bob Pruitt's pond in Little Rock. She smiled inwardly at the thought.

Five minutes later, she was at the front desk, asking the girl on duty how to find a drugstore. The directions were easy, and the girl assured her it was less than five minutes away. Suzy set off for the revolving doors without a backward glance and found herself in a mild dusk, the setting sun casting a pink tinge on the sidewalk and the buildings on her right.

Few people were on the street; it was almost as if the storefronts exerted a giant vacuum that had sucked most of the pedestrians inside. The store was indeed simple to locate. Suzy walked in and followed the signs for hair products, finding the usual daunting array for women (mostly) and men. No one else was in the aisle, and she took her time looking over the choices: Revlon, Miss Clairol, L'Oreal Paris, Pantene, Wella. She read the labels on several and found the instructions were very similar.

She settled on a L'Oreal colorant, Light Amber Brown. She didn't love the color - she wasn't enchanted with the idea itself, to be truthful -- but it certainly seemed a reasonable choice; she picked up the package and walked to the counter, where she waited as an elderly man laboriously counted out change from his leather coin purse. When he finished, he looked up at her apologetically with rheumy eyes and raised his gnarled hands, managing a weak smile. I'm sorry, he seemed to be saying. I can't go any faster.

Back in the room, Suzy went to the bathroom, removed her shoes and her top and read the instructions again. They seemed straightforward enough: rub the dye through your hair thoroughly, allow time to let it set, then rinse thoroughly. She looked at herself in the mirror, sighed as she saw a trace of haggardness around her eyes, and was reminded that she'd stopped wearing mascara; no need to look good for anyone. She opened the bottle.

Fifteen minutes later, when the job was done, she appraised herself again. Well, girl, this is indeed a new page, she thought. She looked considerably different to herself, and that was certainly the first leg on the journey to a makeover. Then another idea clicked in: she'd pull her hair back from her face and keep it that way in a ponytail, another change. Suzy hadn't worn a ponytail since her cheerleading days. Anyone comparing a photo Dean would have with her new look would come up as empty as a roulette bet on black coming up red.

It was after 10, and she realized she needed to get to sleep; the bus would leave fairly early, and she'd want a coffee and a bite to eat first. She called the desk and asked for a wakeup call at 5:30, then ran her fingers hesitantly through her hair. It still felt a bit damp, and she went to the bathroom again and found a shower cap in one of the drawers. No way could she leave residue from the dye on the pillow. Pulling the cap over her head, she winced slightly; it was a tight fit, and vaguely uncomfortable. Well, she'd have to put up with a little discomfort, like wishing for a sweater on a chilly night. There wasn't any choice.

She picked up her book, read the description on the back of the jacket and set it down briefly to go to the window. The sunset over the Rockies was a grand affair in pink and lavender, with the mountains outlined in purple; she admired it for at least a minute before pulling the blinds across. After a half hour in the room's sage green armchair, she put in a bookmark, yawned and stretched before heading to the bathroom to start her evening ritual. Twenty minutes later, she was asleep.

At her first glance, the bus center was more modern and more spacious than she imagined. Suzy quickly located the big scheduling board and saw the bus to Albuquerque posted, leaving at 8 a.m. She had checked earlier online, and it seemed there were only two buses a day on that route; the second – leaving at 7:15 in the evening for a trip of more than eight hours, was entirely wrong – it would have put her in Santa Fe well after midnight.

It was 7:35, and she went to the ticket window and pulled out her wallet. It was a simple transaction, and for $45 in cash she had a ticket to her final destination. She browsed in the newsstand for some minutes before buying a pack of Trident spearmint gum and a small bottle of Dasani water, then walked toward the gate number listed on the board. When she got there, the driver, an affable middle-aged African-American man with a closely trimmed mustache, was loading bags into the bottom storage compartment of the bus. She waited her turn, then showed him her ticket and handed him her suitcase.

"You're getting off in Santa Fe, right, ma'am?" he asked politely.

"I am."

"Very good. Welcome. Take any seat you want." His voice seemed surprisingly high for a big man.

She walked back in the bus about midway and took a seat to her left next to the window; that would be the side that would have the best view of the Rockies as the bus wended its way south on I-25 toward Colorado Springs. The seats, high-backed and cloth-covered, were cushier than airline seats, she thought, and slipped her water bottle into the seat pocket.

Gradually, the bus began to fill and passengers walked by her. She was curious, and she found her fellow riders much as she suspected – a polyglot of people of varying ages and races: older whites, a number of younger Latino families, a smattering of African-Americans, some older, some younger. Far from the older, almost all-white crowd she was used to traveling with, but she smiled inwardly: here was more proof that her plan to stay under the radar seemed to be working.

A few minutes before 8, the bus's diesel engines kicked into droning life, accompanied by the powerful smell, one that took her back to her childhood, when she rode buses to and from school. The driver welcomed everyone on board and announced the stops: Colorado Springs, Pueblo, Trinidad, Raton, Santa Fe, Albuquerque. At 8:01 on her watch, the bus backed out smoothly and started its journey, navigating the downtown streets headed for I-25.

Suzy alternated between looking out the window and reading her book. The sun danced among a flotilla of puffy cumulus clouds, but from her seat she could see only the shadows cast by the clouds, forming dark pools that ran up and along the mountains. Seated next to her, a young Hispanic man stared straight ahead or played with his phone; she sensed he'd have preferred another seat, but this was the only one available.

At one moment her thoughts went to Dean. Poor man, she thought to herself, he really doesn't deserve this – and if things were different, if her secrets had remained buried, she'd still be with him. Theirs had been a good life, and she had real affection for him – close to what she'd had with David, and with Avery in their early years. Am I really an ogre? she mused. The question went unanswered.

As they neared Colorado Springs, the driver pointed out Pike's Peak, approaching on the right. She peered at it, seeing only the mountain's dark flanks - the peak itself was lost in the clouds. The bus stayed generally in the middle lane, occasionally veering into the right lane when it passed a semi and the road ahead was clear. It was a smooth, comforting ride, and she felt drowsiness coming on when the bus eased off the highway for its stop in Colorado Springs – a half-hour stop, the driver announced.

Quite a number of passengers got off at the station, to be replaced by a slightly smaller group that boarded. Suzy read her book, while the man next to her appeared to be busy texting.

About 10 minutes before they were due to leave, she was jolted from her reverie by the sight of two gray-uniformed men walking down the aisle – she saw them only from the shoulders up. Cops. She froze, then looked up again. They seemed to be scanning the passengers, looking from side to side, and they looked grim. There had been no announcement, and the police themselves were saying nothing.

My God, Suzy thought to herself, is this it? It was hard for her brain to register anything but shock and surprise; she'd been cautious, always paying with cash, signing in as Sally where she could. How could they have traced her to this seat on a bus?

Two rows away, then just one. She averted her eyes and pretended to be reading.

"You," she heard. "Where are you headed?"

She looked up and started to speak, then held her tongue. They were leaning over and talking to the person in the window seat just ahead of hers. There was some brief dialogue that she couldn't hear, then they asked the passenger in the aisle seat, a large woman in a black t-shirt, to step out. One of the cops reached over and disappeared from sight, though she heard, "Come with us."

As she looked on, a young Hispanic man with a blue Chambray shirt, wearing a black ball cap, stood up and moved to the aisle. One of the cops, the taller one, appeared to be holding him by the arm as they walked to the front and out the door. As she stared out her window, she saw the cops putting his hands behind his back, hand-cuffing him, and escorting him away; the trio passed in front of the bus and disappeared.

Her heart was racing, and she took several deep breaths. The young guy sitting next to her had his arms folded and was looking down the aisle.

"Wow, that was something, wasn't it?" she said to him.

He turned and looked at her for a moment. "Yes," he said simply, and she made a note of his dark eyes and long lashes. "I been riding this bus for years, and I never saw cops before." He pursed his lips. "Kinda scary."

She smiled and replied, "Yes, scary indeed."

She returned to her book, but it was hard for her to concentrate. A few minutes later, the driver got back in and made an announcement: The man who was arrested was being charged with fraud and had been the subject of an outstanding warrant, he said; the driver apologized for the episode but said that Greyhound policy was always to cooperate to the fullest with law enforcement.

With that, he put the bus into gear and the trip resumed. Suzy noticed clouds of dust billowing as the bus backed out and realized the wind had come up; she watched the leaves in the nearby cottonwoods swirl and flash their pale undersides until the trees were out of sight.

Westchester County, NY

50.

The three weeks since Suzy's disappearance had sent Dean into a tailspin, whirling down like a biplane hit in an aerial dogfight. He hadn't been sleeping well, his appetite slackened, and he was distracted, moody, irritable: even the July Fourth celebration, usually a fine family event with a barbeque at Alex's followed by the glorious sky-painting of the local fireworks, failed to rouse him.

He seesawed between blaming himself for his headlong leap into marriage and blaming Suzy for her secrecy; the roller-coaster of emotions left him tired and sometimes a bit queasy. Alex did his best to try to engage him and help him work through this funk, but it was challenging, to say the least: to Alex, Dean was showing some of the signs of what he presumed was clinical depression.

Suzy's whereabouts were still a complete mystery. Insana had called early in the week after she disappeared to report on the contact with Sally Pritchard. Initially, Sally had been reluctant to talk, but when she realized how much they already knew, she opened up to his investigator, a balding former police detective with a soft-spoken manner who quickly inspired confidence.

Sally had indeed hosted Suzy for two days, she confessed, but Suzy had left suddenly, renting a car in Sally's name and taking off, saying she would call at some point when she had reached her destination. A check of the rental car records then showed that she had dropped off the car at the Denver Airport – and there was no record of another rental. Nor had Suzy called her.

Insana surmised she might have boarded a flight there, but it was only a hunch – and the more he thought about it, the more unlikely it seemed, if only because she would have to use an ID and buy a ticket in her own name. Well, someone would have to check the flight manifests on the airlines that day - a big job, and one he was glad he wasn't being asked to do.

Alex was at his office desk on a muggy morning in mid-August when the phone rang and he saw the call was coming from Atlanta. He answered quickly, and it was Tom Rittenhouse.

"Alex, we got the results from the autopsy, and it showed a substantial trace of a plant-based strychnine. I just can't believe it. Robin and I are livid, understandably – Suzy murdered Dad."

"Oh, man." Alex had been half-suspecting this news. "I am so sorry. This is just beyond the pale. My Dad is a basket case, and this could send him over the edge." He paused. "What are the authorities going to do?"

"My understanding is that an arrest warrant will be issued today on charges of suspected murder."

"Well, alright. There'll be a dragnet out there," Alex said. "Hopefully it will lead to something." Then he paused for a moment. "But is this really conclusive? I mean, without a confession, there doesn't seem to me like there is anything definitive. Some kind of foreign substance in trace amounts might not stand up in court."

He heard a sigh on the other end of the line. "You may be right, but I think the medical evidence is pretty strong. Certainly, we need to press the police or whoever to find her." Alex had told him earlier about Suzy's flight through Little Rock. "Nothing new on her possible location, is there?"

"No, sorry to say. Complete mystery."

"That's what I thought. But – please let me know if you hear of anything. I'll do the same on this end."

"Will do. Thanks, Tom."

As he hung up, a light rain started to fall, speckling the pond. The tears of heaven, he thought glumly.

After lunch, he dialed Alicia at her university office. The call went to voicemail, and he asked her to call him when she could.

About 90 minutes later, she called. After a few pleasantries, he said, "Suzy is still at large, so to speak. But I have other news for you." He paused. "The autopsy in Atlanta showed traces of a plant-based poison. The presumption is that Suzy administered that to her husband."

"Oh, no," Alicia replied with what sounded like quiet resignation. "So, she's being hunted as a murderer?"

"That's right. Unfortunately, the trail is completely cold at this point. We know she dropped off a rental car in Denver a couple of weeks ago, but she's vanished."

"This is awful for your family, and especially for your dad," Alicia said. "It's a little surreal for me, but she's very far in my rearview mirror at this point."

"I know." He waited for a few moments before asking the question that hung in the air like a garish pinata, waiting to be struck. "I wanted to know if you would consider having *your* father exhumed and tested for poison."

The phone was silent for at least 10 seconds before she spoke. "You know, I really don't think so. I – I guess the logical assumption is that she may have poisoned him, too. But there is already one solid case against her. I'm just thinking that that's enough. I'd like to keep my Dad undisturbed." She paused. "Can – can you understand that? I have my daughters to think about, even though they never knew him."

Her answer took him aback. "I guess so," he said slowly. "I just thought you'd really want to know."

She sighed. "At this point, I think I want to leave the past where it is, behind me. Tina – or Suzy – is dead to me now. That will never change. I just want to get on with my life. The divorce is hard enough on my daughters. I'm being very careful about what I share with them."

"I understand," Alex said, though he wasn't sure he truly did. "I'll let you know if they find Suzy. That seems likely, but it may take a little time. She seems pretty good at this."

"Oh, I think she is. Thanks for the call, Alex. Bye."

He'd been dreading the call to Dean, and he procrastinated until later in the afternoon to formulate his script. His father picked up on the third ring.

"Hi, son."

"Hi, Dad. I heard from Tom Rittenhouse, and our worst suspicions seemed to be true. They found traces of plant-based poison and plan to issue a warrant for Suzy's arrest."

"My God." Dean sounded crushed. "This is just so hard for me to absorb," he said slowly. "This wonderful life we had together – it's just gone out the window."

"None of us sensed this," Alex said softly. "You can't be any harder on yourself than you have been."

"No, I suppose not."

"I talked to Alicia in California, and she was adamant that she doesn't want her father exhumed. She says that what's past is past, and the authorities have a good case in Atlanta, obviously."

"Interesting." Dean was silent for a bit. "So, I guess we'll never know about the first husband."

"Not unless she changes her mind."

A long pause. "You can imagine what's been going through my mind if a poison was detected – what if I was next on the list? Did I dodge a bullet?"

"I guess we'll never know, Dad."

"No, probably not."

"Dad, I'm thinking out loud here – what if she is caught and put on trial? Would you go to the trial? It would probably be in Atlanta."

Dean harrumphed lightly. "Oh, absolutely. I want her to look me in the eye, show some remorse. She wrecked my life."

"That's a strong word, Dad. You have a lot going for you here – your friends, us. We're all behind you."

"Yeah, thank God for that." He sounded momentarily brighter.

"Why don't we take you out to dinner tonight? Lisa and me and the kids."

"That sounds good. I'd like that," Dean said, but Alex didn't detect much conviction: his reply had all the enthusiasm of a man headed to an appointment with a dentist. Pulling Dean out of his malaise was going to be a long, slow process, like mounting a set of stairs with a drowsy child on your back.

When the call ended, Dean Perry stared at his hands and felt a lump forming in his throat. His eyes welled with tears for the first time since Marjorie's funeral. He had married a wonderful woman who had deceived him as adroitly as a magician with a practiced sleight of hand, and even if she somehow reappeared, she was a criminal who deserved nothing but scorn. It was bewildering.

Atlanta, GA

51.

Leaning back in his chair with his morning coffee, sweetened with cream and Sweet 'n Low - years of black coffee had aggravated his ulcers, he was sure - Ray Childers looked up when Trevor Trewitt knocked and came in. Trewitt was one of the department's youngest detectives, a college graduate with an earnestness that occasionally brought surreptitious eye rolls from Childers and his fellow veterans, jaded by long years in the trenches.

Tall and lean, with an athletic look tempered by a pair of wire-rim glasses, Trewitt was one of the department's few African-American detectives. He sat down and sighed. "Nothing much to report yet, I'm afraid. I've interviewed the kids, but apart from their understandable anger and resentment, there isn't much to work with. Suzy and Avery had a happy marriage, it seems, and her behavior wasn't that unusual for a stepmother. Not a lot of friction, like in some families – but not a lotta love, either."

Childers was nominally in charge of the investigation into Avery's death, but he had punted the legwork to Trewitt. Childers was happy not to be the lead – the payoff from Baxter still weighed on his mind, and he was compromised to some extent. He knew it. He'd be happy to close the case, which at this point revolved around motive and the actual commission of the act; Suzy's guilt appeared to be a given. But with no leads on her whereabouts, the case still had a local focus.

Trewitt had earlier interviewed the family cook who had found Avery slumped in his chair. A calm, religious woman, she had cried softly in the interview; "Mr. Avery," she said, was one of the kindest people she'd ever known, considerate and generous. She couldn't remember much beyond the obvious from the scene but did remember finding an empty soda can on the floor that she had promptly thrown out after she called 911. Trewitt surmised that this might have been the source of the poison, but there was no way of knowing; the can was probably 20 layers deep in some landfill by now or had been loaded on a garbage barge headed who knows where.

"I'm thinking I should go to New York to interview the husband. He may know something that would shed light on the motive," Trewitt said.

Childers blew out a breath. "I dunno. Sounds kinda like a wild goose chase, and at considerable expense. I would just do a phone interview."

"Um, okay." Trewitt sounded a note of resignation. "I guess it would be an expensive trip without a guarantee of much of anything."

"Right." Childers ran his right hand through the bristle of his crew cut. "But I think you should also talk to the husband's son. He was the one who hired the private dick that looked into Suzy's past and came up with all this suspicious shit. You – you know I don't care for PIs, but he did a good job." At Alex's urging, Insana had sent a lengthy report to the Atlanta PD about his findings.

"Okay, I have the son's number. I think he's a journalist up there, runs a business magazine."

Childers harrumphed. "Then I guess he isn't some nosy reporter. Last thing we ever need is some amateur sleuth" – he made imaginary quotation marks to accent the word – "trying to wangle into this investigation."

"I suppose you're right," Trewitt said, nodding. He took off his glasses and rubbed the lenses with a ivory-colored handkerchief he pulled from his pocket. "I'll try to talk to the husband today. Maybe his son, too."

Childers put his elbows on the desk and looked hard at Trewitt; his smile was an unsettling display of yellowed teeth. "Keep me posted."

"Will do." Trewitt stood and started to leave, then turned back. "Oh yeah, I forgot to mention, the DA's office called me. They're going to hire an accountant to go through Suzy's accounts at Citadel Investments, where she and Avery kept their money. You know, she has millions there – at least seven million, I think, pretty much all from Avery."

"Okay, sounds good." Childers lied – this wasn't a good thing. Any accountant that waded into the financial weeds of Baxter's most notorious client might somehow stumble onto something. He shuddered slightly, like a leaf trembling in a breeze – but then he remembered that the money he'd gotten from Baxter was in cash. Hardly likely to be a part of any probe into Suzy's finances.

"Talk to you later," Trewitt said as he went through the door.

"Right." Childers watched him go, then swiveled his chair to look out the window. He could practically see the steam rising from the parking lot; it would be sweltering day. He felt a twinge of dampness under his collar and pursed his lips.

Trewitt was alright, he told himself; his college degree hadn't given him an air of superiority. He was eager to learn, and he had energy and smarts – though not the kind of street smarts that Childers and his older colleagues had. Those were picked up on the streets, in drug-infested apartments or grimy alleys where most murders turned up. The kind of smarts you get wheedling information from confidential informants, the sort of lowlifes that almost make you wrinkle your nose when you talk to them.

By comparison, the Rittenhouse murder was almost a parlor game, Childers thought: bloodless and clever. It wasn't like she'd blown the husband away with a 12-gauge in a fit of pique. No, this had all the appearances of being carefully planned and executed, with the wife giving herself a solid alibi even if anything was suspected. And leaving for New York had put her many hundreds of miles away. Out of sight, out of mind.

Still, the investigation had elements of risk and uncertainty, mostly in the form of Baxter Dennison. Childers hoped he wouldn't have to pull back Trewitt, like tugging a dog on a leash, if he smelled something fishy. God, he'd be glad when this was over.

Westchester County, NY

52.

The news about Avery's apparent poisoning startled Alex and Lisa like glass shattering on a floor, even though they knew it was possible once the exhumation was ordered. They talked about it in bed that night, in soft voices that simmered with incredulity, as the crickets chirped loudly outside. Now the challenge was how to break the news to their kids.

Jennifer and Jason were well aware of Suzy's flight – and the effect it had on their grandfather, who'd become withdrawn, tired, uncommunicative. It was something unpleasant that they didn't understand, but their summer activities helped distance them from the situation. Still, their parents agreed they needed to put it all out on the table – literally. It was a Friday, and Alex ordered a couple of pizzas that they could share at the dining room table, something he did at least once a month. What teenager didn't want pizza?

When Alex came back with the food, they set everything on the square wooden table and pulled out some plain paper plates and paper napkins. Alex opened a beer, a Sierra Nevada pale ale, from the refrigerator and poured Lisa a glass of Pinot Noir. The kids helped themselves to soda and picked up their slices from the boxes. Rushmore lay at Jason's feet on the floor. He knew better than to beg from the table, but he wasn't above pouncing on any scraps that fell.

Alex took a swig of the beer and cleared his throat. "Your mother and I have something important to talk about. It involves Suzy."

The kids stared at him. "Did they find her?" Jennifer asked.

"No. No one has a clue where she is. But yesterday the authorities in Atlanta concluded that she almost certainly poisoned her husband there – the one she was married to before Granddy. Originally, they thought he died of a heart attack."

"Poison? Wow." Jennifer's eyes widened. She had on a pair of light nylon shorts and a gray athletic t-shirt that didn't hide the chest she was developing. Her hair was tied back in a classic ponytail. Jason, on the other hand, wore cargo shorts and a black t-shirt with an image of Darth Vader.

"Wow is right," Jason said, laying the slice back on the plate. "Kind of like those old English mysteries, where they used poison in the tea, or whatever. The Agatha Christie stuff."

Alex allowed himself a wry smile. "Didn't know you knew about Agatha Christie."

Jason smiled back. "I read a couple of the paperbacks in the library. Pretty cool, really."

"Granddy is taking this very hard, as you can imagine," Lisa said softly. "It's one thing for her to run away, but this is much worse."

"Are they going to be looking for her harder now?" Jennifer asked quickly.

"Yes. They've issued a warrant for her arrest." Alex paused briefly. "Of course, that's complicated because there are no clues to her whereabouts. The trail went cold in Denver."

"Does she know people in the West? Is that why she went there?" Jason asked.

Alex looked at Lisa, who said, "We don't think so, but we just don't know that much about her, or her past." She and Alex had agreed not to share all the results of Insana's probe: the abandoned daughter, the childhood in Little Rock, the name change, the suspicion surrounding her first husband's death. It was almost too much for them, the adults, to comprehend.

She went on, "Like we said, she could be anywhere. She took her passport with her, so she could have even gone out of the country, like to Europe."

"My gosh," Jennifer said. "So, they might never catch her."

"That's certainly a possibility," Alex said.

"What if they did catch her?" Jason asked, his mouth full of pizza. "Wouldn't she go to trial?"

"Yup, that's my understanding," Alex said, nodding. "The trial would be in Atlanta, where the crime was committed."

The table fell silent. "What about Granddy?" Jennifer asked. "I feel there's something more we should do for him."

Lisa looked at her daughter approvingly. "Your father and I have talked about that. We're not just sure what that might entail, but we'll do something. And have you guys involved."

"Of course," Jason said as Jennifer nodded.

"You know," Jennifer said slowly, "there was always something about Suzy that bothered me a little. She was nice enough, but she always seemed kind of phony, like she was acting."

"Yeah," Jason echoed. "You know, pretending to be interested in our school stuff. It seemed like pretending sometimes, anyway."

Lisa smiled. "That's perceptive of you two. There did seem like there was an element of acting, but it's hard to pin it down sometimes, especially when there is someone new in the family and everyone's trying to adjust to each other. It can be hard to sort out which emotions are real and which aren't."

Alex set down his beer. "We wanted to keep you guys up to speed on all this. It's hard for us as adults to understand. But I think it's safe to say that Suzy won't be part of our lives anymore."

As Alicia looked out her office window, the smoke from the fires that had bedeviled Southern California for the last three weeks darkened the sky, which assumed the hue of lightly tinted car windows. Ash was present in the air, but the particles were so fine that they floated, virtually invisible to the eye. Added to the usual smog that hung over the LA basin, it was a double whammy.

She was in the office for the third day this week, nominally to prepare material for the fall semester. But she was preoccupied, restive. The news about Suzy apparently poisoning her husband had left her numb. Her mother was only a phantom in her memory now, as much a relic as a curled old Polaroid, yet the notion that she was a murderer - and may have even murdered her father - was hard to fathom.

She was wrestling with herself about just how - or what - to tell her daughters. They never knew Suzy (or Tina), and it would be easy to keep all this from them. But her other voice told her she owed them the truth. She had a fetish about communication with them, especially after the divorce. Alicia knew from reading, and from several of her friends and colleagues, how difficult divorce can be on children, especially teenagers – like having a comfortable chair pulled out from under them.

One argument for withholding all the sordid details about Suzy was the simple fact the girls didn't know anything about her new life, new name, new husband. Alicia had guarded those details as closely as a poker player holding her cards to her chest. Even if Suzy was caught, and there was national publicity about the case, her daughters wouldn't recognize her name, though there was a slim - very slim - chance that Alison might recognize a photo. If that happened, and the attendant questions tumbled out, Alicia would simply say she'd wanted to shield them from it all.

And then there was the email from last night. It was from Brian, and she sucked in her breath when she read it:

> *Alicia - Hope this last month has been going well for you and the girls. I've been reading about all the fires - horrible. Been hot and humid here - sweltering. You forget about the humidity back in the East when you've been in LA for a long time.*
>
> *I've got some important news: I'm engaged. She's a 37-year-old analyst with Bank of America Securities here; we met through mutual friends, and we've been seeing each other for the past 6 months. She was divorced as well after a five-year marriage.*
>
> *I do feel a little cowardly about putting this in an email - by all rights, I should call to tell you. And maybe I will call. I don't know what the protocols are; this is all too new. I think you should be the one to break it to the girls, but that's your decision.*

I can give you any details you want, of course. She has no children, but clearly wants to have them (well, one anyway). These things get complicated. I want to make this as easy as possible on you and the girls; I don't want to hurt anyone. You know that. But my life has a new trajectory now, and this is an exciting prospect for me.

Anyway, this just happened - I wanted to be upfront about it. No matter what, you and the girls have a special place in my heart. We have a history together that will never be diminished.

Love, Brian

Thinking about it now, Alicia bit softly on her lip and sighed. She thought for a moment, wistfully, about the earlier days of their marriage, when a dissolution seemed preposterous. But it had happened, and now Brian was moving on. She'd realized that she hadn't even had a single date since he left; the notion of a new relationship seemed, well, as wrong now as a thick slab of chocolate mousse would be for a diabetic. Plus, she wanted to allocate her attention to her daughters.

But Suzy? She tried to conjure up a mental image of her mother, and she struggled. Suzy was now a fugitive, but Alicia knew in her heart when she heard the news that her mother would never turn to her even if Suzy knew how to find her. Those bonds had been broken, like frayed ropes whose broken threads danced in a breeze, and they could never be bound together again.

Santa Fe, NM

53.

The motel at the outskirts of Santa Fe was just what she wanted: nothing special, an older property that had mostly surrendered meekly to the passage of time and had recently seen its fifth owner in a generation, a family from Mumbai who had learned in the old country how to run a business. Suzy wouldn't have guessed that the fixtures and the beds were virtually new, and that the kitschy paintings in the lobby – semi-impressionist landscapes that were a bit too blue – had come just the week earlier from a local consignment shop.

In the two weeks she'd been there, the motel had never been more than seemingly half full, with license plates mainly from nearby states like Arizona and Colorado. Meanwhile, she'd gone through the exercises she needed to do to effect a name change. Placing an ad in a local paper had been relatively easy – she'd taken a cab to their offices and been directed to a counter, where she'd read the ad to a bright-eyed young woman who'd helped her refine it and state the particulars. She paid cash for the ad to run in two successive weeks, as required.

To establish herself, she needed to open a bank account that would enable her to take care of bills and incidentals down the road. She chose a branch of a local bank, First National of Santa Fe, that had a sleek look of wood and chiseled stone, and cheerfully went through the process with an eager young guy, his freshly-minted college diploma seemingly tattooed on his forehead, who walked her through the process.

The fact that it required her to present ID as Suzy Perry made her slightly uneasy, but she had no choice – and she knew it would be easy enough to alter that when her name change came through. She started the account with $2,000 in cash and told him more would be forthcoming soon, once she was settled and had a permanent address. He gave her a set of ten starter's checks, light blue, with no name or address.

Two days later, she returned to the bank, produced the debit card she'd been issued and her New York driver's license and deposited a check from her brokerage cash account. The amount, $100,000, gave the teller a moment's pause, but Suzy sensed that her age and apparent sophistication carried the day – and, after all, this was an established community bank, not some check-cashing storefront hard by a pawnshop or standing forlornly in a bedraggled part of town.

Next, she needed a car. It certainly didn't need to be a Mercedes, but she was growing tired of self-sacrifice, the sense that she needed to continue flying under the radar of anyone who might be searching for her. She'd done just fine so far, right? She settled on buying a BMW sedan, used, that comported with her sense of style. She'd driven one in Atlanta for years, pearl blue with black upholstery, that she'd loved.

So, she did some research online over two days, and found just what she thought she wanted: white, two years old and coming off a lease, with just under 25,000 miles. The price seemed good, and she called the dealership to make sure it was still on the lot. A cheerful guy assured her it was, and Suzy took a cab there early one afternoon.

Arriving on the spacious lot, she walked in through the front door and greeted the receptionist – her mind racing back for a moment to the days when David had his dealership in Clayton. Car dealerships hadn't changed much over the years, she thought to herself: huge glass windows fronting on a lot, desks set in regular rows where the salesmen entertained potential buyers. She was directed to a guy sitting at a gray metal desk in the back. He was staring at his computer, and as she walked up she saw the nameplate on his desk, Robert Santos.

He looked up and smiled, his teeth impossibly straight and white; dentures, she thought immediately.

"Are you here to buy a car?" The voice was polished, accented ever so slightly. His hair was dark and slicked back, and he wore a white shirt with western accents – stylized arrows - on the chest pockets.

"I am," Suzy replied, smiling back. "I called about a used white 338i, two years old, and was told it was still here."

"Okay, great. I know the car you mean." He stood up, and she saw he was just her height. "Let's get the keys and take a look."

He walked to a cabinet near the front door and hesitated for a few moments before picking up a set of keys, then ushered her out the door into the limpid sunshine and toward a row of cars to their right. It was the fourth car down, and Suzy liked it immediately: jaunty, modern, with the iconic pair of headlights on either side of the grille. She sat behind the wheel when he opened the door for her and listened politely as he pointed out some of the features.

"Would you like to test drive it?" Robert asked.

"I certainly would. But it doesn't have to be a long drive."

"No, we have a standard route we like to take people on. Ten minutes, tops. Let's you test the acceleration, braking, all that good stuff."

"That sounds fine."

"Okay, let me get the temporary plate. Stay here – I'll be right back." She watched as he half-jogged, gracefully as a dancer, toward the door.

Twenty five minutes later, she was seated in the back office where the finance department hung out. A broad-shouldered man, bald and jowly, walked toward her and extended his beefy hand.

"Darren Echeverria, at your service."

"Hi, Suzy Perry."

He sat down behind his desk and glanced at the paperwork, quickly all business. "I see you want to buy the 338i. Are you interesting in taking the car very soon?"

"I am – I'd like to buy it today."

He looked up and studied her for a moment, as if he was trying to read something in her face. "Do you mind my asking, will there be anyone else in on the transaction? A husband?"

She had expected this. "No, just me. I'm a widow who has just relocated here." The lie slid off her tongue effortlessly, as easily as a brook gurgling over smooth pebbles.

"We have all kinds of financing available, of course, mostly three- or four-year loans…"

She cut him off. "I don't need a loan. I'm prepared to write a check for the full amount."

His eyebrows shot up in surprise. "Why would you do that when you can establish terrific credit by paying off a loan?"

She stared back at him. "My credit is very strong. I don't need to improve it."

"Everyone can stand better credit. I really recommend a loan. Even if you only take it out for a year and pay it off promptly."

She squirmed slightly in the chair. "That may be good for you and your bank, but I choose not to do it." Her teeth were clenched. "I'd rather not take my business elsewhere, but I can't imagine why you wouldn't want cash – and right away."

He looked at her and then down at his hands before looking up again. "If you really insist, of course we can accommodate you. Can you – do you have a cashier's check?"

"I have a check from a brokerage firm in Atlanta where I have substantial assets."

"Ah," he said softly. "But nothing from a local bank?"

"I've deposited a relatively small amount at First National to set up an account, then wrote them a much larger check for cash - but I was told it would take probably two days to clear."

"We would have the same issue." He picked at his sleeve and proffered a half-smile. "Perhaps you can write a check from the First National account when your deposit clears – that would be best for us. It probably means a slight delay – when did you make your deposit?"

"Two days ago," she said firmly.

"Well, it should certainly clear in another day at the latest. Then you can do a cashier's check from them for us."

She was starting to feel something like genuine anger. "You're telling me that I should come back in a day or two, and not write a check today? This is a major nuisance. I – I don't see this as a convenience to the customer."

Echeverria spread his hands and said somewhat sheepishly, "I'm sorry. We have our policies. Of course, we want to make people happy. I think what I'm asking isn't more than just a minor inconvenience. We certainly want to sell you the car." He paused and nodded slightly. "You can write a small check to hold it, just fifteen hundred dollars, and we'll take the rest in the cashier's check."

She sat silently and stared at him, her body frozen in indignation. But she loved the car, and this was the only BMW dealership in town. She looked at him with what anyone looking on would have seen as barely veiled contempt. "And how should I make it out?" she asked frostily.

Ten minutes later, as she walked toward the cab that she'd called, she took out her motel key – the old-fashioned sort that had a real key attached to a plastic fob. As she moved between two cars in the lot, she surreptitiously dragged the key along the passenger door of the car to her right, a black 535i, just below the door handle. She didn't stop to admire her handiwork, a long, jagged scratch very much like the scar on a knee that had undergone surgery. It was their price for her inconvenience.

Back in her motel room, the sun was still strong and she needed to keep the heavy curtains drawn. The air conditioning unit under the window whirred loudly. She sat in the chair, picked up her phone and listened again to the message from Dean, sent several days earlier.

> *Suzy, I know you're on the run somewhere, they tell me probably near Denver. I'm devastated. I want you to come back and let us work through our issues. I love you and need you in my life. I drag myself around every day, just going through the motions.*
>
> *I've had a hard time believing some of the things about you, and your prior life, and your walking away from your daughter. Something must have hurt you very badly. I*

certainly didn't mean to hurt you, but I did want to try to get to the truth, as best I could determine it.

Please call me – I want to hear your voice. You don't have to tell me where you are, just that you'll come back. I want you back in my life. Things may not be the way they were, but we can manage, I know it. Please call.

Suzy felt a pang of something like remorse; she really did care for him, and their life together. It was more than comfortable, and he practically worshipped her. But the news that Avery would be exhumed was insupportable. Dean hadn't mentioned it in his call, but surely he knew about it. If they did find poison, neither Dean nor any other man would want anything to do with her, and there would be a shadow looming over her shoulder wherever she went.

Baxter would probably know about any autopsy, but could she trust him? She'd have to think hard on that one. If he was caught in his little blackmail scheme, she thought, he'd probably sing like a caged canary.

Atlanta, GA

54.

Baxter Dennison was daydreaming, as he often did, during his working hours, which often sandwiched long periods of boredom with phone calls – some urgent, most not – from clients. It was a dog day deep in August, and he thought about the vacation that would be coming up soon to Skidaway Island with his wife, Terri, and son Noah. They had a condo for a week, and he looked forward to seeing Terri lounging by the pool in one of her bikinis – he always did.

He looked down at his tie and smiled. It was dark blue, with small naval code flags on regular diagonals. Just right for the yachting set, even if those types were scarce in Atlanta. Well, people with lots of money liked yachts, didn't they? And hadn't Ted Turner been a big wheel in the yachting world?

Suddenly, his boss, Grant Holloway, appeared at his office door. Trim and tan, dressed in a blue-and-white striped shirt with French cuffs, with nary a gray hair out of place, he was a poster boy for a money manager. But he wasn't smiling.

"Come to my office. We need to talk about Suzy Perry."

Baxter had to suppress a gulp. "Is there anything new since yesterday?" he asked innocently.

"Yeah, there is." He spun on his heel and walked away, and Baxter followed, a little discombobulated. What the hell was this about?

Holloway strode to his desk and motioned to Baxter to take a seat in the one of the black padded chairs facing the desk. Baxter quickly took in the family photos on the credenza behind Holloway, one with the group smiling and happy on a beach with palm trees, and the one with his comely daughter in a wedding dress. Baxter knew the view outside the windows all too well. Though it was only on the 10th floor, it was a corner office with a lovely view of downtown Atlanta on one side and the expressway on the other. The polished wood of the conference table gleamed.

"We have a little trouble on our hands," Holloway began, leaning back and forming a steeple with his hands. "It seems the district attorney wants us to freeze Suzy's accounts. I guess that's pretty routine when someone is accused of murder, but it's certainly new for us."

"I see." Baxter had thought this day would come, but his mouth felt unusually dry. The news about the charges against Suzy had hit the newspapers and television yesterday like a clap of thunder. "Well, as you probably know, she has substantial assets spread over numerous accounts, including IRAs, basically that she inherited from Avery. She's been drawing from a conventional cash account ever since his death."

Holloway's grey eyes bored into him. "They say she disappeared weeks ago. I have to presume there has been no contact with you?"

"Absolutely not.'" Baxter hunched forward in the chair.

"Were there any unusual withdrawals lately?"

"Yes, actually. I checked this morning and there had been two larger withdrawals, two hundred thousand each, a couple of weeks ago." He paused. "That's pretty sizable, of course, but with the portfolio she has, it's not a big deal."

Holloway looked out the window and sighed. "Well, it seems there will be no more withdrawals, at least, since she's a fugitive. Though I imagine what's she's taken to date will tide her through a certain period. Still, not having access to all those millions will certainly put a crimp in her lifestyle."

"I'm sure of that." Baxter tried to radiate confidence.

Holloway swiveled his chair back to face Baxter. "I'd like you to prepare a quick overview of her accounts for me. Printed out, of course. Keep it under five pages." He looked down briefly at the desk, then up again. "I want to be able to show the DA what's out there, and what's being frozen."

"Of course."

"Sooner the better, Baxter. We want to put our best foot forward."

"Certainly. I can have those for you soon, before lunchtime."

"Good." He stroked his chin with his left hand. "And let me warn you, it's a possibility that we may be asked to bring in a forensic accountant to go through her investments. If that's the case – and I really don't know at this point – you would have to be available to help him or her out."

"Of course." Baxter tried not to show any emotion. The thought of postponing any of his vacation for such a task was bad enough, but any accountant worth his or her salt would have to question the regular $10,000 disbursements he'd arranged from Suzy. They would stand out like red flags pinned to a game board, and he'd have to be prepared to say what charities they'd gone to. He'd have to get on it; if this accountant did show up, evasiveness would be futile. He or she would want answers.

About two that afternoon, while he was composing an email to a client, the phone rang.

There was a brief pause after he answered; then he heard, "This is Suzy."

He recoiled slightly and cupped his hand over the receiver instinctively. "My, my. You know they're looking for you."

"Ah. It's official, then?"

"Indeed it is. The news about Avery was all over TV and the *Constitution* today. They tracked down your husband in New York, too. He said he had no idea where you were." He paused. "Where are you, anyway?"

He heard her harrumph slightly. "I'm afraid that's my secret."

Baxter looked at the number on his screen – it was her cell phone, with the Atlanta prefix. No hint there. "Why are you calling? We don't have much to talk about, and I don't like to deal with serial killers."

"Is that what I am?" She paused. "Well, I wanted to know if they were indeed looking for me. I figured you would know."

"Yeah, you're officially a murder suspect in Avery's death, based on the autopsy. No surprise to me, of course."

Silence for a few seconds, then she said, "You may be too clever for your own good. What will happen if they see those – um – payments I've been making to you?" She sounded superior and accusatory at the same time.

"That's my challenge," he said levelly. "The boss told me a forensic accountant may be asked to go through your accounts. I hope not, of course, but I have to be prepared for that."

"And are you?" she asked archly.

"Not yet, not yet." He blew out a breath. "You should know that your accounts are being frozen."

"I thought that was a good possibility." He heard her chuckle. "There goes my villa on the Riviera."

"I've never had a client like you before," he said softly. "I've had rich widows, of course, but no one who did their husbands in. Maybe I should be glad I didn't get on your bad side."

"Oh, you did, with the blackmail," she said coolly. "But you're safe, especially now. I don't expect to ever see Atlanta again."

His curiosity spilled over, like water in a glass under a running tap. "How will you live without all Avery's money? Do you have anything else stashed away?"

"Not really, no, but I'll manage." She paused ever so slightly. "I always do."

"If you say so." He scratched behind his ear. "Suzy, this may be obvious, but I don't think you should call me again. Makes sense in a way. With your accounts locked up, there's nothing to talk about."

"You know, you're right about that. I guess this is goodbye. Don't worry about me – not that you would. You have your own fish to fry, especially if they do audit my accounts."

"Just like you, I'll get by." Baxter paused. "So yes, goodbye. I can't say it hasn't been interesting."

He heard her chuckle. "Thanks," she said softly. "Here's to good luck for both of us."

55.

Four days after the Atlanta DA had frozen Suzy's accounts, a forensic accountant appeared at Citadel Investments. Rachel Janofsky didn't come off like a buttoned-down accountant; she seemed outgoing, self-confident and well-dressed, with a smart crocodile briefcase. Her dark hair fell in waves around her face, and her lipstick seemed preternaturally red. When he was introduced, Baxter even contemplated flirting with her; after all, she was in a position, potentially, to determine his fate at the firm.

Holloway himself wasn't above being unusually friendly to her. "Rachel, we're going to give you a private office and all the access you need. Baxter will give you all the files applicable to Suzy's account. Obviously, take as long as you need."

"Thanks." Her voice was a light alto, with a trace of Georgia drawl. "I would think I could get through this by end of day tomorrow at the latest. I'll let you know where things stand when I leave this afternoon."

"I'll show you where the key areas are – the restroom, the coffee room, all that," Baxter said, smiling. "Then, when you're settled, I can show you how to access all the files."

"That would be great." Her smile was a mere upturn of the lips, with no teeth showing.

"And lunch?" Baxter asked. "There's a cafeteria on the bottom floor, and plenty of other places for takeout around here."

She smiled again. "There's a place nearby that I know well – it will work fine."

Baxter took a deep breath. He realized he had to give her full access to all of Suzy's accounts, which would allow her to look at all the activity since Avery's death. He'd already invented a list of local charities that he would claim the blackmail payments had been given too. Surely that would be enough.

At four p.m. the next day, Holloway called him to the small conference room, where Rachel was waiting with a laptop open. Baxter took the chair across from her, easing himself in as nonchalantly as he could.

"Most all of the activity I looked at seems pretty straightforward," she said. "There were a fair number of trades, but nothing out of the ordinary, I think." She looked up from her computer to Baxter, and he could make out the light freckling on her forehead from the sunlight coming in the windows. "I did see that Suzy had written a couple of large checks on her cash account recently – I gather that came after she took off."

"That's right," Baxter said.

"The one thing that confused me, though, is a series of regular withdrawals, ten thousand each, that started about 18 months ago. I believe there have been six of them. I didn't see them land in her cash account." She looked at Baxter again, and he could sense Holloway staring at him too. So, it had come to this.

"I have an explanation," he said confidently. "She instructed me to make regular withdrawals of appreciated stock to give to some of the local charities she'd been involved with. Of course, that's water over the dam now."

"Uh-huh." There was a note of skepticism, or maybe just confusion. "Do you have records from these charities about the donations?"

"What kind of records?" He wanted to be precise.

"Something on their letterhead, you know, saying they received those funds."

Baxter was ready for this – it was almost like laying down a trump card. "Those would have gone to her, since she was the donor of record."

"Oh, I suppose so." She thought for a moment. "I just think there should be some other kind of confirmation—"

"I do have a list of the charities involved," Baxter said. "I think there were seven or eight."

Holloway leaned forward. "That's good, Baxter, but she needs something more. I think you also need to produce the transactions that generated the donations. That should be simple enough."

Baxter felt the back of his neck tingle. He tried to shrug. "I guess I could try, but I'm not sure I see why it's important."

"I guess because I'm telling you it is," Holloway replied. "Can you do it by the end of the day?"

Baxter felt like his face was frozen. "I have a meeting with a big client in a half hour."

"Alright, by tomorrow morning then," Holloway said. "Then I think we can let Rachel go on her way – right, Rachel?"

"That's really the only loose end I see," she said matter-of-factly.

"Sounds fine with me, then," Baxter said, forcing a smile.

Five minutes later, back in his office, Baxter sat with his hands on his temples, thinking. What the hell was he going to do this time? A conjurer has only so many tricks, and he wasn't sure he had any left.

Santa Fe, NM

56.

The woman who once answered to Tina and Suzy strolled out of the condo complex in Santa Fe toward her car. The sun was already burning in the sky, and it promised to be a warm day for September. The BMW, parked in a marked-off space, lay deep in the shade of a silvery olive tree.

Her condo, like so many nearby, was in tan adobe, with a turquoise wooden door. The late summer grass in front was yellowing and as thin in patches as wisps of hair on a balding scalp. She was starting to feel the rhythm of Santa Fe, which was distinctly western, with broad vistas and distant mountain ranges - so unlike the East, with its tall spreading trees and impregnable walls of greenery.

The name-change procedure had gone as smoothly as she could have imagined; Suzy Perry had proved no more than a brief footnote in her life. Her new name was very different.

As she approached her car, a man was getting out of his black SUV two spaces down. He saw her and smiled. She saw that he was an older guy, tall and lean, with an orange ballcap and sunglasses. He stood by his car door and took her in: the Mexican-style blouse, blue and yellow with cap sleeves, over beige Capri pants. Her light brown hair was cut into fashionable pageboy, clipped relatively short, that showed the nape of her neck. She wasn't young, certainly, but somehow she looked youthful. He was enchanted.

"Hi, I'm T.J. I don't remember seeing you around here," he said as he strolled over to her car.

"Well, I'm new in town and just getting my bearings." Her blue eyes looked at him unflinchingly. She liked his deep voice and his smile, broad and white under a thin silver mustache.

"What's your name?"

"Monica. Monica Mason."

He looked quickly at the ring finger on her left hand and saw nothing. "Well, Monica, if you ever want someone to show you around –"

"Well, T.J., I might have to think about that for a bit. I'm not used to getting picked up in parking lots by strange men." She crossed her arms and stood stock still, her head cocked slightly as she stared at him.

He was a bit taken aback; clearly, she was going to be a challenge. He sensed a certain reserve, and a sophistication that oozed of something. Yes, that was it - money.

"Well, I'm not strange," he said, smiling slyly. "You can ask anyone here."

"Is that right?" She sensed that he was quick on his feet, and she liked that.

"That's right. I hope, Monica Mason, that you might take me up on my offer sometime." His voice was deep and smooth, practiced.

"I'll think about it. I will."

"Well, which unit is yours?"

A half-smile played on her face as she looked directly at him. "A woman doesn't casually give out that information to people she doesn't know."

"I see." This cat-and-mouse game was a bit unnerving, and his face registered his disappointment.

"Ask me tomorrow," she said. And then she smiled at him and turned her face up slightly, like a flower moving to sunlight. It was, he thought, the most beautiful smile he'd ever seen.

www.ingramcontent.com/pod-product-compliance
Lightning Source LLC
LaVergne TN
LVHW091538060526
838200LV00036B/657